Brittle
Joys

Brittle Joys

SARA MAITLAND

A *Virago* Book

First published by Virago Press 1999

Copyright © Sara Maitland 1999

The Psychology of Women by Helen Deutch copyright © Grune &
Stratton, 1944

5000 Years of Glass by Hugh Tait copyright © The British Museum,
British Museum Press, 1991

The Dark Ages by Ruth Hurst Vose, in (ed) D. K. Wardlord *The History
of Glassmaking* copyright © Orbis, 1984

A CIP catalogue record for this book is
available from the British Library

ISBN 1 86049 256 8

Typeset in Berkeley by M Rules
Printed and bound in Great Britain by
Clays Ltd, St Ives plc

Virago Press
A Division of
Little, Brown and Company (UK)
Brettenham House
Lancaster Place
London WC2E 7EN

This novel is dedicated with love to Sebastian Sandys,
for entirely obvious reasons.

I would like to thank:

Stephen Newell, who showed me his glass studio and talked about the choreography of glass making.

Will Anderson and Ford Higson who lent me their wedding.

Joanna Love, Roberta Wedge and others who talked to me with pride about being fag-hags.

Paul Elgie and Phil McIntosh who taught me a number of things I ought to have learned a long time ago.

Janet Batsleer, Richard Coles, Peter Daly, Sue Dowell, Jo Garcia, Harriett Gilbert, Dominic Green, Aileen la Tourette, Ros Hunt, Mildred and Adam Lee, Barbara Loveday, Paul Magrs, Russell and Sue Stewart for various things.

And especially Ruthie Petrie.

For in life we must struggle to hold on to brittle joys.

Augustine, Sermon III

Chapter One

The women were working.

Ellie was sitting at her bench, her extraordinary long red hair, slightly frizzy from the heat, haloed in the light from the furnace. Patsy stood a few feet away, poised, on her toes, her goggles hanging limp against her cotton shirt, like a racetrack gambler's binoculars. Mary, tiny, tough, and stunning, was pulling the heavy metal tube out of the small furnace and carrying it to the crucible, and reaching inside and drawing out the molten glass, glowing, red at the core; she bore it to the marver, kneaded it deftly on the marble surface and offered it to Ellie who received it without moving, or even looking.

The glass on the end of the blowing tube was very soft, bulbous; soft enough to droop off the end of the rod, hanging meekly as though it might fall at any second. Ellie began to turn the tube on the raised wooden ridge beside her bench. At the centre of the glaucous swelling the red colour glowed intensely. Ellie kept the rod moving, with tiny dancing hand movements, never still and never fidgeting, round and round to prevent the glass drooping off. She worked the glass with these circular hand movements and then, watching it with perfect attention, she blew into the tube, little whispers of breath, tiny puffs; and as the glass began to swell it also began to stiffen, standing straight off the end of the rod. And when still glowing red it reached this critical point, Ellie stretched her hand out round it, stroking it. Her hand was encased in a huge wet wadding glove, but still it caressed the glass. The women did not speak; they were like well-rehearsed dancers. With a sudden single fluid movement, Ellie got up and moved around the long pipe, and plunged it deep into the open furnace: a relaxed, fast, totally economical movement. Now, when she was back on her bench, the other two were close, holding flat wooden paddles: Mary was flattening the end of the ball of glass, pushing it in with one paddle and holding its edge straight with another, while Patsy held her board just above Ellie's wrist, to protect her from the heat.

It did not always work; Ellie had scars, whiter whorls and dashes against the whiteness of her arm. And the long scar, down the outside of her thigh, puckered mauve along its inner edge, like an old stretch mark, that she had acquired, years ago, from sitting down on some long forgotten tool, still hot from the furnace. They were always careful – one of Patsy's tasks when they were blowing was to check constantly where everything was, that it was exactly, within half an inch, of where it should be, where Ellie had to be free to assume that it was – but, as Ellie would say laughing, 'You can't be too careful'.

Turning, blowing, moulding, reheating, a tightly choreographed minuet; the three women moved in a tight relationship to each other around the large sparse room. Occasionally Ellie nodded, or waved, signalling yet more precise timings and movements. The vessel grew, full bellied, and now long necked also, a wine decanter from a blob of glass; deep in its base there was the dark red core which reached out tentacles of colour, attenuating into spider's web threads of red, and vanishing into clarity. It was a stock design, quite successful; they would knock them off in a range of colours, the bread and butter of the cottage-industry, the bit that gave Ellie the time and space to grouch about having to do it. But even though this was the fourth time they had repeated this routine that day, there was the perfect stillness of concentration, which framed and structured the continual movement and flow. It was beautiful and it was dangerous; a ritual and a gamble.

Then it was finished. There was a communal exhalation. Patsy snipped with the huge shears. Ellie, with a decisive straightening of her back, nodded towards the cooling oven. Mary, pulling on great gauntlets, took the decanter tenderly and carried it across the room. Ellie watched until her work had reached the table beside the big oven the other side of the studio and had been carefully set down; then she stood up, turned round, smiled warmly, and said, 'Oh Hugo, hello.' She had known he was there. She had just refused to acknowledge it. He moved towards her and they met trampling a pile of shattered glass and exchanged embraces.

Hugo loved watching Ellie working, her rare moments of unself-consciousness. Quite separately he loved the fact that he was allowed to. He knew he was honoured to be permitted to wave at Megan through the office window, and stroll down into the old stable yard without even having to identify himself. He knew how most people would have been caught and steel-pinioned in the efficient office. He was so used to that privilege, along with many others, that he did not even feel grateful for it.

'Mmm, so nice,' she said now. 'Are you well?' Her hair, he noticed once again, was not so much greying as fading. 'What time is it anyway? So, sweet heart, what brings you to these perilous lands south of the river?'

'I heard about Robbie.'

'Oh. Well, it's not too serious this time. They're checking his eyes. Just a day or so.'

'Good,' he said, and then, more tentatively, 'and it's Steph's birthday. I thought you might like someone.'

Her eyes filled suddenly with tears, which did not reach the point of falling. She looked fragile, almost childlike, for a moment. Her eyes always filled so when someone was kind to her; it was one of her most attractive little ways – you had to know her well, for a long time, usually long after you had appointed yourself her knight errant, before you realised that the tears were not an intimate private response, they brimmed universally, for you, for anyone, even the butcher if he had kept some particular delicacy for her. And even knowing this you usually forgot each time and were touched, complimented, moved, unless you were particularly angry with her.

'Bless you. How do you always remember dates?'

'It's one of the things I'm good at.' He grinned, smirking slightly. This was true – he was good at it; at turning up, at remembering dates, events, occasions, at spontaneous moments of support, even at considerable inconvenience to himself. The fact that he often failed to keep carefully organised appointments at considerable inconvenience to others ought to have been balanced against this but seldom was. You had to know him well, for a long time, usually long after you had decided that he was unusually sensitive and tender, before you realised, that it was more to do with excitement than affection; and even then you usually forgot each time, unless you were particularly angry with him.

'You're amazing,' she said, petting his arm. 'We're finished here; shall we go for a drink?'

Mary plunged the glowing rod into the pail of water at their feet, and the still hot glass that clung to it shattered loudly, accompanying the hissing and crackling as the rod cooled rapidly in the water and the glass sharded into sparkling fragments. She banged the rod a couple of times on the floor, to more tinkling and one loud crack, then, glancing to check that it was clean enough she inverted it, leaned it against the doors, pulled her hair out of the red spotted handkerchief she had round her head and grinned at Hugo. Patsy was hurrying, glancing at her watch even as she moved round the studio, fitting the overnight doors on to the kiln openings and retidying the tools.

Ellie surveyed her domain. She noticed Patsy's haste.

'Oh damn, Patsy, are you late? I'm sorry. Leave it. Mary can close up.' Mary did not look pleased. 'Oh come on. Patsy promised her kids . . . I promised Patsy. Go on, Patsy, go.'

There was a pause as Patsy left. 'I'm sorry, Mary.'

'I just wanted to get some drawing done before we closed up.'

'Something interesting?'

'I don't know. I've got this thing about mirrors: I want . . .' Mary hesitated, but the moment of irritation had passed. Mary threw Ellie an it's-OK smile, 'I can draw at home actually, and perhaps later we could talk.' She turned her attention to the furnace doors.

Ellie called goodnight and turned out into the sunshine. Hugo and she walked together up the short alley to the office. She did not look back. After about ten paces it was clear that she had shrugged off work, and as far as he was allowed to know would not think of it again until she came back to the studio the next morning. She was not secretive about it, indeed it was hard to imagine Ellie being secretive about anything, but she seldom talked about the minutiae of her job.

The office, in marked contrast to the studio, was warm and beautiful. There were flowers, growing in pots and arranged in glass vases, and heavy linen curtains and an antique *bureau plat*. On a high shelf that ran round the whole room, an exhibition of Ellie's work was displayed, discreetly but proudly, carefully lit for the best effect. Clear glass vessels and coloured ones that shimmered, opalescent like water or fire: Hugo's favourite – a huge charger, a monumentally simple disc of glass, which was lit from behind – changed colour as you moved across the room, turning from clear purity to greenish translucency, with deep iridescent flashes of pink and gold.

5

Unlike the studio, the office did look like the work-place of a leading craftsperson, who exhibited in capital cities, whose work was commissioned, collected, not just privately but by museums internationally. It had this effect because the studio was run by Ellie, but the office was run by Megan, whom Ellie referred to laughingly as 'my Scottish version of an iron magnolia'. Megan was a little older than Ellie and had the sweetest smile Hugo had ever seen. She ran the office none the less with extraordinary efficiency.

Now Ellie, already unbuttoning the brown cotton boiler suit she always worked in, went through the office to the changing room beyond it.

Megan and Hugo's heads moved nearer together, conspiratorial.

Hugo half whispered, 'Is she OK?'

'I think so. It's good you came.'

Ellie emerged, drying her hands, a baggy silk shirt over jeans replacing the boiler suit. She carried her red leather jacket. 'What are you two muttering about?'

'I was telling Hugo about the V & A,' Megan said almost too quickly: Ellie hated her friends to talk about her in her absence. Whether this was paranoia or a power trip, she needed to control what people knew about her. It ought to have been irritating, this neurotic desire to invent herself afresh, to protect herself from interpretation, and indeed did irritate the people who did not love her. For those who did, it was one of the ways that the tenderness she induced in her friends could be turned into protectiveness. So although Megan had not even mentioned the Victoria & Albert Museum, Hugo looked knowing.

'Yes,' said Ellie, almost complacently, 'aren't you proud of me?' Hugo, who could tell she was pleased, but was unable to make a very positive contribution at this point, grinned warmly and made enthusiastic mutterings. Ellie's glance swept round the room, obviously admiring the samples of her own work: she was transparently open to praise and affirmation – and as easily moved to despair. My problem, she had told him once, is that I desperately need everyone to approve of me, but lack the skills for getting that to happen. She looked along the shelves with a smile. Then abruptly she said, 'Megan, where's the lightning cube?'

'What?'

'That fused cube; the one with the oxidised blue inside.'

Megan still looked baffled. 'You know,' said Ellie impatiently, 'it was up there, next to the big vase.'

Megan stood up, as though that would give her a better view. 'I know which piece you're talking about, Ellie,' she said. 'How odd. I could have sworn it was there.' It very clearly was not however. 'I don't know. It was there. Did you take it up to your drawing room?'

'I don't think so. Never mind. I noticed because it was one of Stephanie's favourite things and I wouldn't give it to her.'

'Oh, Ellie,' a hover of compassion, and then more robustly, 'but not a lot of use in the jungle. I'm trying to remember when I last saw it – consciously I mean. I'll ask Sal. But she's usually so careful.'

'I know. Don't worry about it, Megan, it doesn't matter,' she said, though the cube was rather dear to her – an almost perfectly satisfactory conclusion to a long and complex process of experimentation. One of those rare occasions when she had finally got the technology right and then realised why she had wanted to get it right in the first place: the skill had carried its own meaning through into the cube so that what had set out to be no more than an experiment had become a thing in itself. Not now, she thought, not now.

'We're off for a drink, Megan. Goodnight,' she said and leaned over the desk. Then seeing a sheet of paper, stopped just before their cheeks met. 'What's this?'

'Oh, that; Friedhelm Muller sent it.'

Ellie nodded. Friedhelm was a German architect she had worked with the year before.

'He says he knows it isn't your thing, but the clients want you and he thought the idea might amuse you.'

Ellie liked Friedhelm, and disliked the way he tried to push her into architectural work. Twenty years ago she had been part of the group which had maintained the English craft tradition in the face of American hi-tech architectural glass. She thought the point was made, but still everyone and especially Megan, wanted her to do more cold work – lettering and engraving, and now, it would appear, windows as well.

She picked up the paper and looked at it. 'Megan, I don't do stained glass.' She sounded edgy, 'You know I don't do stained glass.'

Megan grinned slightly guiltily, 'I know you don't do stained glass, Ellie. He thought – and as a matter of fact I thought – you'd like the concept.'

Ellie looked properly at the sketch. It was a very rough outline of a panel of angels; they had wings but no facial features. Instead Friedhelm had blocked in all the angel faces in silvery chalk, and had hand written 'mirrors' across the top with little arrows running to the grey patches. Ellie shot Megan a knowing look.

'Fair enough. Let's see the letter.'

Megan shifted a pile of papers.

He thought, he wrote, that the idea of replacing angelic faces with mirrors so that when you looked at them they were you or your friends or even the room in which you were standing would appeal to her 'post-modernist theological bendings'. It was for a chapel he was designing for some nuns. 'Very After the Council,' he wrote and she could almost hear his ironic chuckle, 'not my usual thing, and I think not yours, but surely rather interesting, no? Especially if the margins are hidden, and the remaining glass a little bit seeing-through. For where the sisters are processing in and out of their chapel, and the angels life-size.'

'Yes,' said Ellie delighted.

'Yes?' said Megan surprised.

'Yes to the idea . . . I wonder who . . . hang on. Megan, show this to Mary will you and say to think about it.'

'But . . .'

'She's got a thing about mirrors at the moment, and I've got a thing about semi-translucency, and you've got a thing about windows so . . .'

At that very moment Mary was putting the furnaces to bed and thinking about mirrors. About those medieval unicorn tapestries and the Lady holding up a mirror – if the mirror frame was made of glass too, blown glass, reaching out beyond the mirror itself, there'd be a confusion. How could she make the boundaries invisible? Why mirrors? Mirrors, functional but not useful, and glass, necessarily glass – mirrors are always glass. Mercury – quicksilver. Mercurial. Like glass, another liquid metal – quicksilver was more like glass than glass was. Her head was humming.

'Mirror, mirror, on the wall,' she muttered.

She must not think about mirrors. Mirrors must wait. Now she was not the princess but the apprentice. Why did she spend three years at college thinking about studio work, and now she was in the studio she could only think about experimental stuff? She felt irritated at herself. She went on with the necessary and impossible task of sweeping the lake of glass splinters which scattered across the floor back into an orderly mountain beside the bucket, near the door.

In the office, Ellie stared at the sketch and said with a flicker of mixed excitement and irritation, 'Just show her, Megan. See if it does anything for her.'

It was only when she noticed Megan's quizzical expression that Ellie realised she had asked Megan to ask Mary's opinion on a design question. Why had she done that? Was that what she wanted? She knew she had been thinking about the angels, not the glass. It was not semi-translucency she had 'a thing' about, it was wings. For a shimmering glimpse of angel feathers, semi-translucent and refracting light, she had moved the whole workshop forward in a new direction: she had given a new significance to Megan's architectural ambitions; she had formalised Mary's capacity to originate work for them all; she had opened a door on new work of her own; she had, even though neither Megan nor Hugo could possibly know it, shifted her own best-kept secret out of the privacy of her head and into the bright public arena of the studio. She glanced again at the sketch, the strength of her commitment making her nervous, and then shied away quickly. 'Poor Hugo, this is a bore for you. I am sorry. We'll be off now.'

Ellie and Hugo strolled towards the river, trying to pretend it was really summer rather than early spring and that they could sit outside and watch the barges on the Thames while the sun struck boldly against the water and fractured into dances of light.

Tell me about the Victoria & Albert then; I didn't quite get what Megan was saying,' Hugo said.

'Oh it's nothing . . .' and then almost immediately, 'you know the glass gallery?'

'We went to the opening,' Hugo reminded her.

'Oh yes. Well, they've just notified us that they're putting a dish of mine they bought a couple of years ago into the permanent display, into the contemporary case.'

'Wonderful,' he said. It did sound wonderful to him: he could imagine taking his mother when she came to town and showing her – 'You know my friend, Héloïse Macauley; look – she made that.' And his mother, who did not really like Ellie, would be very impressed. 'My son . . .' she would say at her WI meeting, 'we had a lovely weekend; we went to the Victoria & Albert Museum to see this glass bowl that a woman I know, a friend of his, has made. She's very famous.' Her friends would be stirred to a prickle of envy at her glamorous life, which might compensate for the fact that the son in question was a . . . you know . . . a homosexual. His mother used all the compensations she could find; what was strange was how she could not acknowledge that there were now more compensations than griefs.

Ellie smiled contentedly. 'It's better than you think, actually; because now they'll display stock pieces in the craft shop there, and then I – I mean, then Megan – will be able to charge more for the pieces everywhere.'

'Even more,' he said. 'That's great.'

He still found it difficult to believe just how much an Ellie Macauley piece could cost. She gave her work to her friends with a sort of casual bashfulness which made it hard to remember. It did not look as though he was going to have to do too much consoling after all.

'Did Megan also tell you I'm exhibiting in Tokyo next year?'

'No. Really? That's neat.'

'Not till the autumn. Do you want to come?'

'So, so. I'd rather go to New York with you in July.'

'Sorry.'

'Why not?' he asked. She always took someone with her when she travelled; it was both gift to them and a succour for her – Hugo was never sure which came first.

'I'm taking Robbie.' There was a pause. 'Do you mind?'

'Jealous, you mean?' but he laughed. 'I'm jealous that he's going to New York, not jealous of you taking him.'

'He's sick Hugo, he's getting sick. It might be his last trip.'

'I know.'

Now, and over and over again, they held hands and walked

in silence. They were both weary of, even bored by, sickness. He wanted to go to New York, he wanted Robbie not to be ill. He was an AIDS professional and sometimes it stuck in his gullet. He made a living and other people died. He did not often let it upset him; he was good at what he did and it was useful and he did it gladly and well. More often he got fretful. He hardly knew Robbie Portland, his name and a few drinks, parties, one night of good but uneventful sex, and that made no difference. Ellie, he thought almost crossly, was too open to people and therefore was too touched by disaster. She did not have to be.

'If he isn't too tired,' Ellie said.

'Yes,' said Hugo.

It was too chilly to sit out really and they went inside the pub; it was still early and the bar was fairly empty. He drank beer, she drank white wine. She always bought the first round, because she was richer than he was, and they might not have a second; they no longer had to talk about it. So he found them a table while she went to the bar.

Now she had laid aside work, she could feel the weight of the day. She remembered it was her daughter's birthday, and with that remembered too the extraordinary joy of the morning twenty-six years ago and the equally extraordinary misery of Stephanie's departure fifteen months ago. She wished she could imagine how it was for Stephanie in the jungle and she wished she herself had behaved better. 'I was only trying to protect her,' she told herself, but was too honest for that to work. At Mass that morning she had cried, real tears of sorrow and guilt. Now she was tired and sad.

She tucked the change into the back pocket of her jeans, picked up the glasses and turned to carry them to the table. Rearranging her features into a cheerful smile, she placed the pint on the table and said, 'I've got a present for you. It's by Dorothy Parker.' Sitting down, she grinned and quoted:

'My candle burns at both ends;
It will not last the night;
But ah, my foes, and oh, my friends—
It gives a lovely light!'

He was delighted. 'Write it down, write it down now,' he demanded.

'You aren't just a decadent, you're a conceited decadent.'

'Yep.'

'And self-satisfied.'

'Go on.'

'And smug.'

'And a masochist,' he said, 'just keep going. I love talking about me. It's my favourite thing.' They were laughing.

'Narcissist.'

They loved to tease each other, especially in public. They enjoyed their combined flamboyance, particularly when it made other people nervous.

'Funnily enough I've got one for you too.' From his bag he fished out a white T-shirt; unfolded she saw the front was simply printed FAG-HAG in large red letters.

'And when am I meant to wear this?'

'To lunch with Judith.'

They both laughed. 'Thank you,' she said.

Emboldened he remembered something he had wanted to ask her for ages. 'Ellie,' he said, 'you know when you're blowing, when the glass is still on the stick and it's beginning to get stiff, and you have to stroke it. Do you find that as sexy as I do?'

She got the point. 'No,' she said shortly.

Then she relaxed suddenly and smiled, 'No, unlike you I don't see sexual metaphors *everywhere*. I tend to see it more technically, to be too engaged with the glass as glass.'

She sipped her wine, and flexed her fingers thinking through

13

the action. 'That's not quite right. Sometimes, not when I'm doing it, but when I'm thinking about it I see it more as a baby's head: that magical roundness, you know, delicate and tough.'

'I still think it's like an erection.'

'You would.'

Theirs was not a simple nor untested friendship. When they had met over ten years ago it had been at the bedside of a dying friend. In the first weeks they had been necessary relief for each other; leaving Mark's flat, weary, they had gone places they could laugh together, a sort of frivolous buoyancy to set against the pain. But at the very end, and not entirely by coincidence, they had sat for eight hours together waiting for Mark to die. Afterwards he had held her while she howled like a banshee; and she had held him while he drank himself sick and sprawled vomiting on his bed. Then they were friends.

'Ellie's Walker,' her women friends called him – and she had many others.

'Hugo's Patroness,' his friends called her, Hugo's moment of self-indulgence, his provider of treats.

She took him to restaurants he would not be able to afford and he took her to louche bars she could not otherwise have entered safely. She took him travelling with her and he introduced her to raffish company, to a wild, an uninhibited sexuality which she wanted to know but did not want to participate in.

For his thirtieth birthday present she had given him a surprise trip to Istanbul; a magical seventy-two hours, a ridiculous amount of which they had spent riding up and down in the lift at the Peira Palace Hotel – lounging on the antique sofa of the wrought iron cage, like budgerigars, and giggling uncontrollably with the lift boy with whom Hugo had had sex.

'You tip him,' she said when they were leaving. 'I'll give you the money but you do it. There are limits.'

Earlier they had tried to select a villa from the frou-frou selection along the waterside. 'Just for autumn; in the spring we'll stay in England for the greenness, and in high summer we'll rent a house in Italy and all our friends can visit.'

'Rent?' exclaimed Hugo. 'Can't we buy one?'

'No,' said Ellie, 'We don't need houses, we need room service. Don't be such a grown up. Houses are hard work.'

'OK,' said Hugo, 'and in winter we'll go to New York. This is after I've won the Lottery of course.' He really did buy Lottery tickets, ritually, each Saturday lunchtime and believe implicitly, and totally, every week from two o'clock until the draw that he was going to hit the jackpot.

The harem of Topkapi was like their lifestyle, too brightly coloured, complex, and crafted – all those little tiled rooms leading off each other with entrances and exits and passages for conspiracies and eavesdropping and endless gossip, sometimes with a cruel edge.

For her fortieth birthday he had given her Judith, whose price was higher than rubies.

They loved each other. The showing-off which they both found enormous fun was also a cover for an enormous tenderness.

Tonight though, there is neither audience nor impulse for them to show off. There is only a peaceful bit of evening.

'Spring is in the air,' he said, 'April is not the cruellest month. I think I shall fall in love next week. Just in time for a summer romance.'

'You say that every spring,' she reminded him.

'I like the thought of walking in Kew Gardens, hand in hand with a sweet young thing and looking at the bluebells. They match my eyes and he, the sweet young thing, will be dead impressed.'

'Rubbish. He'll notice that you, unlike him, have not been to the gym and therefore lack definition. Your eyes are not *that* blue.'

'They are,' he said.

'Nah,' she mocked him, 'like my hair; it's not that red.'

She asked Hugo, in detail, about Robbie's eyes, knowing he would know, knowing that he would tell her, straightforwardly and precisely, however bad the news was.

'He won't be good at being blind,' she said.

'It takes a while,' he comforted her; a strange comfort because he was really saying that Robbie would quite likely be dead before he was blind.

'I'm going to Glasgow next week,' he told her.

'Training?'

'No – organising. Alliance constructing. I'll be there about four nights.'

'Those cute kids in their tiny kilts?'

'No that was Edinburgh; these are more earnest and left-wing homosexuals. They're worried about Ecstasy and Poppers and clubs and taking responsibility.'

'It sounds high minded, if dull.'

'No, it's good. Very good. Anything is better than a movement whose self-defining activity is getting off your tits on dubious cocktails every Friday and not rejoining the human race until Monday afternoon.'

'You're getting old.'

'I am not. When you get old you start campaigning for homosexual marriages and gays in the military.'

'Yes, you are. No reason why you shouldn't turn respectable of course, when you're nearly thirty . . .'

She did not complete the sentence. He lied regularly about his age, and she knew it.

He laughed. 'I'm not turning respectable,' he said. 'I'm a Bad Boy, an urban slut, and don't you forget it.'

'Maybe. But I'll tell you what you really are – you're a boundary transgressor,' Ellie said. 'What turns you on, in the end, isn't sex at all, it's going beyond, beyond what is acceptable, beyond yourself.'

'I prefer Explorer, to "boundary transgressor",' Hugo replied, catching her idea, as he often did, 'or Pioneer.'

'And after you I suppose come the settlers, the cowboys who think the West is still wild, who think they are bad when they're really only naughty. They apply to the land licensing agents: want the law on their side.'

'And what are you, kemo sabi?'

'God,' she said, 'something much worse, tourist I suppose. A spy. A gatekeeper.'

'You're mixing the metaphor.' He was not going to indulge her self-pity.

Patsy was at home with her husband and children, cooking tea.

Robbie was propped up in his hospital bed being teased by Sue, a nurse he knew too well.

Megan was opening the door to the sixteen-year-old daughter of some friends of hers whom she had promised to coach for her A-level history exams: she still liked teaching, though not as much as she liked running Ellie's business.

Mary was still in the studio. The glass sweeping was an endless task, but she had stopped doing it, and was wandering about, fiddling with tools and instruments, and thinking about glass and mirrors. She wanted to be the princess not the sorcerer's apprentice. Boldly she sat at Ellie's bench and dreamed the studio into her own future one. It was identical to this space at first and then she noticed that outside she had substituted hills and woods for back-lane garages. Inside, she had shifted the annealing oven across the floor so that there was space for a raised dais with a shabby *chaise longue* on it, and it was fenced off so the baby could play, and her lover could watch her and watch the baby. At this point she became conscious that the vague lover had the most extraordinary long red hair, frizzed and fading a little. She stopped herself abruptly, got up from the bench, completed her closing-up chores in a most business-like way, and slammed out of the studio.

Hugo and Ellie left the pub. They walked together as far as their obvious routes made sense of. They stood there briefly; the light was fading into blue.

'Will you be OK?' Hugo asked her.

'Yes, bless you.'

'We were meant to talk about Steph.'

'No, you meant to talk about Steph. I meant to avoid any such thing.'

'Write to her, Ellie.'

'I can't.'

Hugo would have pushed on but suddenly he coughed slightly. There was a pause, almost awkward. They both knew why. He had been coughing for months. Shortly after Christmas he had caught a bad cold, and afterwards his cough would not go away. Their mutual determination to ignore the cough made any further conversation more or less impossible.

Ellie knew she must not ask him if he was all right. Early in their friendship she used to say 'Take care' whenever they parted, at the end of phone chats or after evenings out. It was a casual remark with little meaning.

'Don't say that,' he had said one night. 'I don't want to take care, I want to have adventures.'

Now into the pause created by their different but identical privacies, Ellie offered a kiss, and said, 'Well goodbye for now. I'll ring. Have fun.'

He grinned knowingly, and gave her a hug. She walked away from him southwards towards her house in Blackheath, and disappeared into the blossoming blue evening.

He watched her. He loved watching her walk: there was a physical toughness about her body, quite other than sexy. She said it was something all glass blowers had, 'not strength, toughness, we have to be able not just to take the heat, but to love it, like being a dancer, that sort of physical'. When she disappeared round a corner at the end of the street, he turned eastward. Alone he moved extremely fast, chasing his shadow which flowed out in front of him along the pavement. He was always in a hurry, always moving on to the next thing, curious, impatient, governed by a driving energy.

Ellie walked home more slowly. The city really was turning towards spring she thought with pleasure, and here in residential south London the early blossom was opening on the cherry trees along the tidy streets. She was tired; she thought about the V & A and how pleased she was, how delighted Megan was and how entirely and straightforwardly proud of her Henry would be. He would perhaps boast about her to his cronies. Well, why not? She had boasted to Hugo after all. And she did not give the same credit to Henry's achievements, not that simple affirming delight. She must try harder. Even this mild tweak of guilt caused her to think of Stephanie. What could she write:

> *darling Stephanie,*
> *when you were little your head was as round, as smooth, as silky, as malleable, and as fragile as hot glass; but I thought I could caress it without getting burned – I was wrong,*
> *much love, Mummy.*

No. Just a post card:

> *Dear Stephanie,*
> *Happy birthday. It is springtime. Here. What is it like in the jungle? How are the monkeys?*
> *Please write.*
> *Love Mummy.*

She could not.

She pulled her thoughts free and tried to turn them to work. Why could she not manage those bloody Venetian canes? Why the hell did she want to anyway? It was exactly the sort of pretty trick she despised, as opposed to the solid and pure effect she usually strove for. But the fusing had worked . . . and where *had* she put that little cube? It had been enough effort for so small a product without losing it . . . the fusing had worked, and surely the canes could. Must be made to. It was a technical challenge, but also . . . Holding air, holding light, colour inside the glass that was interesting – and bringing blowing and fusing together, and such a strong Venetian tradition, to take that and move it away from the fragile prettiness, into heavier glass, that was what she wanted, old technology for modern effect . . . and Patsy would like it. It was comfortable having Patsy in her head, solid and diligent. Ellie was dependent on her. And on Megan. She was dependent on them and they knew that and liked it, and liked it better than if everyone praised and acknowledged them. She admired them both and loved them even. Patsy and Megan, and Mary; dear God she had a good gang. She planned to make gratitude for them her own Mass Intention next time she went – and knew with a certain wry self-mockery that she wouldn't. She would be praying for Stephanie, or for some friend in trouble or danger.

And immediately she lost these gentle and pleasurable thoughts, and remembered Robbie. He'd be all right. She ought to have gone to visit him though, straight after work instead of loafing about in the pub with Hugo. Of course he would be all right. This time. She'd ring him, she'd ring him tonight, as soon as she got home. Then she thought about Stephanie again, twelve thousand miles away and working under the light of different stars. And the sadness and the sense of failure returned, just as she reached her house.

Ellie and Henry's house was charming. Sometimes the charm got on her nerves. Despite her best efforts, over the years, she had failed to eliminate all elements of 'sweet' and 'pretty'. One could not be a glass blower, a *good* woman glass blower within the British tradition and not be afraid of the lurking prettiness, of dainty decoration rather than hard form. Perhaps, she sometimes thought, it was her fears for her work that had led her to fix any tendencies towards the merely pretty firmly in her house. She rather liked this theory, but knew it was not true: in Henry's house she was never quite a grown-up. Although her brain brought her technical and aesthetic competence to the house, some inner-lurking teenage self constantly took over her decorating schemes, so that she decorated each room to the dictates of an intellectually sophisticated and unusually well off teenager trying to please Daddy. None the less the house was successful; it suited Henry's and her life together. Now it welcomed her comfortably as she opened the green front door and crossed the polished wooden floor of the hall.

'Ellie?' a voice called from further inside.

'Me,' she responded, walking through the sitting-room and into the dark green and scarlet kitchen where the last of the sun still dappled attractive shadows through the little panel of stained glass that ran along the top of the wide window.

Henry was making himself a cup of coffee.

'Good day?' he asked, turning towards her with his usual friendly smile, holding the cafetière. 'Want some of this?'

'So so,' she said. 'Do you remember my friend Robert Portland? Tall, fair, worked for Hammersmith borough? Never mind. He's in hospital.'

'I'm sorry,' said Henry kindly, but a little vaguely as he tried to calculate which of Ellie's phalanx of young, tall, fair men she was talking about. 'You must be exhausted,' he added.

He had decided before she got home that he was not going

to mention Sephanie's birthday. He kept himself always a little distanced from her sadness and guilt: he knew too much about it, as a distinguished psychiatric consultant. He was a good manager, took care of his own carers, but always he held himself a little bit away from grief: there was too much in his life. She subdued her own disappointment as he poured her coffee from the cafetière into the large French pottery cup, and exclaimed with new animation, 'But the good news is I'm going to get exhibited in the V & A. That big chunky dish they bought three years ago, they're putting it into the open collection. Megan's fixed it.'

'Well done you. And I bet she didn't. Megan may be all sorts of wonderful things, but they don't display stuff in the collections just because they're terrified of people's office managers.' There was a pause in which she could see him being complacently pleased for her. He was always proud of her achievements though after all these years he remained slightly surprised by her successes.

'How's the baby with the glass blower's physique.'

'Don't mock. She's damn good actually, though opinionated. And I rather like her.'

'Nice bod.'

'Henry!' but she did not protest much, she seldom did; sometimes she thought he was provoking her when he said things like that and she was scoring points by refusing to be provoked. 'She's a lesbian.'

'Of course.'

Ellie wondered whether he meant *of course* she was a lesbian because that was the sort of person that Ellie would employ; or if he meant *of course* he was sufficiently sensitive to have gathered this from his single, brief meeting with Mary. There was a pause.

She remembered her commitment to wifely affirmation and said, 'How's the hospital then?' breaking the silence at exactly the same moment as he said, 'You haven't forgotten I'm out tonight, have you?'

He said, 'Fine,' replying at exactly the same moment as she said, 'No of course not.'

It did not seem to matter. They moved through the ground rules and the vacuums of their conversation with well-practised grace.

Next Henry said, 'Must run. I'll see you later maybe; don't wait up.' He planted a casual kiss on her neck; but she, acutely remembering Stephanie, turned round and for a brief moment leant against him.

'Cuddle? Please.'

'Sure thing, honey,' he said in a fake American accent.

He gave her a quick squeeze and left the kitchen. She wanted comfort, he wanted not to be there. She wondered if he had forgotten, or was choosing to pretend he had forgotten, that it was Stephanie's birthday. She turned her mind quickly to a pleasant evening alone; she would, she thought, have some soup and a bath and a chat with Judith on the telephone.

She heard Henry in the hall organising himself to depart. She sagged against the limed oak dresser and sipped her coffee, waiting without impatience for the front door to close behind him, for the solitariness to flood warmly over her. After he opened the door there was an expectant pause that went on just too long. She heard him come back down the passage. The kitchen door opened and he popped his face around it, an odd sort of gesture for so dignified a face to make.

'Oops, nearly forgot. Your brother phoned. About five-ish. Can you give him a ring?'

He did not give her time to respond; the face disappeared, his shoes marked out even footsteps down the hall and the front door shut behind him.

'Shit!' said Ellie.

She wondered crossly if he had remembered all along and

did not want to have to listen to her complaints. Even as she wrapped herself around this idea with some pleasure she knew it was not true. She wanted to be angry with someone, fierce and free to compensate for the deep cringing inside her, banishing all thoughts of musing and pleasure. But if something had happened to her mother, Alan would have told Henry, and Henry would have told her, would not have shambled out to play bridge leaving her an orphan. Perhaps Alan had remembered Stephanie's birthday, she thought, racking herself on her own meanness and lack of family feeling. She had to snigger a bit at this blatant attempt to guilt trip herself. Alan would not have remembered and, if he had, the last thing in the world he would do would be to ring her up to commiserate, sympathise or, indeed, express any emotion whatsoever.

'I will have a glass of wine,' she told herself holding herself together, 'I will have a glass of cold, dry Chablis, a delight that Alan would disapprove of – not of the drinking so much as the price, the extravagance. How did she know what Alan would think anyway? She had not seen him in four years and then only briefly on a cold forecourt of a crematorium after the cold service for the cold uncle who had died. It was not fair of her to project on to him such meanness, such lack of understanding. But she did not need to see Alan daily to know that he would indeed disapprove of drinking *premier cru* Chablis on her own in her kitchen. She felt guilty enough, however, not to need this extra titbit.

'I will have a glass of wine. I will take a glass of wine into the sitting-room and drink it comfortably and then I will ring Robbie to see how he is, and then I will ring Judith for a chat, and *then* I will phone my brother.' No, she would phone the hospital, then her brother, and then Judith – for medicinal purposes. Oh damn, damn and shit. Whatever he wanted, she knew only that she would not like it.

She had a glass of wine, bracing herself. She rang Robbie's

ward, but he was sleeping; she left an affectionate message with a sigh of relief. She had to go upstairs to find her address book for Alan's phone number. It had an absurdly long code. The first time she dialled she got the long drawn out number-unobtainable tone and she felt her heart soar, but she was not fooled, and had to dial again.

'Hello.'

'Betty? Ellie here.' There was a silence. 'Héloïse,' she said firmly, 'Henry says that Alan rang. Can I speak to him, please?'

'He rang you ages ago. Henry said you'd be back before six.'

'Yes? Well I got delayed. Work. I'm sorry. How are you?'

'I'm fine,' said Betty carefully, as though looking for sinister traps in Ellie's question.

'How are the children?'

'Just fine. And Stephanie?'

'Oh, fine. I mean she was fine when I last heard from her. The post is a bit complicated out there. You can imagine.' She could hear herself becoming girlie and gushing in the face of her sister-in-law's frosty disapproval, and her own blatant dishonesty, but she was not going to expose so much as a chink in her armour to the enemy.

'Good,' said the disapproving Betty. 'Good. Well, it'll be Alan you're wanting, not me, so we mustn't stand here gossiping all night. Nice talking to you.' Ellie thought she could feel Betty's relief as she turned her face away from the receiver.

'Alan,' she hear Betty calling, 'it's your sister.'

There was a long pause. Alan had doubtless been filling his time with some important activity and would need to demonstrate, by keeping her waiting, that it was somehow typical of her to ring at such an inconvenient moment. She felt, rather than heard, the phone being picked up.

'Nelly,' he said, 'how are you keeping?'

It was not just the name, although that did not help. Did not help at all. She had left her old name, along with so many other things, many of them far more loved, when she had fled south over thirty years ago. But it was not just the name: Alan was a headmaster now, headmaster of the school where she had been so miserable. She could hear the dominie, the man who wanted to keep the tawse, who thought a taste of it would sort her out. Her father, reincarnated in her brother. It chilled her.

'Alan,' she said, 'long time no hear.'

'That's not my fault, Nelly. How are you?'

'Oh fine, and you?' *Damn, bloody, hell*, she muttered under her breath, as though these ancient naughtinesses could keep her safe now. She could feel the hair on the back of her neck pulling itself into the tight plait that her mother had always hoped, and hoped in vain, would 'calm it down'. Another daughterly failure to score against her, that her hair, despite all efforts, tangled wild in the wind, 'wanton' her mother had called it, and once, in a fit of cold anger, 'a red devil's snare'.

As she sat there, cold wine glass in her hand, she remembered a carving she had once seen in California. Some nameless sculptor had created, probably unwittingly a variation on Holbein's *Death and the Maiden*. But here the redwood Father Time was not attempting to abduct or rape the modest young woman. He stood calmly behind her plaiting down her hair.

She knew what Alan wanted now and her breath felt as cold as her drink.

'Betty says your kids are well?'

'Yes. Robbie will do his Highers this summer.' Another Robbie; she preferred her version, despite the fact that he had lesions instead of freckles. Alan described the academic progress of his three children with pride and in detail. She listened dumbly, waiting for the body blow. He did not ask about Stephanie.

When she could stand it no longer she said, 'And how's mother?'

'Hmm, well, that's why I rang you really. No, no, don't worry,' although Ellie had given no verbal indication of profound concern, 'she's well; in fact, she's amazing given her age and everything.' Did 'everything', wondered Ellie with mounting panic, include her unfilial behaviour? 'She's very well. But . . .' even Alan had the grace to pause, 'but . . . well, you know, she can't be left really . . . it's hard on Betty . . .'

And why not on you, you sexist creep? But she was dumb as a sheep before its shearers.

. . . needs a break . . . time for a holiday . . . just making plans . . . when term ends . . .

No, no, no.

. . . a week or two . . . Nelly, be fair, she's not Betty's mother . . .

'I have to go to New York; I've got an opening.' Bad mistake, Ellie Macauley, she told herself; New York and a reference to her work in one sentence. Uppity woman – looking after her mother for a fortnight should sort her out.

'Pick your dates, Nelly, we'll fit in round them.'

'Alan, send her to a hotel; a nice break by the sea.'

'She hates being away from home, it upsets her.'

'What about care in the community?'

'She's not ill . . .' he had nearly said 'enough' but caught himself just in time; this almost made her smile. Almost. They, Alan and Betty had practised all this, she realised, and it gave her a tiny flicker of power. She could hear Betty within Alan's voice. Betty did not want a solution, a sensible arrangement. She wanted to punish Ellie, for being rich and beautiful and appearing on television last winter.

'OK, get her a nurse, a companion, whatever.'

'Nelly, we're not made of money.'

'Alan, damn it, I'll pay.'

She shouldn't have said 'damn', it put the balance of power back in his hands.

'We don't want Henry's money; we want you to do your share, that's all.'

'My money,' she said, but she could hear that he did not believe her; he would think this was some sort of feminist assertion about sharing, a totally unjustified assertion in Alan's world-view. He knew all about male headship in the Lord Jesus. She was tempted to tell him how much she had made in the last tax year, but he probably wouldn't believe that either.

'It wouldn't work. You know she hates strangers. She'd love to see you, anyway. It's been a long time. You're her daughter, Nelly.'

She did not believe that. She believed you claimed your own family: you pretended, in the older sense of the word: to claim, to lay hold on.

'That's not what she said the last time, Alan, and you know it. You stood by and listened while she told me that I was no daughter of hers and she never wanted to see me again.'

'Nelly, come on; that was years ago.'

'She hasn't let me know if she's changed her mind.'

'She's an old lady, Nelly, she's a stubborn old lady, I agree.' Ellie could hear the pride in his voice; for him his mother was a 'character'; in her obduracy, and wilfulness, even in her malice, he saw a sort of magnificence, and deep under everything else, Ellie envied him. 'But she loves you, Nelly; she knows we're asking you and seems really pleased about it. Quite apart from it being your turn, and we want a break and all that, there's also the point that she's old. I can't bear to tell her you've refused, just point blank refused. She won't go on for ever and you have a chance of reconciliation, you know you'd feel better, later . . . if . . . when . . .'

So now it was a favour to her. He would be doing her a favour by letting her come and hang around the old witch while he went on a boating holiday in the Norfolk Broads. She dared herself to say 'No.' To say it boldly, firmly, definitely, absolutely. She opened her mouth and nothing came out.

Alan was not stupid. He sensed her silence, her vulnerability, and said quickly, 'I've sprung this on you, Nelly. I'm sorry, I'm sure. Look, don't say anything now. Just think about it. Ring me. No, I'll tell you what: you've paid for this so I'll ring you. I'll give you a call in a week or so, and we can discuss the details then. OK?'

And what else could a reasonable person do except agree to so reasonable a proposition? Or if not exactly agree, then at least be taken to have consented? His perfunctory enquiries after Henry's and her healths were, as they both knew, minimal necessities before he could say goodbye, put down the phone and go and report back to Betty.

I bet, Ellie thought, from the depths of her beautiful wing chair, I bet they keep the phone in the hallway, in a draughty corner. I bet they have a telephone table, with a Dralon-covered seat, and a little drawer with a fake brass knob to keep the directories in. I bet Betty wipes the phone with a damp cloth, a cloth damp with disinfectant, every morning, in case of germs.

She tried to let her superiority strengthen her. It did not altogether work. They had refused to let their Robbie stay in her house when he had come through London on his way to a school-organised French-exchange holiday last year. They had made sure that she knew this. Betty had rung to tell her that they were finding him a hotel to stay in near Gatwick. Despite the expense, they were running no risks with her morals and other viruses.

Laughing at their telephone table was small comfort.

You don't have to go, Ellie Macauley. You can ring him back and say you are very sorry, your offer to pay for a nurse still stands if they want it, but that you yourself are not going to go all the way to bloody Ayrshire, where even in August it will be cold, cold and grey. You don't have to go.

And suddenly, infuriatingly, she remembered with complete clarity the long ten days when they had thought that Stephanie would die; when the tiny beautiful limbs were so shaken and shattered by the curse of God, the house of demons and darkness. And who had been constant, loving, supportive, quiet, present, prayerful? The old witch herself. Down the path that Ellie had walked when Henry could not, or would not, follow, but her mother had. Dour, upright as ever, her mother had sat in the over-bright children's ward, never slumping on the chair, her handbag ever on her lap, and she had kept vigil with her granddaughter. Unbending, prim, pursed-lipped, her mother had explained to Stephanie what was happening to her, had explained with such patient unembarrassed clarity that Stephanie had survived, survived with fewer scars than most of them did. Her mother, when Henry had wondered whether this was right, whether someone so young had to bear the full burden of their illness, had replied with a prissy smile, 'Plain truth is always better for the young, Henry, than dark mysteries; that is what I've always said, and until Nelly tells me otherwise that is how I shall treat her daughter.'

And she had been right; Stephanie had grown up with only the smallest tendency to treat her seizures as either powerful or tragic, without the tiniest whinge, and had learned to manage, manage well enough to persuade her university to fund her to escape from home into the dark jungle.

It was not fair. Not fair of memory, not fair of Alan, not fair of her mother to have acted so well this one time, and left her with a debt so enormous as to counterbalance all the bad, hateful, mean things her mother had done before and since.

She went out in the end, because she had to.

This was not the soothing spring walk of earlier on; it was cold now, cold and dark. She hesitated on the short flight of steps up to their door and sensed rather than saw the blossom confettiing across the street like snow. She ought not to drive;

vaguely she thought of the Chablis, on top of the wine in the pub with Hugo. She went back into the house for the car keys. She did not think where she was going, but knew soon enough – to Goose Green and the mural.

It was not a long, nor a pretty drive and although she was aware enough of the wine to keep an eye out for police cars in her back mirror she drove confidently – concentrating on that alone.

She felt the strength of her desire coming upon her. Goose Green had been one of the reasons she had consented to south London. Blake as a child had his first mystical vision at Goose Green, when south London had still been rural, when geese had indeed wandered in fields now only ghostly memories. He had seen a tree full of angels, crammed with angels as plane trees in London could be crammed with starlings, the iridescent lustre of their wings muted by the dull greenness of the broad flat leaves. He did not say what kind of tree, but he saw the New Jerusalem coming like a bride down from heaven, and 'bright angelic wings bespangled every bough'.

Bespangled. Ellie sighed, envious. She had never had a mystical vision. In her teens she had tried, she had tried very hard; tried with the passionate commitment of a teenager, beating her fists against the bar of heaven, and in vain. Later as a student she had tried the other ways as well – hash and magic mushrooms, though finding herself too cowardly for acid. Then she had discovered glass blowing and for years had forgotten to bother. Now sometimes she wondered about Ecstasy and the Uppers that the boys used in the clubs and talked about at home. But it was a distant interest, she knew now that for her that would be cheating.

She tried to take comfort in the wisdom of Martin Buber which she had read somewhere and clung on to in the cold night, Rabbi Mendel once boasted to his teacher Rabbi Elimelekh that evenings he saw the angel who rolls away the light before the darkness, and mornings the angel who rolls away the darkness before the light. "Yes," said Rabbi Elimelekh, "in my youth I saw that too. Later on you don't see these things any more." But it was not much comfort, because she had not seen them when she was younger.

Something else, she thought bitterly, getting out of the car and wishing she had brought a warmer coat with her, something else her mother had stolen from her. Her mother and father would never have allowed an angelic visitor in their home. They scarcely allowed dreams. Time-wasting rubbish. A joyful angel would have been told to wipe its feet on the doormat, keep its wings tucked in so as not to break the china, if it had not been expelled on the spot for popish idolatry.

Damn her mother. She was not going to Ayrshire.

The wind was cold and the mural half-lit was as crude as when it was daylight. She did not need to come here to dream of a tree 'bespangled with bright angelic wings'. She walked round, lost, the excitement of coming here worn down by the cold, by her tiredness and by whispers of a foggy depression that lurked, waiting.

Then she felt the too familiar twitchy sensation just above her coccyx, followed by the odd warm glow up her spinal column and there was Angel manifesting somewhere in the region of her *corpus callosum*. Ellie found it slightly sinister that Angel located herself just there so that she could never be quite sure if she was dealing with a rational, objective, verbal perception, or an imaginative, fluid, musical one. She saw afresh Friedhelm's sketches – the angel as herself. But no guardian angel chosen by Ellie for Ellie would have remotely resembled Angel.

'You should have brought a woolly,' said Angel, in her slightly adenoidal accent, as soon as she was settled. This would normally have annoyed Ellie, but now the sense of presence brought her some relief.

'Please, Angel,' she said with unaccustomed humility.

'Please what?' said Angel in a practical bracing voice.

'Please . . . please . . . I don't know please what,' stumbled Ellie. 'Something about "sensible consolations" or mystical vision or *something*. The present comfort of God I suppose. Joy.'

'Joy is a virtue,' said Angel unsympathetically, 'you have to work on it.'

'I shouldn't feel so frustrated. It's not fair.'

'Oh grow up, Ellie,' said Angel. And then in a more kindly tone added, 'Look, you are most unlikely at present to get a mystical vision because you think you know what kind you want, which is precisely what a mystical vision isn't. And you don't need sensible consolations because as a matter of fact you get more than most people, you just don't recognise them.'

'What do you mean?'

'Well, there's me, who might well be described as a sensible consolation, and indeed whom your beloved Blake would have seen as a mystical vision . . .'

'You are not a mystical vision,' said Ellie.

'Of course I am. Or if I'm not you're psychotic . . . schizophrenic probably. You have to be clear about this. You hear my voice – you frequently complain that I'm intrusive or bossy and make you do things you don't want to – so, diagnostically, you've only got two choices: I'm either a physical manifestation of the divine glory – that is to say a mystical experience – or you have a serious psychiatric illness. Henry would probably tell you it was treatable.

'But let's not go into the theology of that now. Apart from me, you also get to work daily in the one medium which is almost impermeable to irony. It celebrates, but doesn't criticise well. Sublimity is its central concern. That has limitations, I'm not defending it, but it does mean that you aren't metaphysically starved like so many people are. And finally, this evening, as you know perfectly well, is not to do with dark nights of the soul, or the absence of glory, or anything else mystical. It's to do with ethics. And since you coped all day with your guilt about Stephanie, and your conflicts about where you stood in relation to Robbie, this is obviously about whether or not you are morally obliged to go and stay with your mother.'

Ellie snuffled childishly, weakened by being corrected correctly.

After a long silence Angel said, quite gently, 'Being loved and being known aren't, as I shouldn't need to remind you, the same thing, but they aren't that different.'

'Do I have to go?'

'You know I don't deal in ethics,' said Angel, 'not that sort anyway. You work it out.'

Ellie could only think of the long wide grey street of her home village; the low grey houses, the wind coming down the hill from a grey sky, and the utter grimness of it all.

'But I will give you something to think about,' Angel sounded quite surprised at her own generosity. 'You modern liberals are very good at the lesser of two evils argument. Admittedly you then tend to move on a little quickly to forgetting that the lesser of two evils is none the less evil. But you're always sloppy about the greater of two goods. The other of which may very well remain a good, but not, so to speak, the necessary or even desirable good.'

It was about being a grown-up, that's what it was about; about her fear of not being a grown-up, of failing to become one. Grown-ups resolved their relationship with their mothers. She had urged it on others: resolve things. 'Speak to your mother,' she had urged Mark. 'Let's call her,' she had said, 'come on, plum-drop, you'd like it really; brace yourself.' That had been a bloody disaster.

'I don't know your mother,' said Angel, 'we're not allowed to consult on that sort of thing, but do bear in mind that it is just as possible that she's a real horror, and a mean-minded manipulative old cow . . .'

Not very angelic language, Ellie thought.

'. . . and that you are as deserving of not seeing her as she is of seeing you. I'm not saying that's true, I'm saying that psychoanalysis has denied that as an option, just like sin in a wider sense, but it *might* be true. And, in any case, if you are only going to go because you think it is good for *you* to resolve your relationship then it's purely selfish anyway and you aren't going to get many Brownie badges, or days off purgatory, or whatever you're into just now for a selfish action of that kind.'

She had been a perfect Brownie, oddly enough. With more little badges than sleeve space. She had flown up from the toadstool to the Guide pack and lost interest overnight.

'There are choices,' Angel was insistent now, 'the choices are there. And, don't forget, it may not be about whether you should honour your mother, your family or not; it may be about who is your mother and your brother.'

Her mother, Alan, Betty, their Robbie. Hugo, Judith. Megan. Henry, Robbie, Angel. Mary. This guilt was just a revenant of pre-choices.

There in the cold night Ellie smiled, then chuckled. She had chosen the day the crocuses flowered.

One teenaged autumn her mother had kindly volunteered Ellie to plant the bulbs for the minister's garden. The manse was bigger than the other houses on the wide grey street. It was set back above the pavement and had a wide smooth slope of grass in front of it. Each year the slope was planted with crocuses. Ellie, fifteen, long legged, angry, lonely, had received the bulbs in bags from the minister's wife. The bags were tidily colour-coded.

Ellie had planted the white ones to read *Ave Maria*.

The yellow ones had spelled out *Viva il Papa*.

And the purple ones announced *Orate pro nobis*.

The worm had turned, the snake was loose in the innocent village, vengeance had sweetened the long winter.

As a stunt it had been spectacularly successful. What she had sown in cold anger, she reaped the following spring in glorious technicolour. The minister's fury, her mother's embarrassment, her school fellows' awe, her father's shock: rich fruits, a harvest nearly full enough to sustain her in the long desert to which she was driven.

Then just when the isolation might have grown too heavy, one of the history teachers, a junior member of staff, a woman who did not even teach her personally, had left an envelope in her pigeon hole:

Dear Helen,
If you would like to come and stay with us until you have finished your exams, you would be very welcome. Don't worry about money, if your parents are obdurate. I haven't laughed so much in years.
Yours, Megan Hamilton.

Ellie had packed her bag that night, and chosen her new family, freely and with delight.

There was no going back from such moments. Out of darkness into light. Her pretend family. When she had first introduced Henry to Megan, who had by then left teaching, left her husband and left Scotland to be an administrative secretary of great skill, Megan had said, 'I'm not sure what to call you. You're older than me, so son-out-law seems inappropriate, but I was very briefly Héloïse's teacher, and her mother, so I am warning you to treat her right.' And she had smiled her infinitely sweet smile.

'With Megan, and the Blessed Virgin Mary,' thought Ellie now, 'who needs psychological maturity?' But the cold remained; the cold of that grim village, and the cold of the April night inside her cotton shirt. Angel had apparently departed. She turned back to the car knowing that she had decided nothing, except that there was something to decide . . .

. . . And as she turned, she turns in the hold, and the wave hits, and the child stumbles forward. The ship has been out of control for hours, the great blood-red sail lowered at sunset, and the sweating oarsmen no longer needing the whip, leaning and straining for their own preservation rather than the Master Merchant's profit. But even in the dark chaos where conflicting shouts and cries, and occasional crashing of waves, and the distant boom of the breakers on the rocks, has been terrifying – even here the Master Merchant does not forget the driving of his stern purpose. He has sent the child to the hold to make sure that all the bales and boxes, the treasures of north Africa, the marketable goods, are strapped down, steady for ballast, not swinging and sliding with the pitching and tossing of his ship. The child is frightened in the hold, the enormous waters are too near; are all around, and balance is destroyed by the force of the waves. The child can feel the ship straining with passion, straining to turn and run before the storm while above the slaves, desperate and courageous, fight with the ship, fight to keep its green painted bow facing into the teeth of the storm. They lose the fight, the ship tears itself from their hands, bucking now like a wild beast in the amphitheatre, like the child's father behind the shed over the body of the whore, turning to receive the wind from the rear like the wild mares of Southern Gaul who are impregnated so and bare foals who run swifter than the wind.

As the child stands nervous in the hatchway the leather thongs around the great box of wrought-iron ware snap, audibly, and the huge box, following the passion of the wind and the ship together, leaps across the hold, carrying with it other chests and bales, and so when the big wave hits, the whole weight of the ship and the goods within it crash together, and as the wave passes laughing, the ship does not right itself into the trough that follows but wallows on its side, broken. The child stumbles forward and is thrown violently against the side beam of the hatchway and breathless, winded, unable to turn, watches as though in slow motion the boxes below spill open. There, there in the heart of darkness there is light, pale light like the moon. It is the magic stuff, the weird stone. It is ingots of glass being brought from Sidon to the glassworks in Colchester. There is gold and lapis lazuli and dark red gems, and silk; there are axe heads and spear points, burnished for the market, crashing across in front of the child and plunging almost eagerly into the rising pool of water in the lower side of the ship. And above the child, behind the child, there is screaming and then the hammer blows as the slaves' chains are smashed, for in the hot sands and the blue waters of the Master Merchant's homeland it is known that the gods will not look kindly on a man who lets another man die a slave, die bound.

The child, drawing breath from need alone, through the pain in the ribs and through the gripping fear, leans down the hold and snatches up a brick of the magic stone. It is greenish, but whether from the sea or from the darkness the child does not know. The child sees in some flash of light which is the cooking fire behind flaring as its flames are spilled into the vat of oil beside it, and in the flash the child sees deep inside the ingot an answering flash of blue flame, dazzling. The child tucks the treasure, inside the grey tunic, and then returning to the urgent business of staying alive, struggles back to the rowing deck.

The next wave breaks not under the ship but over it, and the wave after that lifts the child effortlessly, so that for one moment, suspended within the wave like a fly in amber, the child can look down on the deck of the broken ship settling settling into death like an old lady by a fireside.

And then the water is cold and the treasure is heavy and . . .

'Christ,' said Ellie, still bending down, still moving to get into her car, with the cold wind of the London night lifting the hair on her neck. 'What the hell was that?'

'Sorry,' said Angel, sounding oddly nervous. 'I'm sorry, I blundered.'

Ellie straightened up, furious, baffled, still with the fear – both the fear of the underdeck and the fear of her own fear – but Angel was descending her spinal column with unusual speed, and the straightening only made the pathway through the lumbar vertebrae easier. Ellie was left, panting, bemused, spinning on the corner of Adys Road with the Public Baths across the street and the mural leering down on her. So there really was no choice, but to bend forward again, get into the car and drive home.

She drove slowly, not now because she was afraid of the breathalyser, but because she was shocked. She could still feel the fear of the child, was still aware of huge gaps rending the precise fabric of memory. She feared, felt, knew, that she had not watched the child, but had been the child. There had been no division, no split, between the child and herself, and yet she did not know the child, not even whether it was a girl-child or a boy. It was she who had drowned and she felt her hair expecting it to be wet.

'Oh Christ,' she thought again, 'I'm turning into a crazy lady. They will lock me up and Henry will try out a range of drugs and I won't be me any more.' Then she felt the weight, the smooth weight of the glass ingot, and saw the lightning, the iridescent blue flash of oxides dancing in the core of the greenish glass. She was startled because she recognised it: she knew that glass. It was one of the green glass ingots from the cargo of a Phoenician trading ship which had sunk in Biscay in the fourth century; and was now on display in the British Museum. Important historical evidence in the history of glass, but . . . but what is that glass to her, that it makes her twentieth-century ribs ache here in a car in south London?

She was breathless from shock. It was late, she has drunk too much, it has been a long day, she is tired, she is dreaming, imagining, fantasising. She did not convince herself.

By the time she got home it was so late that it was early again – a cool grey half-light was beginning to uncover a world with form but without colour. She did not know how to do that; it was impossible with glass to have form without colour; form itself, the matter of glass sucked up colour. If, she thought, or tried to think, if one fragmented somehow – sand-blasted? – a surface just so much that it repelled colour without losing translucency, might she be able? . . . she could not pin the idea down, she was too tired. She felt as though she were the only person still awake in the whole city.

This was not true. Mary was still awake, dancing slightly maniacally in a club, watching herself with some pleasure in the mirror of another woman's eyes. Hugo was awake, all the way across London, prowling like a night cat, hunting suc-cessfully, cheerfully, for casual sex on Hampstead Heath.

Ellie parked the car carefully. She went into her peaceful house thinking with pleasure that Henry would by now be asleep, warm and centred in the middle of the bed. Much ear-lier, he too would have crept in silently, not wishing to wake her, just as she did now. She smiled sleepily but affectionately, tiptoeing past his room to her own, sensing rather than hearing his peaceful breathing.

As she curled into bed she knew that Angel was still with her, hovering quite discreetly, almost . . . guiltily. Comforted by warmth but still curious Ellie took advantage of this sheepish-ness and asked her: 'Angel, why me?'

'What do you mean?' enquired Angel.

'No one else is inflicted with a guardian angel.'

'How do you know?'

'Well, no one ever mentions it.'

'And how many people have you told about me?'

The answer of course was none. 'They'd think I was cracking up.'

'There you are then.'

'I've researched it.'

Angel subjected Ellie to a moment or two of scathing silence.

'All right then,' Ellie snapped, 'everyone has a guardian angel. In that case why have I never been aware of you before?'

'Menopause,' said Angel.

'Menopause!'

'Lots of physical changes take place in women at the climacterium, gaining consciousness of your angel may very well be one of them. We're not sure, there is a shortage of data.'

'OK, not "why me" then, but why *you*?'

'Oh don't think you would have got me if I'd had any choice; *we* are under obedience. But, if you are interested, most of my clients have been involved, one way or another, with glass. Probably because of my wings.'

'Your wings?'

'Were they to be material my wings would be made of glass; you'd like them.'

Glass wings. Ellie's stomach gave a lurch, the sort she usually associated with lust. Silent glass wings? Or sweet brittle rustlings?

'Show me,' she demanded and could hear her voice, over-excited like a small child's.

'Don't be silly. We're immaterial. Do the windows, then you might see.'

Ellie's heart shivered, a spasm of bliss.

'But of course, you're half asleep now; this may all be a dream.'

Chapter Two

Tuesday, in Ellie's studio, was the apprentice's day. Regardless of the pressure of work, Ellie tried valiantly to treat that as sacred. Occasionally, she would volunteer to come and assist, especially if she was interested in what they were doing, but it was the apprentice's day; Mary's day now.

One of the commitments that Ellie had made herself when she had left the co-operative to set up as a star on her own, was that her staff would be treated especially well. Her apprentice would be trained to desert her, to compete with her, to challenge her. It was a way of making her feel better about the person she feared she had become. Her work, for Ellie, was a need, but one she had only ever been able to feel 83 per cent good about. The other 17 per cent was stuck in old guilt and had to be propitiated. Tuesdays were part of the propitiation.

When she had graduated, she had been offered a job in America: a high profile job for one of the big commercial producers. In the States, in the sixties and early seventies, contemporary glass had been creating its energies not from a well-rooted craft tradition, but from an architectural and design need: glass that was about light and visibility; water and refraction – glorious and monumental. And there had also been tiny wild studios making it up as they went along, doing weird and wonderful things – creative, imaginative, extraordinary. What there had not been was a sustained craft tradition that linked glassworkers to ceramicists; glassworkers who were disciplined by the William Morris school, which had honoured useful-ness, were dominated by the idea of the usable, solidly lovely, domestic object. The cross-fertilisation had not been equal; American designers had attracted highly competent British-trained workers and had plaited the three filaments together. In the States glass had evolved in all of the existing traditions and had mutated further creating a new art medium.

Ellie suspected often that she should have gone to America then and imbibed that scale and energy and respect for inno-vation. She could have come back to Britain later, and within its traditions been formally innovative, been genuinely original, been great instead of very good. And, of course, if she had gone . . . Oh, God knows what would have happened but it would all have been so entirely different that it was hard to conceive the Ellie who would now exist. All she had was a growing, hurtful, certainty that the forcing weight of crafty prettiness that filled her with such painful suspicion of her own work would have been avoided for ever.

Instead she had fallen in love with Henry and married and lost her way. She had wanted to be a good glassworker. She had wanted to be a good wife. And she had wanted to be a good woman, a useful citizen of the earth and labourer in the vine-yard of the libertarian socialist revolution – which, in those complex and heady years, neither a craftworker nor a wife could be. She had felt drowned in a tide of rising guilts.

The collective had made sense in those terms. They were driven, not by the glass but by the politics of collective work-ing and it had sustained her while she had re-explored what she might do, what she might make. It eased the guilts and helped her establish an identity which she could bear to live with. But she had learned soon enough that she was actually a better glassworker than any one of the rest of them. She did not know who else had known it, or even if anyone else had cared – 'good' or 'better' being élitist concepts in which they refused to deal. They had been purist about everything except the quality of their work, while she was particular about nothing else. For a long time they had not even sold or exhibited under their individual names but always and only The Westbourne Park Studio.

Her marriage had been right for her too, but this had only reinforced her sense of inadequacy. She experienced her failure to enjoy collective working as further proof of her deficiencies. So it took her a long time to work out that she preferred the work itself to the organising of it. Collectivity was time-consuming. She had just wanted to get on with exploring glass.

She had stuck with it on principle, on ill-fitting principle, for a very long time, and her guilt increased. By the end she knew she had exploited their good will, as they sustained her through maternity, through Stephanie's illness and through her growing conviction that she needed more time, more space. They had allowed her privileges that they denied themselves. She started to command high prices, to have people insist on her, rather than the collective's, work. Teetering on the edge of collapse they had all compromised because they needed the money she was bringing in, but it made them bitter and disillusioned. Then there had been, of course, a period when her work had supported the whole ramshackle business, but she had not been able to experience that as a fair trade-off, only as a further source of guilt.

When she left the whole collective had collapsed almost immediately. Jerry had asked her for a job once. She had felt ashamed. When she told him that she only employed women she had done it partly to ease his embarrassment – afterwards it had become an immovable commitment because he would hear. She had known very soon that working in a new and different way suited her, but she was left with a pile of strange conflicts that she hardly knew how to cope with. Her guilts made her edgy, but they never quite managed to persuade her that she had made a mistake.

In becoming a good glassworker, and therefore a bad woman, it had become increasingly important that she be also a good wife. This had seemed easy because Henry was a good man. A radical psychiatrist working out of a soft Laingian discipline, he had sustained for her the visionary drive that she wanted and could only dream of. He was a prophet, a priest of the new selves who would emerge and dissolve all these dilemmas in the white heat of revolution. He was the man who understood all things, who knew the truth and she loved him and took on his convictions so entirely that she barely noticed how his changed. He was the bulwark against her childhood, and against her own lurking madness and infantility and inadequacy. It had worked for a long time, but in that time she had got older and calmer and richer and happier, even if not much less guilty.

She dealt with the guilt in little underhand ways: slightly too generous with her employees; slightly too happy to undersell – one reason why she needed Megan so badly – and to indulge her apprentices; to underrate her own earned status.

Honouring the rule that Tuesdays belonged to the apprentice was a guilt management strategy, but one that had delightful side-effects. Ellie usually spent an hour or so on Tuesday mornings working with Megan, which usually meant little more than agreeing to most of what Megan proposed; discussing the accounts that Megan had impeccably prepared and signing letters that Megan had written. Together they would work out a detailed schedule for the week, to meet the orders from craft and museum shops for the series pieces that were their bread and butter, or to find possible ways to make time and money for Ellie to work on something new. Then, briefly, she would look into the studio where Mary, to Ellie's pleasure, would be sitting at her own blowing bench – although she might well, of course, move to Ellie's undeniably more convenient one the minute Ellie was off the premises. The rest of the morning Ellie might spend upstairs polishing, finishing, wrestling in the cold glass room, or drawing. Then she would go out: to charm potential commissioners, to make contact with colleagues, gallery owners, designers, useful people, or go to exhibitions. And go out to lunch.

Ellie was a woman who lunched.

'Of course you are,' said Judith, 'we all are.'

'But . . .'

'But nothing. Anyway I want To Lunch with you.' Judith could put a capital letter at the beginning of any word she chose, just by wriggling her fabulously low and ginny voice. It was a skill that Judith used and that Ellie envied.

So at least one Tuesday a month Ellie had lunch with Judith. These lunches were quite separate from all the other times they met, chatted on the telephone, played, drank, complained, laughed, wept and went out – to the theatre, art shows, films, meals, trips, shops together – all the stuff of friendship. They called this monthly lunch their Meeting.

'One of the things it is to be a feminist, is to be in a Group,' Judith said, 'and this is our Group Meeting. It's not our fault it's so small.' Judith, of course, was allowed to be ironic even bitchy, about her own and everyone else's commitments.

Judith was Ellie's Best Friend. Their group, which met over delectable and highly alcoholic lunches, was the 'self-defining, self-affirming fag-hags' self-help group'. It had been invented for them by Hugo. It had been a fortieth birthday present from him to Ellie. He had advertised:

Fag-hags, self-defining and self-affirming, seeking support and amusement, contact Box 934. Celebration and anecdotage infinitely preferred to psycho-poop explanations. Sweet young things and other confused bunny rabbits need not apply.

He had also had to ask among his friends. About two weeks after he had placed the ad and was beginning to plough through a pile of replies ranging from the outraged to the deranged, he had met Judith at a dinner party and, while being driven home by her afterwards, late and slightly drunken, he had known by some radiant instinct that she was the very person he needed to make his little scheme work. By the week of Ellie's birthday he had found seven women – two of whom were, as Judith had caustically pointed out 'definitional confused bunny rabbits' – who were prepared at least to pretend to be a fag-hags' support group for an hour or so, and none of whom Ellie had ever heard of.

With the same difficulty and cunning as was always required to generate any successful surprise party, he had produced Ellie at the appointed time and address, and had vanished, leaving the whole thing to Judith's administrative and social skills. The evening, undeniably helped by Judith's insistence on extraordinary quantities of wine, had been a magnificent if surprising success; and quite separately, unplanned – and as Hugo would often remark wryly not necessarily desired by him – Ellie and Judith had become friends.

So Ellie woke one Tuesday, a few weeks after her mysterious encounter on Goose Green, with a warm sense of well-being and optimism: she would get up and go to Mass – a glance at the clock reassured her that there was plenty of time for a long bath first; then she would go to the studio and fall into the rhythm of the day and then, well organised and unhurried, she would cross the river and have lunch with Judith. She stretched with pleasure and listened to the sounds of her house which told her that Henry had already left for work.

Listening for him reminded her suddenly and abruptly that she had to cook that evening, that they were having people for supper. She had not forgotten, it had just not been part of her agreeable waking. It did not matter, she was basically prepared, but it meant she would have to remember all the way through lunch. It irritated her. She got up more quickly than she had planned, and went down to the kitchen where she knew coffee would be waiting, cooling but all set out for her to reheat. Henry was a man of ritual, and Ellie did not count coffee as breaking a pre-Mass fast.

She had just put the coffee into a saucepan to reheat when the telephone rang. She crossed the kitchen to pick it up.

'Ellie.'

'Robbie! How are you, pet?'

There was a pause. It went on a little too long.

'Not good, eh? Oh God, Robbie, you had clinic yesterday, didn't you? I meant to ring you last night. I'm sorry. How are the precious T-cells?' As Hugo had reassured her, Robbie had only been in hospital a few days last time. He had seemed better afterwards and she had lowered his position in her league table of people to be petted.

There was another pause. Her heart sank and his status on that secret list rose sharply, 'OK. Do you want me to guess?'

'Mouth ulcers,' he said.

She replied robustly. 'What an unspeakable bugger. What are they giving you? How bad?'

'Just beginning. It's always just beginning, some damn new thing. Just beginning. Last time they more or less said I'd be dead before I'm blind. Now they're saying I'll die of something else before I die of starvation.' He tried to laugh, and then he wavered, 'I'm so bored of it, Ellie.'

She was bored of it too. And she had taught him to speak about it like this. She had taught him to ask, bluntly and directly for what he wanted.

'Are you frantic, Ellie? Can you come and play with me?' he asked.

'Right now?'

'It would be nice.'

'Robbie . . .' then the coffee boiled. It distracted her for just too long for her to say that she really, honestly couldn't, not today. 'Yes of course, sugar lump,' she said. 'Hang on a moment.'

She grabbed the pan off the ring, although it was past drinking, and came back to the phone. 'What shall we do? I tell you what Robbie, I'm having lunch with someone later and I don't think I can get out of it, but I'll come up as soon as I'm dressed and we'll . . .'

'I want to look at something. Let's go . . . I know, can we go to the Victorian & Albert and look at the fashion bit, in the basement? I love it.'

'Not too tiring?'

She meant it affectionately, but she knew at once that he was annoyed. 'I can still stagger,' he said.

'Fine, I'll see you there. Ten-thirty?'

'Beside the green cloche hat booth,' and rang off.

The peaceful, well-organised day vanished. She felt put upon, and then mean and selfish. She slammed some more coffee into the saucepan and wondered why she did not get a microwave. She would have to ring Megan. Lucky that Robbie was one of the people Megan liked, that would make it easier. Lucky she had brought the fish that they were going to have for supper yesterday, that would make it easier. And she did not have to cancel Judith because whatever he said and however annoyed he got, a trip to the V & A would exhaust Robbie and he would need to go home before lunchtime. She should not feel glad about that, she thought crossly.

Bath or Mass? She looked at the clock. Shower and Mass, just. But her body had wanted a bath. She would, she calculated, go to Mass first, then come home for a quick shower and a chat with Megan. She could sense the space of the morning getting tight around her, squeezing her in.

But, and she managed to be grateful, the Mass itself stood solid against the marching pressures. There was a well-guarded secret to Ellie's inner life. Some critics read a religious inspiration into her work, into the way that she buried colour deep inside her glass, so that it would flash unexpectedly, catch fire from tiny movements of light and angle, but that always made her laugh because really what she most liked about institutional religion was that it was pretty tedious.

Perhaps, she thought wryly, on her knees, as the canon droned on from the altar, perhaps Angel was right, perhaps her work met her metaphysical needs so thoroughly that she did not really even want glimpses of heaven and meaningful eucharistic experiences. She truly desired this slight absence of mind, this quiet drift, this essentially known place.

This was not quite acceptable to either the intensely religious or the secular disbelievers. For them she presented a solidly intellectual faith, lit by a certain high camp flamboyance which was both self-protective and loyal to her Church. Outside of the rites, her faith was flashy, public; she made sure it was mentioned in any interviews; she knew lots of clergy and fed them well and talked to them intensely, about her soul and their emotions; she gave generously to obviously Catholic charities; and she was, in as much as it mattered, a well-known and articulate supporter of advanced post-conciliar Catholicism. But that was not the point: the point was this mild boredom, a blessed and almost certain reward for forgoing her bath to be here. She had noticed that Angel never came to Mass – or if she did at least did not manifest herself; this seemed odd to Ellie, surely angels should use these open-hearted slow moving moments?

So virtuous did it make her feel indeed that, returning home, she allowed herself a bath after all. She took the telephone into the bathroom and dialled the office while she lay in the hot water, and nothing urgent had happened and Megan was in control, and Patsy and Mary had arrived and were in the studio, and they must talk sometime about the Walton Street Gallery, and Megan was concerned for Robbie rather nicely and wanted Ellie to explain about the new problem, and it was all gentle and lovely and getting later and later. Her sense that the world had stolen this day from her increased, making her clumsy and panicked. The clumsiness inevitably reduced her efficiency and she left the house knowing perfectly well that she was going to be unbelievably lucky to be on time for Robbie.

Waiting for the bus raised her anxiety further and her irritability rose with it. Whatever had induced her to agree to meet Robbie about as far across London as it was possible to go? And in a place where there was never anywhere to park? If he wanted museums, why had she not lured him down here to the exquisite scientific instruments at the Observatory, the immaculate and complex brasses and leathers generated, properly, out of the great optimistic project of measuring the heavens? But if it was a long and complicated journey for her to go north and west like this, for him to come as far south and east would be no simpler and much more tiring. She sighed, tried to settle to the view of London, and abide in patience because there was no other choice.

And she did love London; it never ceased to delight her. As the bus lumbered over London Bridge, Canary Wharf shot up the skyline, and the old storehouses and wharves of the south bank of the Thames responded with dignified smiles. Tower Bridge, from this angle, always looked faintly preposterous, too many sight-lines, too many attempts at dignity. She had never seen it opened, she realised with a sort of longing.

And in that half-formed desire there was suddenly another. Just as there had been at Goose Green . . . a moment of total

longing; a longing to be warm and safe, to be dry and warm
and safe, to be warm and dry and not frightened and breathless, to be dry and warm and at home. In the night, it is, and
she is running north still wet from the long swim across the
lagoon, her fourteen-year-old body cold with the water, warm
with the haste and fear of her running. Her tunic clamps itself
wetly to her half-formed breasts and she is terrified. But she has
seen Mr Green's beautiful drawings, goblets so solid and bright,
bright with lead they say, with red lead which makes the glass
brighter than diamonds and heavy.

She has to go north – the Murano glassworkers are the best
in the world and she is one of them, but their glass is thin, brittle, foolish. Inside the tunic, in a waxed bag she can feel against
her naked chest the papers she has stolen, the papers with the
pictures, and she must run, for she is a Venetian Apprentice and
in exchange for the privileges of glassmakers there is the prison.
Free prisoners they are, all the glassmakers of the island in the
lagoon. She may not leave Venice, and she will never go back.
The winter sun will rise over the flat water and the city will
shine, shine gold and white in the early sun and she will never
see it again. The tears that form are warmer than her sweaty
face and colder than her wet body and she does not care.

She has drawn out long threads of Venetian *cristallo*, a glass
more pliable than anyone has ever made since before the world
began; highly-wrought, elaborate, magical. It will take colour
like sugar icing, and still be so fine that the light comes through
the colour like the reflections in the water of the canals of the
Republic in the sea. Her glass, the glass her father teaches her to
make, can twist and curl and contort and baffle and amuse; it is
pretty, witty, clever glass. But now she has seen Mr Green's
drawings of the glass they want in England. Heavy. Solid. Cut
like jewels are cut. Not playful, exuberant, airy, coloured, but
serious, and so clear, so clear, so clear that it must be engraved,
cut, pointed, cold-worked or else you might not see it, but

through it, like the Sacred Host through which the holy can see straight into the heart of God in Heaven. Glass like that.

Her father says this glass gets sick and dies. He says there is a wickedness in it, because Protestants make it, and God's wrath is upon it; inside the glass there is a sickness, and shadows work their way, not into the glass, but out from its invisible frozen heart. Glass sickness, her father says, and serve them right for trying to compete with the glass of Venice, the glass of St Mark the Evangelist. Her father says this glass gets sick and dies, but she does not believe him.

Her father says it is ignoble glass; that it is for the northern bourgeoisie, not for princes and nobles, not for gods and angels, but for fat businessmen who eat raw beef, and do not know that all glass is made in honour of the Virgin, the Holy Mother. She does not believe him.

She does believe him and it does not matter. It will be heavy in her hand and the walls will be thick but still perfectly clear. The glasses will be heavy, stable, dignified. It will be glass you can hold, turn in your hand, turn while you talk and think, turn heavy, filling your hand so that the weight of your thoughts, and of your wines will be resting there, solid with meaning.

She wants . . . ah, she wants, she wants so much to make that glass, and to be free, free of the binding traditions and free of the stultified frivolity. Heavy as lead and bright as diamonds. So – wet, cold, sweaty and scared – she runs; she runs through the night, her face towards the mountains, and the pictures of the glasses that Mr Green has sent, sent with stern letters saying 'Heavier, thicker, stronger, more, more solid. More.' She will cross the whole world, wet and frightened, to find the man who can make glass look like this and offer him all the skills of the lagoon, all the secrets of Murano and he will show her how to make his glass and she – when she is no longer cold and frightened – will be happy and beautiful and rich.

But now she is only wet and cold and frightened.

She is . . . she is Ellie, sitting on the top of a London bus. Except that here on the bus it was not cold or wet or frightening, so it was at the same time a disorientating sensation of being somewhere, someone completely other: a stranger in a strange place.

Ellie came back to herself. Her skin was still cold, goose-pimpled but her shocked hand found that her hair was not wet, not dripping. And once again she knew what that glass was. She knew the pictures that she had been carrying . . . no that the apprentice girl had been carrying in the small waxed bag – they were now in the Sir John Soane's Museum. They were the instructions and designs from Mr Green, the London importer, to the Venetian artists. They were English orders that the Venetians had been unable or unwilling to fulfil. Unable or unwilling to the point that English glass had been forced to evolve, to develop, to invent the new lead crystal to meet the desire of a new strong market.

What Ellie had not known, and now she did, was the moment in the night, the long exhausting swim from the island and the strange mixture of cold and warm in the northern Italian summer night. The intensity of physical sensation. That was not history it was biology, autobiography, or insanity.

Ellie was shaken, by the fear, the haste, the strain. She was, in the bright London morning, out by a different river, sweating with the adolescent, even if she was not dripping wet with her. There had been no gap, no split, between the apprentice and herself, and yet she did not know that young woman. It was she who had run away and she felt her lungs heave although she was sitting quite still.

By the time she reached South Kensington Ellie was actually late and she hastened down the museum stairs, flapping slightly, apologies rushing through her head and piling up on her tongue. She was late, but Robbie was later and she felt aggrieved, even before she had whisked herself around the whole fashion department to check that he had not wandered off, needing somewhere to sit down, or simply bored of waiting. He was not there; even as she tried to calm her breath and admire the hats, slightly too reverentially displayed in the glass cages, she knew she was peeved. He had wanted her to come; he had inconvenienced her. He was rude.

She tried to deny her irritation by arguing it away. She lectured herself about the particular emotional complexity of having a terminal disease that made you so hated in some places that you had endlessly to test the love of those who did not hate you. But despite her efforts to persuade herself that she was professionally interested in some bugle beading on a huge Edwardian hat, she knew she was angry with Robbie mainly because when he arrived she would not be able to allow herself the relief of being cross with him.

At about this moment, in the studio, Mary and Patsy were settling in to work. Mary loved these Tuesdays and knew she was lucky to have them. In any other studio, at the very best, she would have had to share independent blowing hours. But Patsy, despite instruction from Ellie, seldom wanted to take the chair and was happy to be servitor, gaffer, footmaker, as required. Today Mary felt newly comfortable and with the new confidence she could feel curious.

'How did you get into this?' she asked Patsy, as they got themselves organised.

'I worked in a factory, mould blowing. I was pretty good, but it got very boring. I heard Ellie talking on the radio one morning, she was just setting up the studio, and talking about the shortage of women blowers. So I wrote to the programme and said I'd like to come and work for her. That was that.'

'Don't you want to . . .'

'Be an Artist. No thanks. I don't get it, frankly: sometimes I dream, but no. I like to do my job, collect my wage packet and go home in the evening to my family and sleep tight.' She laughed. 'I like being here. Ellie is a good studio boss and Megan makes sure you get paid. I tried once before, you know, working in a studio, but it was a nightmare – they thought they were all wonderfully creative, too creative to be good mannered or efficient, or sometimes even safe. They expected everyone to design and blow and want to be famous. In the end, for all the talk about Equality and that, I think they despised me. Ellie sort of knows what you can do and she values that. They . . . I felt that they valued themselves so highly that they couldn't believe anyone wouldn't want to be like them. And, well, you know, it's quite glamorous here; and fun. I like working with other women.'

'Do you like her, Ellie I mean?'

'Sure. I mean, I like her as a boss. She's, outside the studio, well, she's a bit of a film star, isn't she? So intense and stuff, but to work for, it's good. It's different for you, isn't it? You'll move on. You'll want to be a partner, have more time; you'll get to hate the series stuff, you'll start to feel she's keeping you back. I've seen it all, you're all the same. But for me it's a good job; and I'm good at it. Why, don't you? Like her.'

Like her? Some evenings as she walked home Mary knew she loved her, and despised herself for doing so. Héloïse Macauley, she would mutter, I'm not going to be bound to a witch-woman like her. She's straight. Married. Mary did not have the time for that. She was not a child. And Patsy was right: Mary knew her own ambition, her lust to have what Ellie had. Not just that extraordinary touch with glass, that reaching after the technically possible, not to show off but to use. She wanted Ellie's lifestyle too – she wanted people to say 'Mary's extraordinary' in the way they said 'Ellie Macauley, she's extraordinary.' She wanted to hear the faint tone of resentment, of pique, when men said it, and the less faint tone of admiration, of delight, when women said it. But she did not want Ellie to gobble her up; she did not even want to think about whether she *liked* her.

'Do you,' she asked Patsy abruptly, 'know anything about blowing glass flat?'

'Flat? What do you mean?'

'Like medieval stained-glass windows. It was blown glass, not moulded.'

'Oh yes, I remember. I don't know . . .'

'Do you think we could try?'

Patsy was pleased. Mary had put the 'we' in the right place. They settled down to work.

When Robbie finally did arrive, over half an hour late, Ellie found she was not cross with him. She was moved to compassion by his thinness and by the dark flowers of his lesions. She knew too, even as she saw him shambling down the stairs that he was not late because he was rude and exploitative; he was not late, this time, because he had got too exhausted to manage; he was late because he was Robbie, who long before he had even had his diagnosis, had been chronically and unashamedly late.

'Sweetheart,' she said hugging him. He leaned against her, like a child, flopping into her embrace. He became more and more like a child, as he lost weight – more delicately boned, more waiflike. She knew that people seeing them together would think she was his mother. She hated that; and in fact he was nothing like young enough to be her child, but she could see the tender sympathy she, rather than he, was offered now when they went somewhere together and encountered a stranger knowledgeable enough to interpret the dark stains that were beginning to destroy his features. Mothers were allowed to suffer most: they were the 'innocent victims'. She knew that neither Judith's mother nor her own would suffer as much as they themselves would if the other were dying. She was not Robbie's mother – the idea was insulting to him, to her, to Robbie's real mother and to Stephanie; none of them needed substitutes.

'Ellie, darling.' He did not apologise for being late; he probably did not even think of it and she remembered, with some odd relief, how angry his unpunctuality had made Tim. The first time she had met Robbie he had been late and Tim, anxious to display his new lover to his old friend, had been irritated.

'It's about the only thing that makes me wonder, Ellie,' Tim had said. 'Can I really be serious about someone who will never, ever, ever, be on time? And worse, will shamble in shortly and not even bloody notice that we've been sitting here for hours awaiting the honour of his company?'

And she, then, had said, 'Perhaps that's his charm – you really want to be loosened up.' Which had probably been true, as a matter of fact.

Tim had died last year, more prompt to the end than his lover.

Now Robbie smiled at her, raising his head from the soft curve of her neck where he had snuggled it.

'How goes it?' she asked him, as casually as she could manage.

'Fucking awful, really. Can we not talk about it now?'

'I was admiring the beaded cloche when you arrived.'

'Glass beads, a special treat for you.'

'I noticed that.'

'Which reminds me, Ellie. How can you be so modest? I'd have been yelling from the roof-tops.'

'What?'

'After we'd talked this a.m. I was chatting to Maurice on the phone . . .'

'Maurice?'

'You know, that cute Greek-looking bloke who works with

your friend Hugo; he's an old mate of mine and I wanted to go through some of the info stuff, like not with some medic. So I said I was going to meet you here; and he said, "To see her new bowl". And I said, "No, hats." And he said, "She's a weirdo, that woman. Didn't she even tell you she had a new bowl in the museum?" And you didn't, did you?'

She was touched and also embarrassed because Robbie would now have to feel obliged to go and see it.

'Well, come on. Where is this glass thingy gallery anyway?'

She shrugged her shoulders.

'Ellie, I want to see it. I demand to see it. Take me to your bowl.'

'Dish, really. Or platter, "platter" is rather preferred in the profession.'

'I shall drop this inner knowledge deftly into my next conversation.' And he would, she thought.

The glass gallery was as high up as fashion was low down. Glass needed light as immediately as cloth needed dimness. It took them a very long time to climb the stairs, and Ellie dared not even ask him if he wanted to use the lift.

The gallery dispelled her mixture of discomforts. It was a place of joy, of sparkle and delight. It appeared to be deserted as they approached, filled with light and colour, empty of people. But as they came right into the room they saw a child trotting down the glass staircase. He came to rest less than a yard from them, gave them a radiant choirboy smile, then turned immediately. With his hand gliding along, rather than holding on to, the banister he jogged up again. He was about nine years old, wearing jeans, a very white T-shirt and trainers.

At the top he leaned over the rail and called to an invisible person below, 'Mummy, this is wicked. Do you think Jacob's ladder was like this?'

In the night Jacob slept, his dreams made fretful by the wound in his hip, tossing uncomfortably, facing the fact that he has stolen a blessing from his blind father, and an inheritance from his hungry brother. And even as he sleeps and frets, a stairway is set up, a ladder between heaven and earth, a ladder of iridescent stone, a glass staircase, shining as lava shines after cold rain has smitten its still glowing surface, a stairway and all the hosts of heaven climb up and down it, coming and going, and singing as they climb. Jacob in his wrestling has forced open the breech, and there is a passageway that will never be destroyed, a passageway for ever between heaven and earth. Ellie felt a warm flush of delight between her breasts.

Robbie sighed and said, 'Wow!' and then lest he should have over committed himself added, 'how fabulously camp.'

The child turned towards them with some curiosity and started down the stairs again and Ellie, feeling completely at home, neither visitor nor tourist because the works of herself and of her colleagues were on display here, said to the boy, 'How odd, I've always thought that too. And it's one of my favourite Bible stories.'

Her voice brought the boy to a halt, just a few steps from the bottom of the staircase, less than a yard from Ellie, grinning with pleasure. It also brought the invisible mother out from her concentration on Egyptian glass scent bottles, and she emerged amused smiling at Ellie. Then she saw Robbie's face, and the smile froze.

'Dominic,' she said sharply, 'come here and stop bothering those people.'

Ellie was still smiling, opening her mouth to say, 'no bother' or 'it's fine' or something like that, in the complicity of mothers who are both pleased and slightly shy when their children make friends with strangers by doing clever things like quoting biblical stories, when she felt Robbie's arm grip hers.

The woman edged round them so that she stood squarely between Robbie and her child. The morning turned cold and sad.

'The thing is . . .' Robbie began over the cup of coffee they went and bought as soon as they had taken a cursory glance at Ellie's platter, now enshrined in craft history. Dominic, still glowing hugely with delight, and his mother had departed rapidly, and on his part reluctantly. He had waved as she had dragged him off down the passageway.

'The thing is,' said Robbie, 'that she was not pig-ignorant and I can't pretend she was. She knew. She knows enough to recognise Karposi's when she sees it, so why doesn't she know that it can't hurt her precious.'

'More "ess",' Ellie said, a shade too quickly, 'her precioussss. She's a Gollum.' And when that did not make him smile she added, 'She's rude, pet, just rude. Hate her.'

'He was such a cute kid and so . . . Hey, I really liked your . . . he groped for the word she had given him, . . . your platter.' He smiled at her invitingly. She was meant to make it all right, she was meant to find the magic thing to say that would soothe the hurt, that would redeem the morning.

She compared the gallery they had just seen with one in New York where they were going in the summer. It was not quite good enough, but it was the best she could do. At least he knew she was trying. Soon he was tired. She could see him wilting. He had used up his limited credit on the energy bank, and, quite tenderly, she offered to pay for him to get a taxi home. He accepted.

Outside, on the monumental steps he tried to apologise. She stopped him, 'Don't, sweetheart, please. I will not have lovely lovely you made ashamed. She was an asshole.'

He smiled and kissed her and she hailed a taxi for him, and then another for herself. Glancing at her watch she thought she might just about be in time for Judith.

In fact they arrived at the same moment outside the small Italian restaurant they often used for these lunches. Their greeting was extravagantly demonstrative. An undeniable factor in their friendship, although one they found it hard to discuss, was that they looked fabulous when they were together, their very different styles creating something unexpected and glamorous.

'Kiss me like that,' said Judith coquettishly, 'and everyone will think you're a lesbian.' Judith was.

'Rubbish,' said Ellie. 'No one ever thinks that unless it's shoved down their throats. They'll assume you're a visiting American agent, and, deceived by my faintly arty appearance, will wonder whether they did in fact see me on the TV in some sitcom last month.'

'Do I look like an American agent?'

'Of course you do. A very successful one. Only successful, high-powered and ambitious American women look like you.'

'You only think that because you assume all Jewish women are American – I mean all professional ones. Lots of people look like me.'

They did not though. Judith had a particular elegance; Ellie had long thought it was the elongated thinness of her wrists that gave her every gesture a remarkable distinction. Always, regardless of whatever she was wearing, there was a slight floppiness to her cuffs as though they felt shy at lying too snugly against such lovely bones. Her ankles were the same. For a long time Ellie felt that if she had looked like that when she had been an adolescent she might have grown up quite differently; but once when she had said this to Judith, Judith had roared with laughter and shown Ellie a photograph of herself as a teenager. She had been a slightly podgy child, her hair cut very straight and square with a hair-slide fiercely shoving a fringe off her forehead, and an unmistakable air of mild dim gloom about her.

'Though in fairness,' Judith had said, 'anyone would look like a depressed coypu if they had to have their photograph taken to celebrate their brother's bar mitzvah – we didn't have any of that trendy liberal girlie stuff. Oh no, Ellie, I invented myself; you didn't have to; you just had to stand around with that extraordinary hair and wait for someone to come along and cast you as the romantic lead.'

'Rubbish. You have no idea what it was like in the Borders in the fifties. You know, this surprises nearly everyone, but my colouring is actually very common. Look at any primary school photograph from those parts of Scotland and you'll see at least half a dozen children with carrot tops, and a fair handful as dark as mine. It's supposed to be our Viking genes. So the colour was boring and the curls were wanton. My mother cut them short lest I be inflamed unto vanity.'

So, now, they welcome each other with flamboyance because they know how successfully they have remade themselves, escaped not just by the skin of their teeth, but with all their sails set fair, running out of harbour towards the open seas for the new worlds they discovered in their twenties and have pioneered with such glee, such hard work and such success.

Judith was a fundraiser, one of two partners in an independent consultancy which she had set up three years ago. Along with professional and social success, she also had an enduring and sweet relationship with an Italian woman who lived in Venice, and consequently did not interfere with daily life and provided regular holidays in all that loveliness. She had a chic little flat in Primrose Hill, and a wicked sense of humour.

They swept into the restaurant together and the young waiter cheered up at the sight of them. He knew they would tease him, but nicely; flirt without him feeling threatened and leave him a handsome tip. He showed them to their table with a flourish that made other customers glance up briefly curious.

'Gin,' said Judith. 'Gin first and then the menu. With tonic. Twice.'

'Not me,' said Ellie, feeling disgruntled again, 'we're entertaining tonight. I'll just have wine – white, dry, a glass now and then we'll see.'

'Tired?'

'Not really, but fed up. Robbie's sick again and we went out this morning and someone was horrid, you know. And I have eight people for dinner. So far as I know they're all straight. I'm being a good wife.'

'Well, don't look so weary, you're dead good at that stuff.'

'I know I am, Judith. That's half the problem. And Henry will be pleased and avuncular and everyone will notice that I'm eighteen years younger than he is and aren't we a charming and interesting couple. "He's so brilliant and, you know, they say she's very talented." Do you know in academia they have something called "pedigrees": neat family trees of people who were people's research students, even unto the third and fourth generation.'

'Like who's slept with who if you're gay.'

'Not like that at all.'

'I know. I, on the other hand, am also going out to dinner. I'm going to Paul and Keith's and we will have far too much to drink and tell each other infantile jokes in very bad taste and I will lurch home happy and pissed long after you have done all the washing up, and snuggled down on your chaste couch. And I bet I have more fun.'

'I bet you do too.'

To cheer her up Judith performed for her. 'Business first, Ellie. I am currently working on the historical section of my thesis, *The Natural History of the Fag-Hag*. Well, the unnatural history really, being totally socially constructed.'

This was an old joke but it never ran dry.

'I am looking in particular at the Christian martyr model. The women who think they are fag-hags but are really just looking for a lion or two to get them into heaven quickly. I am planning to take Elaine Morton as my case-study for this section. What do you think, oh venerable academic supervisor?'

Ellie laughed, 'I think you are a total bitch, Judith. I often

wonder just how malevolent Hugo was being when he introduced us. He knew I was seething with guilt then, and I think
he was baiting as much as teasing.'

'Oh come on, Ellie,' Judith responded, 'not malevolent,
ambivalent. Even the nicest gay men are a bit double edged
about fag-hags, and can you blame them? They're all so sexually arrogant that they are convinced we must want to have sex
with them, so they're terrified. Or else they realise that we
don't and then they're offended. The very political ones tend to
do a bit better, but at the heart of every gay man is a
misogynist, not surprisingly, and all one can do is be grateful
for the ones who are beginning to grow out of it.'

'What about the babies who go dancing at The Fridge on
Saturday nights?' Ellie enquired, 'they *do* want to sleep with
them.'

'They're not fag-hags, they're "sweet young things," the post-
modernist, post-feminist version of the Southern Belle. I'm
talking about the deluxe model, the real McCoy. Us, Ellie,
wonderful us.'

Ellie interrupted, 'As your thesis supervisor I have to point
out that one of the ways you can tell a fag-hag is that her first
lover is always a gay man.'

'Watch It,' said Judith.

'Damn, yes, sorry.' Ellie looked sharply at Judith who would
be completely entitled to take offence at this, but luckily
appeared not to have done so, but to be amused in a slightly
less than kindly way instead. 'I meant of course the heterosexual fag-hag. And anyway I at least was once a sweet young
thing.'

'And have you Grown Out of It?'

'Yes, alas. Well, mostly.'

'There you are. Now and again doesn't count,' said Judith
firmly. 'Falling in love with gay men does not make you a
fag-hag it makes you an idiot, a self-indulgent nincompoop.'

And they both grinned a little wryly, recalling specific occasions of self-indulgent idiocy in their lives.

'What a comfort you are to me. OK, now we've cleared up these minor points of methodology, I had better hear the details of your new research.'

'Well,' Judith put on a rather pompous academic voice, 'I am starting with the background context.'

'Very professional,' said Ellie.

'The history of fag-hags has been somewhat obscured, like so much of women's history, by prejudices of various kinds. I shall not, here, fill in the long centuries of development (*see* footnote 39d), but start only with the late 1960s.'

'You mean with your own self.'

'Don't interrupt. In Britain in 1968, as one of the major reforms that was generated by those exciting and liberating years, male homosexuality, between consenting adults in private, was decriminalised. Even in the continuing political struggle for complete legal equality for all homosexuals, the enormity of that victory, and its importance in all our lives, should not be minimised.

'However, it cannot be denied that the 1968 legislation had a side-effect: it put the classic fag-hag at risk. The vital niche she had filled in the life cycle of social intercourse became semi-redundant. The early 1970s, with the emergence of women's liberation and gay liberation, weakened her position still further. Many fag-hags diverted their not inconsiderable energies into feminism, which was healthy for them. Gay men learned to prefer their own company and, having hated themselves for their dependence, gladly forgot their centuries-old debt. By the middle of the next decade the fag-hag, although her plight excited little attention from the ecology groups, was in serious danger of extinction. Although she still hung on in certain rarefied and closeted environments – one thinks of the operatic and student communities –'

'And the Church.'

'Now who wants to talk about themselves? But you're right. Let me see . . . Although she continued to function within the operatic, religious and student communities, the fag-hag did not wholly flourish there. If one were a Darwinian gradualist one could point to her evolutionary failure and see her, like the dinosaur, as being non-adaptable and consequently on her way out.'

'This is impressive work, Miss Davidson.'

Judith sipped from the gin that had appeared at her right hand and continued portentously, 'But one is not necessarily a Darwinian. When it comes to evolution one may be a catastrophe theorist: catastrophe theory does not accept the traditional gradualist mutation, adaptation or extinction. It posits instead sudden environmental catastrophes, which so change the ecological situation that while some species abruptly become extinct, others are enabled to make fast evolutionary leaps forward, ensuring their survival and rapid development. In the middle of the 1980s such a catastrophe occurred within the ecosystem of the fag-hag which created an environment highly favourable to this declining species and, with certain minor adaptations, she has flourished again in the last ten years. The catastrophe I refer to is HIV/AIDS.'

'Judith!'

'Over the top? I'm sorry. It's more or less impossible to say this with anything even approaching the boundaries of good taste, but we, fag-hags, are doing terrifically well in the present situation. It's not just that we're particularly well adapted to raising funds and pouring out time and energy. There is something in our relationship with PWAs. And I do not just mean the business of turning up in hospital wards in glamorous hats and smelling of Paco Rabanne *eau de calandre* though that should not be minimised. I mean something about need. Mutual, symbiotic need.'

Judith could walk extremely near to a perilous edge. Occasionally she wobbled.

Ellie reached across the table and patted her face gently, 'That was dead classy, Judith. Someone in particular?'

'No I've just had a week of it . . .' she pulled herself back from the precipice, 'which reminds me, darling, do you want a commission?'

'Paid?' Ellie knew from bitter experience that it was always best to clarify these things with Judith. One of the reasons that Judith was so successful at her work was because she could inspire people with such enthusiasm that they found they had volunteered for appalling amounts of work without even notic-ing. On the other hand, she was entirely honourable: once it had been established that you were talking professionally she was thoroughly professional herself and fully aware of her friends' worth.

'Paid. Very paid. Though, frankly, I haven't got this one in the bag yet. We've a client, a reasonably commercial organisa-tion, which is setting up a design competition; very high profile I hope. We need a flash sort of award, TV catching, and I thought to myself, all things considered, what could be more appropriate than a nice, big Héloïse Macauley piece.'

'Lettering, they're bound to want lettering.'

'Well, you can do lettering.'

'Of course I can do lettering, Judith, I just don't like doing lettering. Actually, if they can pay, I'd love a commission. Anything to get away from the bloody decanters. Why don't you give Megan a ring?'

'She's deeply suspicious of me.'

'Can you blame her? "*Oh, Megan, Ellie promised, just a little something for our auction.*"'

'I never do it unless you've already said.'

'I know you don't, Judith. That's not the point. You asked why Megan treated you with suspicion; I'm telling you.'

'You let her boss you about too much.'

'No, I certainly do not. I ought to let her boss me about a great deal more, actually, then I'd be rich and famous.'

'Richer and more famous.'

'I'm not richer than you, so shut up.'

'You're not *meant* to be richer than me. You're an Artist. I'm a Nasty Capitalist Jew.'

Their voices were rising, although they had not noticed. Several other lunchers looked up at this point; a tiny *frisson* of nervousness hovered in the air around them. They sensed it, caught each other's eye and giggled complacently.

'Speaking of which,' said Ellie, only slightly more quietly, 'my brother has summoned me to take care of my sainted mother this summer.'

'Speaking of what?'

'Money. I said they could put the old cow in a home if they wanted to go on holiday and send me the bill; outraged virtue quivered down the line. I shouldn't be able to afford it. I could hear him thinking "poor Henry", along with a particular undertow of "male headship in Christ Jesus", which, in Alan's opinion, Henry shows a lamentable failure to exercise.'

'You'll go.'

'No, I won't.'

'I bet you do, Ellie.'

Ellie felt discouraged. If even Judith thought she'd go, she probably would. The clarity that she thought she had established with Angel's insistence started to evaporate.

'I don't see that. I don't want to go. I've made them a reasonable offer. I'm frantically busy. I'm going to New York later. My mother has disowned me for ever. I haven't been there . . . I haven't even seen her for nearly ten years.'

'This is true. None the less you will go. Your problem is that some people get a positive charge out of behaving badly. I do for instance. But you don't. You never succeed in behaving properly, but you don't get any emotional benefits from your own badness – except of course having people like me love you. I'd call it a diabolical combination of Catholic and Protestant guilts. So you will go to Scotland this summer because you won't be able to live with the guilt of not going; and it will put you in a piss-awful temper; and you will want us all to be deeply sympathetic, which is unfair; and we will all be deeply sympathetic, so it's not worth talking about now.'

Ellie looked sulky; Judith's narrative was horribly recognisable. 'Well, you're wrong. I won't go.'

'*On verra.*'

They moved on fast frothy chatter. Almost nothing was out-of-bounds and almost nothing was too serious.

'How's *La Carissima*?' Ellie asked at one point; this was their pet name for Judith's absent Italian partner.

'Divine, of course. I'm going over for the weekend and she'll be here at the beginning of next month.'

'Shall we have a party?'

'I thought they bored you – cooking dinner parties.'

'Who said I was going to cook?'

'I did. You always do, because you're good at it and I'm not. It's because you're a heterosexual fag-hag, unlike me.'

'What? Isn't that just a teeny-weeny bit essentialist, or am I now being punished for my earlier blunders?'

'No, no. It's sociological. Haven't you noticed? Lots of trainee fag-hags can cook; lots can't of course, like me, but lots can, and they are usually straight. All those sweet young things who have, through the unmappable workings of what you would call 'grace' develop, at a crucial moment, both a turn for camp humour and a deep love of cooking for people. They also have to be a bit bright, of course, so they notice that heterosexual men always exploit good cooks, and that women who can't cook tend to despise women who can; they tend to prefer talking to being reminded of their feminine failure. So then they have to start cooking for gay men and wham bam there you are. Fag-hagged. Whereas lesbians have a completely different route of access; I shall have to research it.'

'I thought explanations weren't allowed.'

'Socially constructed causes, explanations, whatevers are allowed; it's only psychopoop drivel ones that aren't.'

Judith asked later, 'How's the sweet young thing, the sorcerer's apprentice, settling in?'

'Good. I mean she's going to be good. She's also greedy, which makes a nice change. She's not venerative or grateful, and she still thinks I'm better than she is. It won't last. But I like it. Some sort of colleague perhaps. Usually the ones that can blow don't want to make anything, and the ones that are artists can't take the heat, or can't get down to work, or are so sensitive or whatever. Actually, Judith, it makes me happy. It makes me happy to go into the studio and know that someone other than me is generating some of the energy.'

'You need loyalty more than you need that.'

'Actually, you're wrong. I know what you mean, but I have surprisingly little difficulty with loyalty. I've got Megan.'

'Whose loyalty is above the price of rubies.'

'Yes. Don't mock. I've got Megan and I've got Patsy.'

'And your faithful lads.'

'I'm talking about work, Judith.'

'All I'm saying is I wish my particular predilections ran to your delightful young men. Babies instead of Daddies.'

'No one could require more loyalty than you get from yours. Plus David, of course.'

'I'm not complaining, Ellie.' There was a pause as they each contemplated with smiles their own and the other's delightful array of homosexual friends.

'Yours have better manners,' Ellie said generously.

'They also have a tendency to die eventually.'

'So do we all.' Her stomach turned over. 'So do mine.'

Judith reached out her long wrist and touched the back of Ellie's hand. She had been brusque with her about her mother, but mainly because she knew that if she made Ellie feel bad enough, guilty enough towards her friends about going, there was a small chance that she would not go. Now she was sorry. Ellie stimulated sympathy, excited tenderness; Judith could never quite work out why but it was a nice feeling. When Judith felt mean she always did something that made her feel nicer.

'That commission,' she said, 'it's for The Haven.'

'Judith! Why didn't you say? You didn't even say they were employing you.'

'David really.'

'Phooey. And you know it. You should have said. Of course I want to do it.'

'I didn't say because I don't want to be in Megan's even-worse books. If I had, you'd have said you'd do it for free, wouldn't you?'

Ellie grinned, perhaps a little sheepishly.

'OK. This way they'll pay you, and you'll get a load of publicity, and Megan will love me and if you want to give the money back to the most conspicuous Red Satin Ribbon Cause of the moment you can. And you'll get to come to the party.'

'Oh yummy, yummy. Why didn't you tell me?'

'Secret negotiations. We're only doing the Grand Opening. They'll have their own fundraising committee.'

'For which you have already volunteered. And no doubt you and David are offering them a special knock-down price, in the first place.'

'It was Judith's turn to look sheepish. 'Why do we do it?'

'You mean, why do we like them so much?'

'They soothe *La Carissima's* jealous Latin heart.'

'Liar. That's the same as saying that Henry is relieved that I am kept safe from the evil machinations of macho men when I'm cavorting about with Hugo.'

'Well, and you are.'

'Oh I know, I know, fag-hags are women afraid of their own sexuality. All they really need is a real bonking by a real man; that would sort out their little ways.'

'Watch it!'

They are laughing now. They draw joint breath for the marching slogan of the Self-affirming Self-identifying Fag-Hags Group.

'If you're looking for causes, you're looking for cures.'

They laughed and ate and laughed; it always turned into a very long lunch.

'Talking of cures,' said Ellie, 'I'm thinking about making a window.'

'Cures for what?'

'Professional inertia.'

Judith looked quizzical. 'You don't do architecture, Ellie; you're always telling me that you don't do architecture.'

'It's for a church.'

'Well, maybe. *Même que . . .*'

'This is special.' But suddenly, even here, even to Judith, she could not talk about the angels. 'And Mary's very keen on . . .'

'Mary!' Judith almost shrieked. 'And as of when does some two-bit baby-dyke make Studio policy for Héloïse Macauley? And you're telling me you don't have a problem with loyalty.'

'It's not like that.'

'What is it like then?'

But she cannot tell Judith what it is like. The iridescent flutter of glass pinions beating on the doors. Angels with glass wings processing up glass stairs, singing silent songs.

There was a pause, then Judith said, 'I'm going to give you some advice that you won't want to hear. Write to Stephanie.'

For a moment Judith was afraid she might have gone too far. But Ellie, aware that she hadn't given Judith the full picture, drew a deep breath on the pain and found a laugh at the bottom. 'And if that isn't psychopoop drivel . . . No Mary is not a replacement daughter, she is not . . .'

'Sorry,' said Judith.

'Anyway, you want me to do lettering. Megan wants me to do buildings. Friedhelm Muller wants me to do windows. Blowing things is old hat. Inflation is out this year – it must be the New Labour.'

Which opened up politics, and Lottery arts funding, with which they were both professionally concerned.

'More coffee,' said Judith eventually.

'No, I must go.' Ellie turned, looking for the waiter and made bill faces.

They paid. The waiter brought Judith's mac and held it out for her with an almost deferential air, and a special charmingly coy smile. 'You do not look like a feminist,' Ellie said sternly, then added 'I failed to notice your new garment in my political horror at your attire. God, it is b-e-a-u-t-i-f-u-l.'

'It is, isn't it?' said Judith shamelessly.

'And you wanted me to notice, or you wouldn't have worn it at all. I failed you. I'm sorry.' They knew each other very well.

'Never mind, you're making up for it now.'

Outside they hugged warmly, and mid-hug Judith saw an approaching taxi with its light on, cast a flying kiss on Ellie's forehead and departed, heels clicking. Ellie was still standing on the pavement warmed by real pleasure as well as good wine, when Judith had been carried away round the corner at the end of the block.

Ellie, unlike Judith, used public transport. She walked towards the tube station increasingly conscious of her dinner party. Whether she wanted to be or not, Ellie was a cook. She was very good at it and now she felt lumbered with it. Boredom, it seemed to her was an odd emotion. There was never any warning as to when comfortable habit and easy competence would shift into tedium.

It was the bloody menopause. It gave her a manifesting angel, hot flushes and tedium. She was only forty-eight, she argued plaintively, she did not yet feel like a grown up. She refused to be menopausal. She tried to withdraw her memory, her imagination, but clear and painful on a white page in slightly too small a font size she saw vividly:

Successful psychotherapy in the climacterium is made difficult because usually there is little one can offer the patient as a substitute for the fantasy gratifications. There is a large element of real fear behind the neurotic anxiety, for reality has actually become poor in prospects, and resignation without compensation is often the only solution.

Rubbish. That was rubbish. There had to be another way through. She could not face thinking about it. She refused to face it. No, her silly mood was just ordinary boring boredom. There were too many things not to think about.

My dear Stephanie,
I had lunch with Judith today and she had the nerve to suggest that I was over-indulging my new apprentice – who is called Mary, and is very talented – because I was missing you so much. Isn't that ridiculous?
love from Mummy.

Dear Stephanie,
Judith says I am replacing you with Mary, my new apprentice. How would you feel if that were true?
best wishes, Mummy.

'I'm going mad,' Ellie thought, panicked. And then some deep pride seized her. Whatever happened she would do this dinner party, she would do it with grace and charm and please Henry, and indeed herself. And if she did not like it, it was no one's fault but her own. Henry did not force her into these things, she could have said 'No', she could have told him she was too busy, too tired, too uninterested.

She forced herself think about the bass; the *loup de mer*, the sea wolf. She deliberately recalled the extraordinary beauty of fish, which were made of glass, tiny slivers, scales, of glass. The lightning flash like oxide deep in green, green glass of the sea bass from the ocean, shifting, shining, silver-blue light in dark green. The fish that she would grill and flame this evening had come from the haven under the ice. She disciplined herself to think about her favourite thing of all, the miracle at the beginning, the reason why she loved God and glass: ice floats.

Ice floats. Life, all life, at least on this planet, depended on that. Ice is the only substance whose solid form has a lower density than its liquid form. As water freezes its molecules organise themselves, for to be solid is to be organised, as glass never is. The pattern in which they organise themselves inevitably means they squeeze ever more firmly, trap even more securely, a shard of air between themselves: a fragment of air that cannot escape from the nesting crystals that secure it. And because the air is there, embraced so closely, ice floats. Its floating, like a blanket, keeps the water underneath it warm – the floating coldness of the ice is, a down jacket, a snuggling duvet, a blanket to the warmer water beneath it. Ice floats; and icebergs float, the polar ice cap floats, clinking ice cubes in a gin and tonic float. Because of this extraordinary chance, improbability, blessed luck, or divine providence, the world stays warm enough and wet enough and biology, organisms, us, humans can live on it. An exasperated scientist had explained this to her years ago and had ended by saying almost pettishly, 'I try never to think about this actually, Ellie; it's about the only thing I know that forces me to wonder just occasionally about the necessary existence of God.'

Ellie, in gentle gratitude, had not pushed the theological point. It did not make her wonder about the existence of God, that had been settled for her too long ago, faith was a habit of mind and heart, she never bothered to doubt the existence of God. It did, however, delight her, reassure and amuse her. Things do not always behave as they should. Glass is a super-cooled liquid, its crystal lined up disorderly, and that was why it could expand stretch grow under her hands and lips.

She thought about the glassy fish swimming in the glassy water under the glassy ceiling of floating ice and she felt better.

When she reached Greenwich, she bought sheaves of flowers from the stall by the station exit and walked home – tall, red headed, lovely in the spring evening, carrying a huge bouquet to the grave of a dead self – a self who would once have enjoyed the sight of all this magnificence crossing the road with long strides.

But the corpse remained efficient and charming – by the time Henry came home she had converted all her tiredness and worry into order and decorum. The table was laid and Ellie had changed and arranged the flowers. She wanted Henry to be impressed, but although he was pleased and benign he was not remotely surprised. Henry was the opposite of a new man, not an old thug, but an unreconstructed gentleman. Compared to many of her friends' younger partners, he was immensely helpful about the house; a washer-up and handy with the vacuum cleaner when he had to be – though sincerely preferring a daily who came when he was out; tender and attentive to Stephanie when she had been little; profoundly supportive of his wife's career. But somewhere, deep down, this came into the twinned categories of his pleasure and good manners. He would not have been able to conceive of the effort of thought and skill that this pleasant house, this delicious food, these swathes of daffodils and tulips looking so casual in their glass vases, represented. He enjoyed it, he appreciated it and he thanked her – but he thanked her for the wrong things.

Ellie had long ago stopped noticing this. She saw his gentle control, his benign certainties, as solutions. They simplified things. They created structure and order and direction. When she did not know what to do or how to behave, Henry, without ever saying anything, provided the answers. She reclined on that security.

It was a problem, Ellie teased herself, in marrying above oneself. Henry was posh; he thought he liked informality, he just began his notion of formal several rungs higher up the ladder of style than she did. He liked his house to be calm and serene, his wife's cooking and more particularly the whole ambience of a dinner party to be slightly more up-market than her natural tendencies directed. He wanted urbane sophistication masquerading as effortless relaxation; yes to eating in the kitchen but no to paper napkins, and no to no napkins at all – they had to be linen and ironed; yes to French cheeses still in their greased paper wrappers, no to nursery food and giggled confessions of culinary cheating.

For Henry a dinner party meant a civilised thing, a special kind of behaviour. He never said that people shouldn't talk about religion, politics, money or sex; and in fact they talked about all three with great *élan*, but also with a kind of decorum, a gentle and abstracted wisdom. He and his friends knew lots of interesting things, but things in the end weren't interesting.

Tonight was really his party – they were entertaining a visiting American colleague and his wife. Ellie had added a smart gloss – a sophisticated and urbane Vatican diplomat; and a woman friend of hers, a journalist whose husband was doing something about bridges in Saudi Arabia and who loved to be asked out to dinner.

She relaxed when the guests arrived and began to enjoy herself. They were agreeable people, all of them, ready to be pleased and willing to be pleasing, clever, confident, successful.

She liked their groundedness; the sense they had, though none of them would have articulated, that the world and its values were basically safe in their hands. She liked the ease and the warmth and the gracious manners: they might not be as exciting as her own friends, they might be clay not glass, but both substantial and fineglazed. She was not schizoid, she thought, just greedy. She wanted this too.

After duly admiring the wonderful aroma of sea bass flamed in fennel, the woman journalist wanted to pick people's brains.

'Have you seen this case? John Holland, the Newcastle serial killer. He's saying that his guardian angel told him to do it. Well, last year there was this programme, I'm sure you remember, about some Danish doctor who doesn't think there's anything wrong with voice hearers, they just have to learn to manage them. What do you think?'

'Traditionally,' said the priest, 'we – the Church – had a really good system: on a totally arbitrary basis we either canonised voice hearers or burned them.'

'I thought we used to test the Spirit by observing the fruits,' said Ellie. 'Shouldn't we still do that?'

'You can't "test the fruits",' said the American psychiatrist, 'not of angelic voices. The fruits aren't there. Angels do not, in any meaningful sense, exist; therefore anyone who communicates with them is delusional.'

His wife, slightly too quickly – their marriage is in trouble, thought Ellie knowingly – said, 'Over 70 per cent of Americans currently believe in angels. If they're all deluded . . .'

'They don't all hear their voices though, do they?'

'I've got one at the moment,' Henry said, 'and I hate it. I don't mean her, she's rather fine, very persuasive, and apparently totally benign, but . . . She's clever, she knows there's a problem, but . . .'

'Clever isn't really relevant, is it?' said the priest. 'When it comes to morality, I mean.'

'It helps in our line of work,' said the American, 'There's something wrong with yours if it doesn't.' He smiled elegantly to take any possible sting out of the words. That well-constructed, placatory expression made Ellie hate him suddenly. Feeling the surge of hatred, she realised that she was frightened. Was she expected to say, 'Well, speaking personally, I have an angel, a rather tiresome one as a matter of fact, who jabbers at me constantly, and I don't murder small children.' She wanted them to talk about something else.

But the journalist said, teasingly, smiling at the priest – safe, Ellie thought meanly, to flirt with a dog-collar – 'Bertrand Russell said he could never become a Christian because there was nothing in the Gospels in praise of intelligence.'

'His loss. But actually God created intelligence so . . .'

'And stinging nettles.'

And Karposi's, Ellie did not say. Robbie's blotched and decaying face would not be welcomed by these people. She had a sudden longing for Hugo – and imagined his evening: his meeting would be finishing and they would be adjourning to the pub, just as bright, just as witty, as these people, but in an atmosphere charged with emotional tension. If someone there thought you were an idiot to believe in angels they would not smile deprecatingly when they said so; but nor would there be a horrible ripple of social unease, as opposed to philosophical disapproval, if you said you did believe and what's more the angel you knew best had sinusitis. Hugo would get a little drunk, but then so would they, and he would either end up talking politics all night or picking someone up and either would constitute an evening well spent.

'It's not the same as stinging nettles,' she said, not missing her hostess cue even as she imagined the blond and ideally tattooed young thing that Hugo was very likely eyeing across a bar: 'You can argue that stinging nettles are a consequence of the Fall – but we wouldn't want to do that with cleverness.'

Her priest grinned at her, 'It's more like the freak genetic chance of red hair. We wouldn't want you not to have it, but it won't get you into heaven.' Safe, Ellie thought meanly, a flirt with a married, middle-aged wife, if you knew she was a Catholic. But it made her bold nonetheless.

'It might get someone else into heaven though, mightn't it – speaking hypothetically of course – if they found in it an image of the beauty and brilliance of its creator? Intelligence likewise.'

'Jesuit.'

'Yes,' she said and caught herself smiling a well-constructed placatory smile. She wished that Angel would manifest, all glass wings and glory here in the dining-room and shut them all up, especially her. The conversation moved on. And the elegant texture of the dinner with it, the two perfectly matched.

Meanwhile Hugo was having almost, but not quite, the evening that Ellie had imagined for him. After his meeting he, with several colleagues, had indeed adjourned to a convenient bar. And there quite by chance he encountered Mary. He greeted her warmly and brought her and the woman she was with over to join him and his friends.

This gave her real pleasure. She felt a little smug, partly because the woman was obviously impressed that Mary knew them, and partly because they were somehow the sort of people that she had hoped to get to know before she came to London. These men were neither disco bunnies, nor slightly camp older arty cardigan-wearers – the two sorts of gay men she had known from college. They were slightly scary, leather jackets, shaven hair, plaid shirts, but they talked fast, loudly, and assumed in each other a radical sexual politics that did not need a flirtatious or even camp undertone to assert its own practice. Gay men had not come like this before, and it excited her.

She was in buoyant mood anyway, from the excellent day's work she had had. This week Patsy had, for the first time,

made a real effort to work technically on Mary's own ideas and
they had established a new working partnership. Meeting Hugo
here just added to that. She was alight with charm.

'This is one of Ellie's people,' Hugo said, introducing her, and
they had all smiled warmly at her, welcoming her in that
framework, the smiles more affection for Ellie than entrance-
ment at her.

'Not,' she said.

'Bad luck, then,' said someone.

'So, she owns people does she?' Mary felt that this had come
out a little more aggressively than she meant it to. 'One of
Ellie's people.' She did not like that. On the other hand she did
not want to seem sulky or unsophisticated. And she did want
to find out more about Ellie. So she applied an efficient little
grin, making her question cheeky rather than rude.

'No,' said someone else, 'people own her. She gives herself
away.' It was said quite flippantly. 'It can be tiresome sometimes, being given too much present when you didn't want it in
the first place.'

'Watch it, John,' said Hugo.

'It's all right for you, Hugo, you're really good at handling her
'little boy' stuff. But I don't always want to have my T-cells
counted tenderly, by some red head old enough to be my auntie,
if not my mother, in the middle of Quiz-night at Central Station.'

'That is fucking unfair,' said the same person who had said,
'Bad luck'. 'And you know it.'

Hugo was obviously annoyed with John. He turned from
his friends and focused on Mary. Ignoring everything that had
been said since she had asked her question, he had smiled at
her and said, 'Feeling devoured? Ellie is an old witch and don't
you forget it.' But his eyes were laughing. 'It does put you in a
very special gang.'

That made it all right. They were in the same gang, she and
Hugo. He had even included her in an implicit disloyalty, the

kind permitted only to the loyal. Mary thought perhaps she ought to protest at the word 'witch', even though she could see it was loving, but she was both curious and slightly awed by him, and did not quite dare enough to correct his verbal politics. She liked him and wanted him to like her.

Someone bought her a beer. They were welcoming, effortlessly including her, on Hugo's say-so, on the strength of her association with Ellie, on account of her own conspicuous beauty. She began to relax, and therefore to be cute and sharp, which was lucky because in that company her loveliness would not have given her long credit.

The man who had said 'Bad luck' to her denial of being one of Ellie's people, and who it transpired was called Phil, sought her out at one point.

'I wanted to clarify. After John's crabbiness. Me, I'm an Ellie fan.'

Mary was a little annoyed; she did not want Ellie to be her passport here as well as at work. She was not used to gracious dependency, nor to the sense of being a member of this vague extended family, a sort of second cousin by social pedigree, instead of blood. But she quickly realised that Phil would tell her about Ellie, would tell her things she wanted to know and which could not be extracted from Megan, or even from Patsy.

'How come you're all so crazy about her?' Mary asked, trying to open up some territory for exploration.

She got a distinctly baiting grin. 'Jealous? And of whom? Do I detect another victim of her charms? I'll tell you one thing, she is totally straight. To the best of all knowledge a faithful wife and mother.'

'Mother!' exclaimed Mary startled by the immediate success of her strategy, 'I didn't know she had a child.'

'In which case I shouldn't be telling you.' He grinned conspiratorially, and she knew she ought not to encourage what was obviously treachery. She grinned encouragingly.

'Well,' he said, 'she has a daughter. But last year they had an enormous fight, and Stephanie flounced off and has never been heard of since.'

'Am I allowed to ask why?'

It was bold. He grinned and said, 'Almost certainly not. You should get Hugo to give you the full details. But . . . Well, Stephanie, who frankly is a spoiled brat in lots of ways, but so clever and . . . Really you would have to know her to understand. Stephanie is crabby, and strange but very very funny – seriously, on a good evening she is one of the wittiest people I've ever met, and that's part of it. Ellie dotes on her. Well, Stephanie got this incredibly fancy degree from Oxford in social anthropology or something and . . . Oh, Henry is involved in all this too. Have you met the good Henry?'

He looked at Mary and she nodded. They both raised their eyebrows, sharing but not mentioning an incomprehension. 'Well the two of them got busy and got Stephanie this fancy job and she was livid, and even Ellie knew she sort of had a right to be, except . . . So anyway Stephanie suddenly announces that she's off to Borneo, on a field research project. She announces this, for the first time, in the middle of a party, ambushed them with it. And, it was funny really, Stephanie made it extremely funny, what she is doing her research into is these monkeys – there's this big debate about whether or not the mother monkeys murder their offspring . . . It was pretty spectacular actually, because Stephanie was so witty about why she was specially equipped to research infanticidal mother monkeys, having been Ellie's daughter. God it was funny, and very public and we were . . . everyone was laughing at Ellie, and she . . . she lost it . . . they had this amazing fight, right there in public. Really screaming at each other, not nice, not funny. And afterwards Ellie tried . . . she cheated really . . . she tried to get Steph taken off the expedition. I mean she went behind her back and . . .'

'But . . . but that's outrageous . . . I mean, how?'

'Steph's an epileptic.'

'Shit!'

'As you say. She hadn't told the expedition people. Ellie thought, really believed, it wasn't safe. She was in a right state. But actually Steph won. So she vanished to South-East Asia swearing she would never talk to either of them again and to date has kept her promise.'

'I never thought she had a child. Ellie, I mean. Damn damn. Now I have to be totally jealous of her.'

Hugo joined them suddenly and Mary abruptly changed the conversation. She had a strong feeling that he would not approve of her discussing Ellie, and Phil's smooth acceptance confirmed her decision.

'Your friend John doesn't like women, does he?'

'Not a lot,' said Hugo. 'Do you like men, then?'

She laughed in his face, 'Dykes who don't like men, don't drink here.'

'Not bad. She's getting to be quite the London sophisticate, isn't she Phil?'

She knew he was teasing, and that she was not meant to be offended. On the contrary it was a compliment to be included in the badgery snapping that they all indulged in: a gossip of a fierce and nimble kind, a high camp without simper, that she admired and was slightly shocked by. But she felt frustrated, tangled in Ellie's web. She drank her beer, gathered in her friend and prepared to leave. Hugo's farewell hug cheered her up, and she went into the night buoyant with the promises of her new life.

He saw with pleasure that she had satisfied his friends. He'd invite her to supper some evening, a step forward. She was fun and cute.

He smiled at the considerably cuter young man drinking the other side of the bar.

'Neat tattoos,' John murmured in his ear.

'Go on, surprise me!'

At much the same moment, after Ellie's dinner party had moved to the sitting-room and the conversation had fragmented, moving between couples and the larger group, the priest, taking a cup of coffee from her, said abruptly, 'Ellie, do you believe in angels? Not theologically, but effectively?'

'Is that a serious question?' she asked, suddenly sharp; ashamed, as though he had caught her out picking her nose. She would have turned the question, but there had to be a place, however small and wobbly, where she took her stand. She drew in a breath, letting herself be inspired. She said, 'Yes, I do.'

'Lucky you,' he said and she knew he meant it.

But later still, while the party was breaking up and he had accepted a lift back across the river from the journalist, she heard him say to Henry, laughing, as part of his farewell: 'I hope you get your angel communicator sorted out. Don't be fooled by theological persuasiveness – I'd ask her for a feather at least.' He was laughing, mocking the poor woman, behaving like a grown-up. He had no right to envy what he was not prepared to run any risk for.

Afterwards she and Henry tidied up together; she loaded the dishwasher, while he hand-washed their beautiful eighteenth-century wine glasses – a collection slowly gathered, not matching but each one exquisite and all from the same forty years: blown in England, engraved in Holland, the mismatching so deliberate and so lovely that it pleased rather than frustrated Henry. He was replete with pleasure, delighted with his party.

She asked him, squeezed delicately into domestic chat and gossip about the guests, 'What will you do for your voice hearer? The angel one?'

'I hate voice hearers,' he said, 'I really do. They push the whole issue too far. I don't know. Drug her, I suppose. That's what we do.'

'You didn't used to.'

Henry when she had first met him had been a radical – with a passionate, almost religious, conviction he had held the ground that named insanity as the sane response to an insane world. The Bird of Paradise – and no need to take acid to get there. He clung, just, inside the system, working in a large institution, but genuinely because he believed that there he would meet the ordinary, the sad ordinary people with neither money nor spectacle to offer. He had been Ellie's knight in white armour. His medical coat, required by his hospital, more tabard for her, displaying his colours, than shield against germs and insanity.

'No I didn't used to,' he said, 'but actually we never made anyone better, did we?'

There was a pause. She was not sure whether he was confessing or boasting or both.

Then he said, 'Drugs control schizophrenia. They really do.' There was another pause, and then he said, 'They control epilepsy.'

Squatting down, feeding the plates into the plastic-coated grill at the bottom of the washing-up machine, she froze. She wanted to say 'Sorry' and knew that would be inappropriate.

She had never worked it out. She was unspeakably stupid. She had thought him distanced from Stephanie's illness, right from the start she had thought him cold and critical – while for him it had been a different challenge.

'I wanted it to be shamanic,' he said, a slight self-mockery colouring the words, 'I wanted to believe in the inspired voices of another order, I really did . . . all those Native Americans. And, actually, it was just a little kid getting her face cut up.'

And then, lest they had gone too far into a place where they did not want to be, he reverted quickly; 'Voice hearers, though, are rather in the middle. It is dangerous – even the most benign voices seem to turn dark so suddenly and you have Peter Sutcliffe, or this Holland fellow. But sometimes to get the voices to shut up you have to drug people so far . . . like commissurotomy, you know.' They are back on to epilepsy and they both know it. Left and right brain studies were one of his special fields. Commissurotomy – severing of the *corpus callosum*, the band of connective tissue between the left and right hemispheres of the brain had been a effective treatment for epileptic fits, but unfortunately it so distorted perceptual processing that the confusions were now held to outweigh the advantages. She remembered suddenly and with great clarity that she had first been attracted to him when she had heard him explaining to someone that chopping a person's head off was a 100 per cent effective cure for headaches, but that didn't make decapitation a useful clinical tool.

'I'll drug her,' he said now, without anguish, addressing an interesting problem, 'I'll drug her for her and our safety and I'll still wonder if they didn't handle certain mental illnesses more effectively in the Middle Ages.'

'They burned witches, as the Monsignor told us,' she reminded him.

'We're on each other's side,' he said laughing.

'So we are.' Now she could never tell him about Angel. Never. As an option it was closed.

He finished drying the glasses, hung up the cloth and put the kettle on. Suddenly, she said, 'I think I must have left my notebook in the car.'

'Yes?' he enquired. 'Do you want me to get it?'

'No, I'll go.'

She slipped out into the road and felt the night, damp and warm under the street lights.

'Angel,' she whispered to the cherry trees; she so much wanted contact, needed connection.

Angel said, 'You did really well tonight so I'll tell you an embarrassing secret: Almost all angels like gay men better too. We have a soft spot – I mean for those sexually active liberated ones. Queers. Angels like queers.'

'Angel!' Ellie was annoyed to find that she was slightly shocked, as though an angel ought to be a little bit homophobic. 'Why?'

'We identify I suppose; they're more like us than most of you are.'

'Yes?'

'Well you know; no begetting, no permanence, lots of highly enjoyable experiences which aren't forced into a social framework, which aren't built on for something else, built into anything. Oh it's hard to explain. Something to do with camp, of course, but more . . . look, angels adore sex. We aren't fixed by gender, even Milton knew that, we're free, we're what you would call promiscuous, though we think of it as generous; we don't trade delight for anything else, and we can't make it permanent even if we wanted to. We love sex, and when it comes to bodies we are inevitably a bit voyeuristic. A bit! And who else gives us . . . Let's just say gay men frolic. Angels frolic. We have that in common. Pride marches, for instances, are one of our favourite things: they make us happy. Where else do you see thousands of humans celebrating only the fact that they *are*. You don't get heterosexual Pride, do you? Of course we have a soft spot for them. A pretty gay man on his way to a bar on a Friday night, ideally before he has got E-ed up or drunk, is your average angel's idea of heaven.' Angel paused, 'To coin a phrase,' she added quickly.

Restored and delighted Ellie laughed out loud.

Chapter Three

The morning after the dinner party Ellie got to the studio a little late. Everyone was already in place. Megan gave her a reproving smile as she passed through the office to change into her boiler suit.

Patsy was sweeping the floor when Ellie came down the alley and into the studio: as usual the shards of glass were sparkling on the rough pile that they were swept into by the door; they caught the morning light and gave Ellie pleasure.

'You shouldn't be doing that. Mary should, if she didn't do it yesterday.'

'I gaffered for her, we were both working.'

'Not the point, Patsy. You're meant to be training her, not indulging her.'

'Well, she'll do it tonight. I want to get off promptly, it's parents' evening. GCSE choices.'

'Fine,' said Ellie cheerfully, 'so long as she does. I exploit you quite enough without her adding to it.'

They both smiled, knowing this was true and knowing too that it was basically acceptable to them both.

Patsy went a little further. 'Ellie, it's not like that, you know . . . I really like her . . . she's nice . . . we had fun yesterday. She's good, good to work with.'

'OK. Where is she?'

'Upstairs. What's the plan today?'

'Megan needs three, even four, more of the decanters . . . the ones with the red and gold octopuses. Fun, eh?'

'Great.'

This was a joke. The two of them shared a dislike of these decanters; Ellie felt they were outdated now, did not really reflect where her work had got to, and therefore in the long run would not prove good for her reputation. Patsy found them dull. Unfortunately they were enormously successful. We need a new line like that, Ellie thought, and, quite suddenly, she visualised a wide fruit bowl, with handles – handles and feet, Patsy would like that, they had not done any handles or feet for ages – and different-coloured thread work. She must do some sketches, talk to Megan. She forced herself to focus back on the present.

'We could do three, I should think, this morning, nice easy straight through sequence. We both know that – and Mary, I think. We could do them before lunch if we're lucky. And this afternoon, if you're in a calm mood, I'd like to have another go at those damn Venetian canes. Just you and me. Mary can do some grinding or something. Upstairs.'

The last time they had experimented with this technique, she and Patsy had ended up in a weeping fight, frustrated with each other and with the whole project. Patsy grinned, 'Well, I'm not premenstrual this time, anyhow.'

'Me neither. OK. Look, you get the moulds for the decanters sorted, and the red metal into the oven; I'll run upstairs and have a word with Mary and we'll try and get started in . . . hmm . . . twenty minutes? Half an hour?'

'Three-quarters, better. There's a bit of sorting out here still. Oh, Ellie, that reminds me: you know that little bowl you did, the one with the blue stars, that Venetian copy?'

Ellie nodded.

'Did you take it home?'

Ellie looked blank.

'I wonder where the hell it is then.'

'It'll be somewhere.'

'Oh yes, I just wanted to check the pattern – they were rather good canes and I didn't make notes.'

'Oh, Patsy,' almost a reprimand.

'Yes, I know. I'm sorry. Well, I'll find it.'

'Sure. Let's say forty-five minutes then. That'll give Mary time if she wants it. What was she up to yesterday?'

'You ask her, Ellie.' A tiny but clear shift in Mary's direction and Ellie could not help but notice it. Of course she wanted them to be friends, a support group for each other, but she depended on Patsy's loyalty too. She had Megan. Fair's fair.

'You did have fun, didn't you?' For a tiny moment she envied them. Their liking each other was not a disloyalty. It ought to be a relief. Patsy had really disliked the apprentice before Mary; and Patsy was extremely skilful at disliking someone in a slightly cunning way that never gave you anything to complain about. The envy, she realised, passing through the door and up the rather rickety stairs to the workshops, was not about their liking each other – it was about the fact that they had clearly had a playful time yesterday. They could afford it; they didn't have to think of commercial ideas, and the choreography of their production. They didn't have to earn her salary as she did theirs. Like a mother, she thought crossly.

As she climbed the faint irritation fell away and she thought of Patsy with affectionate gratitude. It was Patsy who daily reminded her about the value of pernickety, well-thought-through craftsmanship. Craftpersonship. It was easy to get carried away and all fancy, and Patsy kept things grounded in the practical – if you want to do it, let's work out how to do it. And safe. Megan had pointed out to her recently how low their breakages were since Patsy had come; how few accidents with glass or with hands they had. Ellie could still remember the burn in her thigh, a stupid foolish moment when she worked for the collective and no one had really taken the sort of care that she now depended on Patsy to take. Knowing it was being taken she, Ellie, could run creative risks.

It was inconvenient having all the workrooms upstairs. She knew now, what she had not realised when she had moved in, that it was her dislike and lack of interest in cold working that had caused her to fail to notice this inconvenience. She wanted the grinding and cutting and engraving and stuff to be invisible. Now, she was growing more interested in those processes. She was getting curious about surfaces. Perhaps she could distress the outside of these fruit bowls; sink them into sand while still molten. Would the coloured threads she had seen in that first flash of vision, would they have to go on afterwards? Would that re-smooth the blasted surface? . . . Sometimes Ellie wished she did not have so much technical curiosity. The actual techniques of glass . . . she still hadn't got them under her belt, she knew she never would: the science and the rigour and the practicalities and the long long history coming so close together all heaped up and entangled.

Mary was in the drawing room, but she was not drawing. She was standing looking out the window; tiny and tough, her back to Ellie. She did not turn when the door opened, so Ellie did not see her particularly stubborn expression, and only thought how lovely she was.

Mary was plotting.

Mary had had a somewhat unusual childhood. Her parents had been joyful middle-class hippies, never worn to sordidness but high-spirited and peace loving and vagrant. Her mother had hair that flowed, the colour of primroses, down her back and twined in wanton tendrils across the pillows of her many lovers. She loved with abandon – with a greedy longing to have everything: freedom and laughter and an end to all oppression and to hear the whales sing on their long journeys and to see the Bird of Paradise. She never grew out of any of this, nor became ground down and weary, nor political and fierce, because – spectacularly – she managed to die in child-birth.

The fact that this was brought about entirely because she wanted to give birth 'naturally' under the light of a full moon, and stubbornly ignored all advice to the contrary, was forgotten very quickly by Mary's father, and Mary never had to learn it. Her mother remained always for her the lovely flower child of devoted photographs.

Her father, who until her conception had been merely one in a running string of romantic relationships, was the ideal man, born at the ideal moment in time, to be a single father. He had received a tiny baby in the dark from a dying woman and found in that gift a sort of magical trust. He had been then a young and promising poet: a troubadour, an alchemist. He could look at anything and turn it to gold. And because of the long demanding business of mothering a baby, coupled with being a man, he became a very fine writer, but he remained, perhaps because of the extraordinarily delightful experience of bringing up a child, somehow carefree in every respect except in his devotion to his daughter. Mary had had what many people would call a ramshackle childhood, but it was also a blessed and golden one.

Her father, being now under the spell of early feminism, did not think for a moment of abandoning the baby to the willing arms of either of her grandmothers. Mary grew up with two prosperous and besotted older women, both longing to provide her with all the delights she had been deprived of by her father's loving, but eccentric, attention. Meanwhile he changed nappies and did the night feeds and wrestled with sieved spinach and whether or not to buy Barbie dolls – and so he knew those tiny intimate moments which bind a parent to its child. Being a man, however, he was disproportionately rewarded for what when women do it is just their duty; he received admiration and help and support and love for raising a child, so he seldom felt disadvantaged.

Since Mary's mother had not actually been a great love, his mourning, though often sentimental, did not become his life's work and he did not project the memorised virtues of the dead woman on to his child, nor blame her ever for the death of his previous beloved.

He continued in his sexual casualness, within a context which was not predatory but friendly. Since her mother was not around to be pained by this, Mary did not have a dark secret to deal with, but an entirely above-board selection of kindly women to be, never stepmothers, but fairy godmothers, who seemed to come and go at their own whim and did not inter- fere because they had nothing to be jealous of, while she stayed in the secure centre of her father's life.

And most importantly, he felt rewarded in complicated ways when at seventeen his daughter told him she was a lesbian. Subliminal jealousy was dealt with for ever. And he loved her. He really loved her.

Mary arrived in Ellie's studio as a very particular, and still unusual, kind of person. A woman of considerable talent of which she had been brought up to be proud. A woman with a confident sexuality which had not been won from her parents aggressively or competitively, nor given to her on a plate. She was innocent and untrammelled in the curious way that those whose passage through childhood has been straightforward and happy often are. She believed that gender was something to be transcended, that it didn't matter; talent and energy mat- tered but gender was an accident. She never had to see her parents fight, and her infant years were brightened by a father who fathered, a father who – by force of circumstance and his good will – mothered.

But she had never encountered either the good mother or

the wicked stepmother. Without even knowing it she wanted Ellie to be both.

She admired Ellie's work more than anything – and knew her own would be better. She was not at all surprised that she had managed to become the apprentice of this woman whose work has been an inspiration and illumination to her. She loved women and knew nothing about mothers. She expected to be loved and admired and to get whatever she wanted.

She had inherited from her parents a thread of gold. She knows she is a princess and therefore she is entitled to have everything she wants.

Looking admiringly at Mary's back, Ellie said, 'Morning,' and then when there was no reply, she asked, as she asked every Wednesday morning, 'How did yesterday go?'

Usually Mary talked to her about the work. It was part of their arrangement, but she was under no obligation to do so. Now she said nothing. Ellie felt no irritation at all, only sympathy, when she added, 'You know you don't have to tell me. It's up to you. But do say.'

That's not 'owning people', Mary thought with some confusion. Perhaps she wanted to be owned. 'Mirrors,' she said abruptly.

'Mirrors?' Ellie repeated interrogatively.

'I'm trying to think about mirrors; Megan showed me those pictures, the architect's ones for the stained glass with mirrors in. I . . . Ellie, I want to do those windows.'

'No,' said Ellie. The word was like a little explosion. Ellie was surprised at herself, only yesterday she had been telling Judith about the windows. Mary turned round sharply, and Ellie interpreted her mulish expression as shock at the rudeness of her response.

'I'm sorry, I shouldn't have said it like that, but I don't want us to do architectural stuff.' In her own 'us' she knew the reason for her snappishness – Mary had said 'I' not 'us'. 'That's not what I do. It isn't, I mean, it isn't for me, real glass. Cold cutting and leading and painting. I do blowing, hot work, craft tradition stuff – I know it isn't very avant-garde but it's what I do, and you know that.'

'But listen Ellie, I want to do them with blown glass.'

'Blown glass?'

'The earliest stained-glass windows were done with blown glass. And not painted; coloured, but not painted. Solid chunks of colours.'

'I'd forgotten that,' said Ellie, suddenly curious. 'I don't know how to do it though. You blow and then flatten and then I think you split them. What happens about the pontil mark?'

'I don't know,' said Mary. 'We'd have to learn. Perhaps you could have a little navel in the centre of each piece. I was thinking very solid strong colours, and, like you do, oxidisation, refraction, those things so that when you walked past it would flash. And mosaic, canes, all those things.'

Damn it, Ellie thought suddenly, was this why she had been wrestling with canes and burying blue iridescence deep inside fused cubes? She felt excited. At the same time she was listening carefully. She knew that Mary was grasping for something, was having a new idea, a new glass idea. Ellie tried to hold herself still, not interfere, not interrupt, be available, be there. But the stained-glass windows could be very high profile for them . . . for Mary herself if she wanted it. And Mary must know that. Ellie was impressed.

'We . . . Patsy and I . . . we were trying yesterday, just messing, experimenting . . . but we didn't know how to . . .'

'We could find out. And with modern hi-tech we could reduce the amount of lead, so you wouldn't need those very heavy lines. It could be . . . It could be beautiful.'

Mary was saying, quite hesitantly, 'Then, the mirrors . . . there would be movement in the glass and movement in the mirrors; and the two would be . . . And I don't know shit about your churchy stuff but, you know the Matisse chapel, where everything is done together. We could . . .'

'Steady on,' said Ellie, but she was smiling. Glass chalices, glass patens. Glass mirrors in the silks of the vestments. She was running fast through her extensive mental data bank. 'I can't think of any glass church ware. But you'd expect some . . . Except for the wickedness.'

'Wickedness?' Mary was startled. On the one hand she could sense Ellie's enthusiasm and she needed that crucially, but she also wanted to keep a hold on this, it was her idea, hers.

'The wickedness of mirrors and glamour and vanity. Don't worry, I was thinking aloud. So that, I assume, is what you were doing yesterday, blowing flat glass? It does seem strange. How did you get on?'

'We gave up. We hadn't a clue actually.'

'Nor have I – we'll have to do some research.'

'We did do some work. And then Patsy showed me how to make canes instead. Millefiorí – pretty. She's pretty good, isn't she?'

'She's good at pretty – it drives me up the wall.'

'What?' asked Mary.

'Pretty glass.'

'But lots of your stuff is lovely.'

'Yes, I know. I hate it. Pretty is the endless temptation of glass you know – blown glass anyway. Sand casting perhaps is different but I don't enjoy it. Glass inclines to be pretty – it can't be ironic; prettiness is the great temptation of glass, like natural is the great temptation of clay. But I don't believe it – in pretty and natural and that stuff.'

'Natural?'

'They're always reactionary terms – pretty. Glass has to be beautiful, transcendent, technical or . . . not pretty.'

'Transcendent!' said Mary pettishly. 'I think *that* is a necessarily reactionary term.'

Ellie laughed, quite affectionately, and said, 'Please don't sulk, because we've got five bloody decanters to do this morning.' She knew she'd said three to Patsy, but she was pushing Mary now, irritated still. Excited and irritated. If she wanted to do the windows she must not mind that Mary wanted to do them too. It was good, not bad.

'Look,' she said, drawing a breath. 'I don't know. This studio isn't set up to do those windows. Frankly I'm not sure I'm set up to do those windows. Architecture scares me, and . . .' Ellie could not bring herself to confess to Mary's youth that she was safe with what she did and this could change her whole standing, change the league that she played in. And if she was not interested in that; if she were really satisfied with what she was doing, then why had she told Megan to show Friedhelm's letter to Mary? Why had she told Judith about the invitation? Did Mary give her courage, or steal her power like every sorcerer's apprentice? 'We'll have to think. You think about the logistics. I'll think about . . . I'll talk to Megan.'

'Really?' Mary asked. It was more than she had hoped for.

'Really, but only if you get a move on now, and we get these decanters done.'

Mary pleased with herself scampered down the stairs. Ellie paused trying to keep a track of her feelings. And then she felt the pressure, low on that flat bony plane at the bottom of her spine; an upward movement like a cool channel, but upwards, against gravity and good sense, like a fountain through her vertebrae. She felt her spine straightening, her shoulders moving back to take the beauty of Angel's passing into her. There was a sweetness in the spiky bones of her neck, a shudder of coolness uninvited in her brain; a shimmering, perfectly timeless moment. Then there was Angel comfortably located in the front centre of her head and speaking in that infuriatingly nasal voice.

'St Gregory says that the sinner, if she really commits herself to her sinful act, "sins eternally", for it is an immortal creature who commits herself.'

'I bet Gregory didn't say "she",' Ellie muttered back.

'Don't be such a clever clogs,' said Angel, 'just watch and pray that you enter not into temptation.'

'Which temptation?'

'So you are aware of the problem?'

'Not now, Angel.' Ellie shook her head free, and followed Mary downstairs. Her bench waited for her; Patsy and Mary waited for her, poised and committed to the morning. They were ready and, with synchronised energy, the three of them abruptly shifted gear. Work. They moved into the dance of the glass, and there was no need to speak. There was a wonderful confidence – they had faith in each other. There were those days when nothing goes wrong. They did four decanters and when they were all laid gently into the annealing chamber, Ellie glanced at her watch and smiled with a pure pleasure.

'You're both wonderful,' she said, and knew instantly that it had been so good because Patsy and Mary were now friends and far from that being threatening to her, in any way at all, it was an added gift, pure bonus.

'Patsy, do you want to take lunch now? Mary? No, you and I can trot upstairs and have a look at what that needs doing to those little jugs – so you'll know what you're up to this afternoon.'

'Ellie, please, can't I have the afternoon off? Well, not off really – to start that research; maybe go to the Craft Council.'

So easy to say yes; Mary looks suddenly sweet, very young, very charming. How can Ellie be so mean? She refused to be seduced by such manipulative charm. 'We've got to get those jugs off.'

Mary's face fell transparently.

Kindness. Dependency.

'I'm sorry. Look, give up your lunch hour and if you do the jugs now, you can take off when you've finished.'

Ellie caught Patsy's eye and remembered that she had been insisting that Mary did her share of the chores, that Mary had to clear up tonight. 'It's OK, Patsy, I haven't forgotten you want to get off early too: I'll scivvy this time.'

Was that a reasonable, though generous, balance, or had Mary exploited her? If the latter, would Patsy mind? Was it her responsibility anyway? Did she care? 'Right,' she said, 'let's get a move on.'

Megan appeared in the workshop doorway. 'Have you got a minute, Ellie?'

'What for?'

'Baubles.'

'God, not already.'

'Yes. Distributor wants to know how many so we can agree a price.'

Mary, still annoyed by the refusal of her research, looked impatient.

'Megan, come up with us and we'll show Mary the pictures and see what thoughts she might have. This is a money earner, Mary, and in that sense a bore, but it's a good one; better than the decanters anyway. Glass Christmas tree baubles, sold – mostly in Germany and the USA – for outrageous prices, but they're pretty and we usually have fun doing them.'

'I don't get it,' muttered Mary, 'one minute you're snapping my head off about pretty and the next we're making Christmas tree trinkets.'

'Mirrored glass,' said Ellie suddenly, genuinely inspired; no longer trying to propitiate Mary. 'There you are, those mirrored baubles; we weren't allowed them as children – my mother thought that they were (a) frivolous and probably blasphemous and (b) dangerous and wasteful since they broke, shattered and might cut the cat's paws. But – I've always done clear ones, with fancy bits inside, but . . .'

And unable suddenly to endure the crossness in Mary's face

after such a wonderful flowing morning she said, 'You see, that makes research into a commercial proposition, so of course you can take the afternoon to research mirroring and blowing and stuff, but you'll have to convert that into commercial designs, not just grandiose fantasies, OK?'

Mary was almost reluctant to give up her sulk. 'What about the jugs?' she asked.

'The packer isn't coming till Friday, we'll fit them in somewhere.' She heard Megan sigh. 'No, we will, Megan, honestly. So, leave them now, Mary, and push off. Megan, have you got anything you need me for because Patsy's gone to lunch and she and I are going to work this afternoon.'

She came out of the huge doorway into the sunshine and stretched; she pulled the plait she often twisted her hair into for work, free of its elastic band and, with Megan, walked away towards the office. 'Did Judith ring?'

'No. Robbie did, and I said you'd ring back later.'

'She will. She's going to commission.'

Megan looked wary.

'No, properly. She says. A competition prize – a big something – charger, bowl. Charger I think because of the lettering; commemorative.'

'You don't like lettering.'

'Megan, please; no, I don't like lettering, but I can do lettering – you're always on at me to do lettering, to do big pieces, cold cutting. To do high publicity display items. It's not that I don't like lettering, it's that you don't like Judith.'

'Actually Ellie, I like Judith very much; and you know I do, but I think she bosses you about and I don't believe she'll pay you properly and I don't believe it because she never does. She crosses over – between private and professional, and I don't like that.'

Ellie suspected she was being reprimanded for giving Mary the afternoon off.

'Look, Megan, you negotiate it. She has said her clients will pay. Get a good deal for us – something that will buy me enough days to try and learn how to do this bloody closed cylinder stuff with the canes – which, if I can get it down, will be extremely profitable and something new – and I want to, so I agree we need money, but just bear in mind I do want to do this one. It's for The Haven.'

Megan's red ribbon fluttered encouragingly on her bosom. Ellie had given her an enamel one for her last birthday, but Megan more often wore the older simpler model, the little gold pin much more neatly managed than most people's. Megan smiled now, understanding and supportive, and at the same time completely conscious that this could indeed be a high profile, media-worthy commission.

'How was Robbie?' Ellie asked, peace having been made.

'All right, I think. He didn't say much.'

They went into the office in silence; and then, in that serene space, relaxed. 'We had a really good morning,' Ellie said.

Megan had bought them both lunch – a pasta salad tidily laid out on plates with metal forks, not plastic. As usual, Ellie perched on the edge of Megan's desk, while Megan occupied her own swivel chair.

'Don't indulge her, Ellie.'

'I don't.'

'She's . . . she's too good at getting what she wants.'

'This time she wants something that you want, Megan,' Ellie said; and then more tentatively; 'If I said that you should contact Friedhelm and say we might be interested in doing his windows, what would you do?'

Megan paused, her fork halfway to her mouth. 'Hypothetically? I'd contact Friedhelm and say that you might be interested in doing his windows. If you mean what would I think, I'm not sure. I never direct artistic policy here and you know that. And I don't know much about stained-glass windows anyway – what sort of technical expansion we might have to take on. Ellie, you know I believe you should tackle that sort of work, but it's a big step; and a big surprise.' She popped the forkful of salad into her mouth, chewed and swallowed it and said, 'So I'd do what you told me; I wouldn't know quite what to think; but I'd feel extremely excited.'

'Megan,' said Ellie, 'please will you contact Friedhelm and say we might be interested in doing his windows, and that I have some ideas about further uses of craft tradition studio glass within his overall design context.'

'But that will be expensive . . .'

'. . . and very provisional at this point. I just don't want him commissioning George Langley or some American stunt engineer while I think about it.'

'He'd rather have you.'

'I know,' said Ellie. 'Which is the point. I mean, I won't have to compete.'

'Coward,' said Megan, but with pleasure and affection.

'I'm going for a walk,' said Ellie, 'hold the fort. And if Patsy gets back before I do ask her to set up and I'll be right with her.' She was suddenly pleased with life.

It was spring. The sun was shining. It was good to walk. She knew she was excited. Mary had tossed down a gauntlet, a challenge. She was up to that. And when she came in Megan was smiling happily – not just contented by Ellie's interest in the windows, but in addition Judith's assistant had rung and proved more than satisfactory on price, timing and scale.

'I'll do some drawings then,' said Ellie, relieved.

'No hurry,' said Megan. Just as Ellie was leaving the office she said, 'Did you find your cube?'

'I haven't really looked. Why?'

'No big deal, I suppose, but Patsy was in a bit of a flap because she can't find that little bowl. She needed it because, as usual,' Megan's voice tightened slightly, 'she hasn't done her paperwork. Apparently you wanted to do some more. They're quite small, Ellie, but it would be a good line perhaps. Anyway she seems to have lost it.'

'She said.'

'But it's odd. We don't lose stuff.'

'Oh come on, Megan, what about the shears?' They had once lost a pair of glass shears under circumstances that had become funny in the retelling, although it remained completely baffling.

'Not the point. The little cube, this bowl. No one could possibly have wanted the shears, we knew that, but these are pretty things, not valuable but . . . precious . . . but I don't want . . .'

Ellie did not want either, she wanted to get to work. 'I'd hang on, Megan. You know what I'm like. And Mary doesn't really have the shape of everything in her head yet. They'll be somewhere. I'm not sure the bowls would work commercially anyway, Megan. That mosaic work's a bit trying, making the canes is really time-consuming, and you could not really charge enough because they're so small. I did have an idea for bowls though. Big blown ones. For fruit, or something, with handles.'

Megan smiled. 'You'll probably never get away from those decanters, Ellie. Unless you do the windows. But sure, why not try? Go on with you, then. I've got work to do.'

Ellie went up the alley-way feeling wonderful, love behind her and work ahead. She paused with a strong sense of physical pleasure in the huge doorway. Patsy came clattering down the stairs at precisely the right moment and with real collegiality and joy the two women went to work.

Suddenly it was radiant spring, the blossoming April moving smoothly into a deep May – bright and green. Hugo and she walked, one late afternoon, up to the Greenwich Observatory and across the park. Hugo was in love.

'You always fall in love in May,' Ellie teased him affectionately.

'Of course,' he said, 'a summer romance, new clothes, holding hands in Soho Square. Warm enough for sex without the
duvet: so it's worth having someone stay overnight. A necessity
of life for your well-adjusted urban homosexual.'

'Will I like him?'

'Probably not. He's too young for you. In fact, he's too young
for me, but so sweet and so filthy minded.'

'How young?'

'Take that severe expression off, not that young.' Ellie really
did not like it when his passing partners were under-age: she
was a keen supporter of an equal age of consent and not at all
worried about legality, but she found very young men boring
for her and she could not eliminate worries about exploita-
tion.

'I've never had a lover more younger than me than you are
than Henry,' Hugo said challengingly.

'I should hope not indeed, you'd have to be into school
blazers. But perhaps that's why . . . perhaps it's me I don't quite
approve of.'

'Henry . . .'

'I entirely approve of Henry.'

'You can't have it both ways: you can't disapprove of me
having twenty-year-old lovers and not disapprove of an even
older Henry acquiring a twenty-year-old wife.'

'Something about commitment, maybe.'

'Permanence is it now? Everything is OK if you are stuck
with it for ever, but not OK if you can change your mind.'

Once again they were walking on the edge, pushing each
other, risk-running.

'All right then,' said Ellie, 'it's about your desire to dominate.
You like being the boss too much.'

'Look, Ellie,' he said, 'I don't think you understand about

sexual dominance – it's never that clear who is dominating whom. Haven't you noticed: I have casual sex with people my own age, and I fall in love with babies? So I'm vulnerable to them more than the other way round. And you don't know, and I'm not going to tell you, who does what to whom, and even if I did, you still wouldn't know who was dominating.'

'Fun with spanking and manacles, eh?' She was never able to imagine it; she had a distinct feeling that, for her, such highly constructed sexual activity would push her giggle-factor too high. However did one move from the 'come back to my place' to the dressing up and tying up business? Hugo assured her that it worked perfectly well, there was a dance, a ritual of organisation, a careful code, but she was never quite convinced.

'No,' he said. She knew she had been warned off.

'I'm making these beautiful bowls,' she told him, 'far sexier than your sweet young thing.'

'Bet you.'

'You bring him to supper and I'll serve you pomegranates and figs in the bowl and we'll see.'

'Figs is cheating, they're sexy even without a bowl.'

'Bring him to supper,' Ellie said, 'it had better be soon, before it's all over.'

'Catty.'

'No, realistic and experienced. By the way, would you like two tickets to the opera for next Wednesday?'

'Can't, alas. I'm off to train trainers. All next week. Midwives.'

'So why "alas"?'

'I'd rather go to the opera. The whole thing . . . I'm . . . frankly, Ellie, I'm getting bored; and the midwife thing always stinks, the gay v. gender politics and . . .'

'This is not like you.' Her concern flickered.

He ignored it. ' . . . And we all know the midwives' boss has invited me because it's cool to have a gay man do the educating, but at the same time someone will pull the womanly mysteries number and who do I think I am trying to teach them their job, and . . .'

'And some of them will be lovely women, whom you will like a lot, and the most important, the best educating will take place in the pub after hours and you will in fact prove genuinely useful.'

'So I will. Thank you.'

Work too was going well. The prototypes for the fruit bowls had taken time but were, for the moment, pleasing both to look at and to make. Megan was persuaded, and was now busy persuading would-be stockists of the decanters that the bowls were a superior alternative, even managing to replace a couple of entire orders.

Ellie's design for Judith's commission pleased The Haven's sponsors, and pleased Ellie more. It had developed into a wonderfully heavy piece; and after some effort she had convinced everyone that the engraved lettering should be around the pedestal so that the interior was as smooth as a font; the surface opalescent, shimmering very slightly, the tones of water in a dream; she began to feel a passion for it, waking in the morning with the weight of it in her hands.

Megan as instructed had contacted Friedhelm and he was buoyantly enthusiastic; and, Ellie caught herself thinking, he did not even know Mary existed; he wanted her, Ellie, and she in her generosity could allow Mary some minor part in the enterprise. Friedhelm came to London and Ellie remembered just how much she enjoyed his wide-ranging intelligence. She took him and Mary out to dinner to discuss the project. Mary was charming and modest, and Friedhelm discreetly smug.

'The sisters are really wanting you, Ellie. They are wanting very much to have women, and to have Catholics also. But I think they are wanting you, for the glass not just for that.'

'Why are they having you then?' Ellie teased him.

'Ah. Of course I am the best. But really for the nepotism.' He smiled at Mary, including her in his warmth. 'My aunt, you see, is the Superior Mother. They are going back, the sisters, to an old monastery, in the Neuelande. Old building, new chapel. It's very good.'

'We must come and see it, the site. For the light,' Ellie said. 'Mary, have you been to Germany?'

'No,' said Mary, 'I haven't been to a convent either.'

'Never?'

'Never.'

They both looked surprised. 'You'll very much like the sisters,' Friedhelm said, grinning; and Ellie laughed knowingly. But Mary did not feel patronised, she felt excited, and also surprised and almost moved by how much this man liked her employer, her boss. Ellie was now telling Friedhelm that he had Mary to thank for her involvement in the scheme. 'I wouldn't have dared without her.'

'Ja. It's a big move for you, Ellie, I know that. But I think it will be good. I think you are brave and not stupid. This is not usual.'

'Not usual?' Mary asked, curious.

'I think not, for a – what is the word? – established? For a craftworker so established as Ellie. To do the new thing, and not a little one. When I am the architect it is never a little thing.'

Ellie glowed. 'The time's right,' she said, 'I've got your authority and Mary's eagerness. We'll send her to Leibnitz next month, and you can talk about me then, so long as it's flattering. Mary, can I trust your loyalty?'

It was not the sort of question one would ask in public unless one was confident of the answer. Mary was aware that she was being given a precious gift, even if Ellie was hyped up, excited and emboldened by the adventure of it all, and by the wine and the party atmosphere.

After that supper they found they were working extremely well together: their good will and energy were infectious and embraced Patsy effortlessly The studio became enormous fun; all three of them graceful, confident and comfortable with each other. A halcyon phase, which they were all capable of appreciating.

One particularly lovely sunny afternoon Ellie arrived home almost completely contented. They had had a good day working with the Christmas baubles. Ellie had been amused by Mary's efforts to get her head and hands around the technology; then suddenly hitting a rare moment when showing off, where technical competence and long hours of practice all came together, Ellie and Patsy had made an extraordinary Venetian curlicue ball, filled with twisted canes and asymmetric loops and threads of glass pulled so fine that the colour faded from the bold cobalt to a purity of sky-blue so delicate that it collected and refracted colour as well as light from elsewhere. It ought to have been hideously coy, like too much contemporary Venetian glass; but its technical skills overrode any tendency to prettiness. Mary, impressed, had gasped 'Can I do that?'

'Yes, of course,' said Ellie, and then caught Patsy's eye. They both laughed wryly. 'Probably not,' Ellie amended, 'not because you aren't up to it, but because I doubt that we are. I don't think it can be done again. Megan will have a fit.'

'Surely . . .' Mary wanted to argue.

'Do you know,' asked Patsy, pleased as Punch with herself, with Ellie, with the bauble itself; 'do you have any idea how many times we have tried this, how many tearful fights we've had with each other because it wouldn't behave?' She held it on her gloved hand with a kind of triumphant humility.

'Have a go, though,' Ellie said, getting up from her bench and offering it to Mary. They had enjoyed an hour of pure laughter, during which all three of them failed even to blow a properly spherical glass ball, and it had not upset them in the least. They had all been very delighted with each other.

Ellie arrived home still entranced and finding Henry already in the kitchen extended her pleasure to him effortlessly. He looked so distinguished, she thought, and relaxed, leaning against the worktop, smiling slightly at the evening and watching her.

He often stood so. In her more complacent moments she liked to think he was admiring, quietly and calmly, her competent and calm grace. Except in the studio where Henry never came, she was not always physically graceful; too many times as she did things there would be an element of fluster, of straggliness. But this evening, in her kitchen, she was graceful, competent, integrated.

She bent down to get the milk out of the fridge.

He said, 'It's my sixty-fifth birthday in September.'

'I know,' she said, turning her head to smile at him over her shoulder – she would take him to Venice for the weekend, a surprise trip; and they would walk hand in hand along tiny back canals while he looked for mannerist paintings and she mourned, while trying not to remember, the decline in Venetian glass. They would eat wonderful meals and drink too much wine. It was a secret, she had not told him yet. Now she thought she would also give him a party and make a layered meringue cake with coffee and almonds which he loved, but was convinced was bad for him. It was; but some things that were bad for you were good for you sometimes, so she smiled over her shoulder and then casually turned back to her reconnaissance.

'There's something I want for a birthday present,' he said.

'Yes?' She was a little curious, because this was unusual for

him; he did not go in for birthdays and had the greatest difficulty in remembering that she did – she wanted breakfast in
bed and silly gifts and to be taken out for extravagant cocktails
at the sorts of bars they never went to; or to be driven into the
sunny countryside for dinner in restaurants beside rivers where
the food was better than she could cook. She wanted them to
act out the tender movements of romance even in her forties,
even when they had not had sex for over ten years.

'Yes?' she said, benignly.

'I want a divorce.'

She did not turn round, she saw her own hands still in the
fridge, quite still, and felt the world stop turning.

'Is that a joke?' she asked.

'No,' he said.

'Got yourself a bimbo?' It came out more sarcastically than
she had meant, but it was the beginning of a process of understanding and persuasion. She could cope with a bimbo, with a
mistress, with another woman. A latish version of the famous
male mid-life crisis. They did not need to get divorced for that.
He was a man of too much integrity. A smile, almost tender,
formed on her face, even while the icy contemptuous amusement of the question hung in the warm kitchen air.

But it was to the sarcasm, not the unformed and unex-
pressed tenderness, that he replied.

'No,' he said, 'I have finally found myself a grown-up.
Annabel is fifty-five and she's offering me a chance, a last
chance, to live a normal life.'

'Well, fuck you,' said Ellie, still not looking at him. She was
in a state of advanced shock; she did not want to hear this and
refused therefore to believe that she was hearing it.

'She does, Ellie, and she loves me and she's capable of doing
so. I am belly sick and bored with your immaturity, your inability to relate to normal human beings and your bizarre perverse
neurosis and your strings of little queens who are dying of

nasty illnesses and who exploit your infantile desire to play mummies and daddies without any of the responsibilities.' He must have practised it for weeks – ten days later she would be laughing with Judith about the astonishing skill of his offensive.

She remembered thinking that. She could not remember what happened next. Something must have happened between when she remembered thinking that and when she heard him yell in both pain and anger. Using her fish gutting knife which, so far as she could remember, had been lying on the draining board beside the sink she sliced his face, a long savage wound from the base of his ear right down past his chin bone and there was a rip in his sweater and he was looking at her stunned and furious and as shocked as she was.

It was a single slash, a beautiful white line, and then the skin was pulling apart, opening up, and the white line filled with red and then suddenly there was a remarkable amount of blood. Pouring down his chin, splashing their lovely Mexican tiles, red on the kitchen floor, red on the linen drying-up cloth that she snatched up, even before she had put the knife down, and clamped to his face. There was no blood on the knife, she noticed distantly, she had been too swift, too clean in her avenging fury and now she felt none of those things, only the panic that accidents and other violence provoked in her.

And they were getting into the car.

And they were driving to the accident and emergency unit.

And at the first set of red lights she said sorry for the first time. 'I'm sorry,' she said.

'You should be,' he muttered from inside the drying-up cloth.

'Yes.'

'You're insane.'

'Yes.'

Insane, and frightened, and deeply ashamed, but with all these things she could still hear a tiny muted undertone of satisfaction, of complacency in his voice, and that gave her back her anger.

'How did it happen?' said the sweet young nurse, peering tentatively under the drying-up cloth and being taken aback by the depth and extent of the wound.

Ellie waited.

'My wife slipped, the kitchen floor was wet, she slipped and fell. Carrying the knife.'

'Oh dear,' said the nurse, 'very nasty.' Like the disease her friends had, according to him. But how nice to be middle class, and safe from too much investigation. How nice to be female on this occasion if she is honest; a working-class male person who had slit his wife's face open with a fish knife would have had the nurse calling the social workers if not the police and she is aware of this even while the glass bubble in which she is enclosed, in which she has been enclosed since he said the word 'immaturity', anneals, hardens and holds her.

'I'm afraid we're going to have to stitch it,' said the sweet young nurse.

They were both somehow reassured. They were good at this. In the early days of Stephanie's convulsions, before they had learned better and the drugs had begun to control things, they had too frequently, too painfully found themselves here, with some different sweet nurse, young or old or inbetween, saying as gently as possible, 'I'm afraid we're going to have to stitch it.'

Ellie held Henry's head gently, firmly, efficiently, and the doctor admired her grace. He put in neat clamps, a line of them like the legs of a monstrous caterpillar crawling down Henry's face.

The doctor said, 'This will hurt like hell in the morning, I'll give you something.'

The doctor said, 'You're not going to be able to shave for a while. Not that side anyway. Do you fancy a beard?'

The doctor said, 'It's a lovely clean cut, you shouldn't have much scarring.'

The doctor said to Ellie, 'Are you all right? This must be pretty scary. Don't blame yourself too much, accidents happen.' She felt Henry's face twitch under her hands, but could not be certain whether it was an impulse to tell the truth or pain or a deep-rooted, if rather malevolent, grin.

The doctor said, 'There you go, sir.' Sir. Dear God, where the hell did Henry get his authority from?

She drove them home, both exhausted. She could not sense his mood, but knew that somewhere that smugness remained. Because he could excite such passion in the wife he was disposing of, or because he had already calculated that she had given him grounds for a divorce even if she would not give him the birthday present he wanted?

In his bedroom, she helped him to get as comfortable as possible. She brought him a glass of water and the doctor's painkillers.

He said, 'That was pretty childish.'

'Yes,' she said, 'I'm sorry.'

'I'm sorry too. That I broke it to you so casually. I really didn't think you'd mind that much.'

He felt some guilt too, then, as well as the complacency. That, as much as his upper-class self-confidence, might explain his ease in lying at the hospital.

'How long?' she asked. 'How long have you been with . . . Annabel . . .?'

'Three years. I've known her longer than that though.'

'Why now?'

'Her husband died.'

'Oh.'

There was a silence. Henry broke it, 'Ellie . . .' She knew he was about to ask her for something: for sympathy, approval, forgiveness, apology, admission that she had indeed been a pseudo-wife – for something, and she did not want to give him anything, not now.

'Not now, Henry,' she said. 'It's late and I'm too tired. You too I expect.' She thought about giving his forehead a goodnight kiss and decided against it.

She stood irresolute at the door for a moment. 'Goodnight,' she said finally, 'sleep well. Shout if you need me.'

She went to her room, pulled her shirt off over her head and dropped it on the floor, stripped off her leggings with her socks still tangled in them. Somewhere as she did this the glass bubble which had seemed so tough around her began to crack. She crept into bed, pulled the duvet over her head so there was no chance that Henry would hear her and began to cry. She did not know if she was crying because he wanted to divorce her; or because she had slashed his face with a fish knife, fish wife, Billingsgate, oh, sweet Jesus. She shook with misery and shock and shame and guilt and anger and love and sadness and pain and loneliness and fury and grief. Loss. Mourning. Death. At which she was expert, as she was with a fish knife, gutting, gutted, guts.

The glass bubble sharded, disintegrated. There was no sign of Angel, no flowing movement in her spine, no comfort, no consolation. She was a crazy lady, sick inside, crizzled.

Telling people was embarrassing. The fact that Henry wanted to leave her felt shameful, but the fact that she had cut his face with a fish knife was embarrassing.

When she told her, Judith whooped with laughter and sent her a first edition copy of the *SCUM Manifesto*.

When she told Hugo he stopped dead in the street dumbstuck for a long moment. Then he held her in a gentle hug, which she knew meant concern and commiseration.

When she made her confession,

'. . . and especially since my last confession which was two months ago, I accuse myself that I, on one single occasion,

slashed my husband's face open with a fish gutting knife, so
that he needed to have twenty-three stitches in his cheek . . .'
she heard a sharp intake of breath. She had never managed to
provoke a personal reaction through the grille before.

Ellie and Henry tried to talk about it.

'I don't see,' sobbed Ellie, over and over again, 'I don't see
why you need a divorce.'

'Not need, want. I want a divorce; I want to marry her.'

The poison welled up. 'You're married to me. You've been
fucking her for three years. You don't need to marry her just to
get laid.'

Henry left the room with a painful mixture of offended dignity, and paternal compassion.

Sometimes Ellie would try to explain, almost as much to
herself as to him, why she would not, could not, do what he
wanted her to.

'I can't consent, I'm not allowed to consent. From my
Church's point-of-view. I couldn't bear to be out of Com-
munion; I can't just let you.'

'Given the things that you do do, and think and say for that
matter, this feels like a pretty childish avoidance exercise.'

He was so cold, so suddenly icily distant. She would not give
him what he wanted, and so he was withholding everything
from her. But she had sliced his face open, and moved herself
outside the normal range of human considerations.

Annabel invited her out to lunch. Ellie went in something
approaching high spirits – impeccably dressed and claiming the
moral high ground: the injured, but noble victim of another
woman's selfish whims. She practised beforehand, in front of a
mirror, saying cruel and clever things: saint to Annabel's whore,
mummy to Annabel's adolescent, wife to mistress, priest to
Annabel's Magdalene, the woman who understood Henry to
Annabel's optimistic ignorance.

It did not work. Annabel was undeniably sweet, but clear and firm, and Henry had betrayed Ellie to her – she knew too much. She was kind, and properly sorry and not stupid, and too much older than Ellie, too professionally successful for Ellie to be able to patronise her. She was obviously very much in love with Henry, and definitely the sort of woman Henry had to marry. Not a bimbo.

She was a grown-up. She chatted to Ellie while they waited for their first course; displaying a considerable and real knowledge, contemporary craft being something of a hobby of hers. She was civilised. She would, thought Ellie viciously, expect her, Ellie, to give them a fruit bowl, an original piece, for their wedding present. She felt more and more infantilised with every mouthful of delicious pepper salad, as though she were being taken out to lunch by her aunt for a treat.

Without thinking Ellie had ordered fish. When she picked up her knife and started to run it along the main bone, she saw the split in Henry's cheek, white and clean before the blood welled out and, quite suddenly, she lost control. She shoved the plate away from her and stood up; her chair fell over behind her and she did not notice.

'Fuck you,' she shouted in the small discreet restaurant. 'Fuck you.' And then with a fierce and horrible venom, she leaned across the table, her mad face only inches from Annabel's shocked one, and hissed at her. 'Until two weeks ago he was living with me. There has been no irretrievable breakdown and I won't play-act: it will take him every damn minute of five years. I'll take you both to the cleaners, and you can see how you like it, bitch.'

She swept out of the restaurant, and caught up with herself on the next street, in floods of wrenching tears, howls of misery which had passers-by stepping aside rather than be contaminated by her deranged passing. It did not prove cathartic. She could not even bring herself to tell anyone about this episode.

She felt she was on the edge. There was a chasm. If she slipped over only Henry could rescue her and now he would not. She did not want to be divorced from him. She was his wife. It was who she was.

'Stay, please stay, please,' she begged him, ringing him on the phone at work, and was humiliated by her own cringing tone.

'It won't change anything, Ellie.'

In between these grovelling fits she moved in a strange terrain where every step felt like too much effort. This desert was, she knew, how it was to be a grown-up; no wonder she had decided, chosen, to be what Henry called 'immature'.

She discovered that she was also frightened that, without Henry, she would not be able to cope; simply be incapable of managing daily life. Right from the beginning of their relationship, for over quarter of a century, Henry had taken care of her. Henry had been the only person to know she needed taking care of.

No one understands, Ellie thought self-pityingly.

My dear Stephanie,

I hope your father has had the decency (if one can use the word in this context) to write and tell you his 'news' – the two of you will be feeling very close, I dare say. Since excuses for moral failure are now so prevalent I am sure the two of you will happily be able to establish a gene for desertion and betrayal so that none of it will be either of your faults. I hope too that you are amusing yourselves together working out all the ways that it is my fault. I would really like to know, and think now that I have a right to know, whether the two of you have been in communication throughout the last year.

I am feeling very sad and lonely actually; it would be nice to think that I had taught you at least your duty to care; even if I have failed to give love any real emotional practice in your life.

> *I do hope you are well, as I continue to love you very much,*
> Mummy

Inside the depression, and beneath it Ellie had an escalating fear of her own insanity. A Voice Hearer; she was a menopausal nutter:

> 'Usually there is little one can offer the patient as a substitute for the fantasy gratifications . . . for reality has actually become poor in prospects, and resignation without compensation is often the only solution.'

Sometimes it was tempting – the darkness called she could so easily step towards it, embrace it. She could be ill; she could go mad, then it would not be her responsibility any more. It was there, madness was there waiting, all she had to do was consent. Then someone would take care of her, would drug her into silence. She needed someone to take care of her.

Yet when the maddest moments came they had nothing to do with consent. At Goose Green, on the bus . . . losing herself, being quite clearly and absolutely someone else, some other self, without will or volition. She was her, she was Ellie and she could not, would not consent to be anything else: she was not a child in the hold of a Phoenician merchant ship; she was not a Venetian apprentice on the run; she was not . . .

. . . The priest, his hands shaking with fear, raises the chalice, the magical chalice, the treasure of this cold fenlands church, the *diatreta*, which is the green of fresh peas, in reflected light and glows violet pink in transmitted light – he raises the chalice for all the people to see. The chalice from the green western hills which the hermit princess, the prophetess Alfreda, daughter of Offa of Mercia, had given them in gratitude for their hospitality when she fled her father and sought the true and silent fatherhood of God. The chalice which they have been forbidden to use by the Holy Mother Church, but which now they use, because the Danes are at the gate, their dragon ships seen in the sunset and they are coming, encouraged by their fiercer gods who have more sense than to die peacefully and forgivingly. There will be blood and rape and death before the dawn and the rising sun will see the smouldering ruins of this proud house.

The ordinary chalices of gold and silver will not avail against the blond strangers who hunt in packs. They will not prevail now, and the huddled people have turned by common consent to the old magic.

The priest elevates the glass chalice and sees its heart catch fire. It is high above his head and his wrists are tense when he hears the low roar of the war horde outside and above that growling thunder the first screams of a small child. He hears the silence and his wrists respond with fear. He feels his fingers jerk, a spasm of horror, and then he feels the chalice filled now with the blood of Christ, feels it slip, slip through his tremulous consecrated fingers, and smash, smash on to the tiled floor, the sacred blood of the Saviour, spraying up, staining the very edge of the white tunical and the shards of glass, pea green and magenta, tossed out on the red flags. A long moan of fear and loss shakes the congregation, for they are all damned now: the Danes will kill them tonight, and they will wake in hell for eternity. The use of glass chalices is forbidden and they chose to disobey and they are punished. But the priest looks only at his hands, and prays to a more ancient god, the winter god of the villages where still they bury their dead with household treasures and dance at the foot of the yew trees during the longest night. The gods have fought here, Christ and Thor have fought along the bones of these fingers, and the priest is not certain who has won. He knows though that the beautiful glass chalice is broken, and when he gathers in the pieces, there is green and pink, but there is also the red of blood, Christ's blood and blood from the cuts to his clumsy and sacrilegious hands . . .

. . . But there were no glass chalices, Ellie thought, still sitting in her bed and looking at her own hands, clumsy, sacrilegious perhaps, but not blood-stained. There were no glass chalices. She was an expert on the history of glass, and she knew there were no glass chalices. It suddenly mattered enormously. With slightly shaking hands she reached for her standard history of glass and thumbed the index: *chalices* p. 87, it said:

> The spread of Christianity meant that after the late seventh century goods were no longer buried with the dead in Britain, northern France and the Rhinelands. Although the making of glass vessels did not cease altogether, the industry existed only for the production of everyday items. The use of glass chalices was prohibited by the Christian Church in 803, and again in 813 and 895, as well as by Pope Leo IV (847–855) for fear that they might be broken. This prohibition robbed glassware of its prestige and led to its closer association with commoner materials like wood, pottery or tin.

She was terrified, now, and crying. Being terrified made the whole thing worse, not better.

> Although the Church forbade the use of the glass vessels for ritualistic purposes, it encouraged the use of glass for windows, so the monasteries began to concentrate more on stained glass for their abbey windows.

'Angel,' she cried, 'do something. Get God to do something.'

But apparently her madness caused even Angel embarrassment. Ellie could sense Angel's odd shame, a sheepish and sly evasion. Angel only said, 'Try intercession.'

And when Ellie was exasperated added crossly, 'Prayer is extremely effective. Don't you understand, it doesn't even have to be a prayer, a *thought* when it is genuine and strong, has an effect. And if you humans seldom, if ever, have direct experience of that, it's because your thoughts are never *real* enough.'

Ellie knew that was true. The glass bauble they had made only a few weeks ago had been a real thought. The still missing oxydised cube had been a real and effective thought. It happened sometimes. Of course, she believed it, it was her stock in trade, every serious craftsperson must know that, even if they did not have a vocabulary to say it.

But she did not know how to think herself sane, and good and lovely and secure any more. So there was nothing else to do but get up and face life in a house where there was no pot of hot coffee waiting ready-made for her.

There was no escape from the wearisome day, she could not even curl up and die, because on top of everything else Robbie was ill again, and she had to go to Kentish Town and visit him. By mid-morning Ellie was driving, or trying to drive, across Tower Bridge. The traffic was heavy, solid, standing and creeping when she noticed nervously that the little needle of the temperature gauge was moving, slowly but steadily, towards the right. Angel was suddenly present again. Ellie felt distraught and short tempered: 'Why don't you get to work on that then, if intercession is so brilliant.'

'That,' said Angel, 'doesn't need prayer; it needs you to remember to put water in.'

'Henry . . .' began Ellie, crossly, and stopped. 'Oh, go dance on the head of a pin!' She got some relief from her own wit.

'Can't,' said Angel, 'no room.' And before Ellie could draw breath to remonstrate, added 'They were wrong, the schoolmen; the answer is not infinity.'

Ellie roared her engine. The traffic jammed entirely. She

slumped down behind the steering wheel, unbearably frustrated and irritable.

'Look,' said Angel, in a quite different tone of voice.

The tide was high, the sun shone brilliantly, the river swept gracefully, up past St Paul's, and the water, ruffled up by a stiff breeze caught sparkles of light and bounced them off the walls of the Embankment, the sides of dirty barges, and in and out of the barrier of shadow that the upper, laced web of the bridge had laid down on the water over fifty yards away. There was, beyond the dancing tongues of fire in water, light in shadow, a faint mistiness, despite the opalescent blue of the sky. A thousand thousand candles, tiny double tongues of pure light.

Ellie burst into tears. 'He's going to die, Angel.'

'Yes,' said Angel, quite gently. 'Try not to envy us in heaven.'

Half-blinded with tears and the refracted light from the river, startled by a blaring horn very close behind her, Ellie revved the engine and quite automatically noticed that during the brief pause the accusatory pointer of the temperature gauge had dropped back to normal.

'Don't thank me,' said Angel, 'I don't understand about cars any more than you do.'

'Did you intercede?'

'None of your business,' said Angel.

'Oh, leave me alone,' Ellie shouted. Angel obeyed demanifesting painfully fast. Then Ellie missed her.

She found Robbie was a great deal more ill than she had realised and she had the tiresome task of getting him organised to go back to hospital. She had a sense that this was going to be the last time, but he did not seem to share that awareness. Hospital visiting under these circumstances was tiring, time-consuming and self-revealing, but she did not feel she had the energy to pay proper attention.

And she had to; all the way across London a regular basis, when she had no sympathy to spare for anyone except herself.

Did she need him as much as he needed her? She did not like the thought.

'Plum drop,' she exclaimed arriving in his room after he had been there about ten days.

He smiled. He was very tired and he was happy to see her.

Someone needed her; she drew a perverse pleasure from that and hated herself for it.

'I want to go home,' he said to her, as she was drawing herself together at the end of the visit. 'Can I go home?'

'Mmm . . .' she considered it sensibly, 'tricky I should think. Some of this stuff . . .' She swept an experienced eye around the room and its equipment.

'I'm quitting,' he said.

'Oh damn, Robbie,' she said, 'are you sure?' The tears sprang up, the inexhaustible well that each time she thought had dried up, that next time it would not hurt so much and it always did. Or worse, it didn't. She knew she was business-like now. She knew her own limitations; and the drowning sense that she ought to keep something in reserve in case it was needed by someone she loved even more than she loved Robbie. She was running out of the strength to do this, and yet she might need it . . . She wanted to tell Hugo to test now, so that she could calculate how much energy she could spare for Robbie's dying.

At the same time this was important for Robbie. Robbie's choice, that ought not to be monitored or measured against anyone else's. There was no point in her having been here, no point to the four happy days they had spent in Paris less than eight months ago, no point in all the long years of friendship and giggling and affection, no point unless she would stay there and hear his choices and then do what could be done to have them work for him.

'Are you sure?' she asked. She did not argue. It had gone on a long time.

'Yes,' he said and her tears flowed over. Floods of them, for him, for her, for them all and for the time ahead.

'I'm sorry,' she said through the tears.

'No,' he said, 'it's nice to be cried for.' He was crying too, but quietly because he was too tired for anything else.

'OK,' she said. 'Give us a couple of days to get it laid on.'

He muttered something and she bent down to hear it. He tried again, 'When Ellie Macauley lays one on, it stays laid.'

'Thank you.'

She sat there for a while, holding his hand, grateful that he was one of those people who liked to have his hand held. It was a hard discipline for her with people who loathed that. When he fell asleep she left the room and went down to the nursing station.

'Sue,' she said to the nurse, the wonderful nurse whom she wished she did not know. She did because Robbie's partner, Tim, had died here eighteen months ago. Robbie had been scared – and later angry, betrayed: they had both wanted to die first. Early on they would joke about it, drawing lots and producing a complicated black comedy of merit, to decide who would have the privilege. 'If I clean the loo *and* the fridge, can I die first?'

'Ellie?' Sue responded warmly.

'He wants to go home.'

There was a silence. 'To die,' added Ellie, just in case it wasn't clear.

'Yes,' Sue said. 'He's very tired today. He hasn't said so to me.'

'I think he wanted to know if I . . . if we . . . if it could be managed.'

'Can it?'

'How long?'

'For heaven's sake, Ellie, you can never guess. Not very, I'd say.'

'If he wants to, we'll manage. I told him.'

126

'OK. Look . . . he may talk about it this evening now, and if he doesn't and it seems right, I'll ask him in the morning. But if he's going it should be soon.'

'Yes,' said Ellie, and a wave of tiredness overwhelmed her. She started to cry again. Sue started to cry too. They wrapped their arms round each other and sobbed. There wasn't much else to do.

They took Robbie home two mornings later. The room was so full of medical stuff that it looked like a hospital anyway, except that his cat slept on the bed with him. So much effort just for that.

'Megan,' Ellie said, 'Robbie's dying.'

'Oh, Ellie.' Megan said nothing more, she just reached for the diary, and then in a coolly efficient voice said, 'Actually, it could be worse. We'll take it day by day.'

'I'm not sleeping there,' said Ellie, 'a friend of his is, and his mother's coming down.'

'Good or bad.'

'Good, I think. They've got the number here anyway.'

'Fine, I'll be prepared. Let me know where you're going to be.'

'Well,' Ellie said, to Hugo on the phone, 'you can come to New York now if you like.'

'Don't,' he said. 'Don't be like that.'

'Don't you want to come then?'

'Can't you just say it? Can't you just say, "Robbie's dying"? What am I meant to say? "Oh goody. Oh lucky little me." Whereas if you'd just say it, I could say "Oh poor Ellie, I do love you and isn't it all fucking bloody awful", which is what I want to say, instead of you sniping with me about New York. And, before you get wound up, yes I do want to go to New York, and thank you very much.'

'I suppose it's good that we still get angry.'

'Jesus, Ellie, don't make it sound like a therapy session.'

'I'm not getting anything right today, am I?'

'Oh, I'm sorry. Do you need a long distance hug? Shall I come over?'

'No, I'm fine, honestly. Don't worry.'

But she knew the real reason she did not want him to come to Greenwich was because of what Henry had said about her 'strings of little queens who are dying of nasty illnesses and who exploit your infantile desire to play mummies and daddies without any of the responsibilities'. She was angry with Henry, he would not comfort her himself and he would not let her be comforted, and she knew too that she was taking her irritation out on Hugo because she did not want Henry to divorce her and perhaps if she were sweet and good he would change his mind. She felt drained. 'I'm fine,' she reiterated to Hugo now, 'I'm sorry I was tetchy, Hug. I'm tired.'

'Poor Ellie. Let me know if there's anything I can do.' But he was cross with her. He loathed it when she called him 'Hug', and made cute jokes, and then did not want him to come and comfort her in the only way he knew. He was irritated with her for being so sad and needy and unamusing, and he did not like that in himself.

Ellie found herself wishing that Robbie would just get on with it. He died, very early on Thursday morning, less than a week after they brought him home.

Megan, when Ellie told her, immediately rang Hugo, and he came at once.

He stopped in the office for a briefing. 'Bless you,' said Megan looking up from her desk. Hugo shrugged his shoulders, indicating that there was nothing to thank him for.

'How's Ellie?'

'I don't know yet. She's here, she's working. She wasn't there at the end; just bad luck I think, but she minds.' And then suddenly her face broke up. 'He showed me a new lesion one day, quite casually; he said, "Look, Mrs Hamilton, it's like a map of the new world." And I said, because I couldn't think of any-thing else to say, I said, "I do think you should call me Megan," and he said, "Just because I'm dying, Mrs Hamilton? That would be a new world," and he laughed at me.'

'Oh Megan,' said Hugo surprisingly touched.

She smiled, slightly self-mockingly, 'And who said you could call me Megan, young man.'

'You did.'

'That's fine then.'

They laughed, and Hugo went down towards the studio and met Ellie in the doorway. She leaned against him, and he held her. 'He just got too tired, Hugo.'

'Yes,' said Hugo, his arms tightening round hers. 'Or tired enough.'

'I wasn't there. I wish I had been. I went home about mid-night, I was exhausted. His mother rang there, bless her. So I went to church and lit a candle.' She knew Hugo wouldn't like that much, but also that he would tolerate it.

She told him the whole story: 'It was good, really. We always seem to be telling ourselves that it was a good death and it was time; no one says "merciful release" any more but we might as well, you know. There are no good deaths really, not good AIDS deaths anyway, because no one should have to be there in the first place. I suppose that's unbearable. But it was good. Gentle. Not like Tim's. Do you remember Tim's? That was tough, brutal. Tim was from hell: truculent, resistant, paranoid, angry, the lot. Furious with Robbie. And Robbie was so hurt and frightened. This was a doddle.'

She did not like sounding like that and went back to the story, 'Mike – Mike Turney, do you know? – and some friend of Robbie's called Simon from way back, were there; and Trish came just a bit before I left and was what I think one calls "a Tower of Strength".'

'Trish?'

'Oh, Tim's sister; she's a nurse, a good friend. I think she's thick as two short planks myself, but . . . but, well, it wasn't for his penetrating analytic intelligence that one loved Robbie anyway. And his mother was fabulous. Very calm. Very generous with herself. You know, she wasn't trying to claim Robbie, or the death, as *hers*. She did all the right things – like leaving the room when other people came, and making sure she knew everyone's names and how they were connected. I rather admired her. But it was hard too, because she adopted me somehow as her ally, because I was older and so on, as though I was there for her. Not as someone who might need help, but as a quasi-official support-giver. I resented that a bit. She couldn't quite figure it out. But she was great really, and you know how awful they can be . . . remember Mark's mother!'

Hugo knew Ellie needed to link the whole business of Robbie's death back into her own history, a history of too many similar deaths, to make it both like and different from them. He too was experienced at this. He picked up on 'mothers' and added to the collection.

'Or Jamie Crighton's. Did you encounter Jamie's mother? She just wanted to take her darling "home". She could not accept that he was at home, his home. She wasn't loathsome like Mark's mother, she really wasn't, but she was quite unable to see why he was better off where he was, you know?'

'Oh God, yes. Well then, this was easy. And she could talk about Tim. She asked me on the phone this morning if they could have "a funeral like Tim's", and how did she organise it? I was pleased, but I did point out to her that her family might not like it. And she said, oh she'd thought about that and perhaps they would have two funerals – one here in London and one in Norwich – but we, his London people, had a right to have first go, something like that. That's quite impressive.'

'And you, were you "impressive"?'

'I don't know. I was so tired, Hugo. I was reeling. You know what I sort of like about myself is that I can stay, that I can stay there in those situations, very simply be there, and I was finding that I couldn't, not really. And then I got angry. He was such a bunny rabbit, wasn't he? And I couldn't get my head round it. Round my anger on his behalf, I mean, because it sort of suggested that if he hadn't been such a sweet person, it wouldn't have been so shockingly unfair, and that can't be right. Like it was normally it's God's judgment on homosexuals and junkies, but he should have been exempted. I couldn't shake the anger.'

There were things she could not tell him though. That she had tried to work out who would do this for her, and realised that there was no one. And worst of all she had been bored. That was frightening. Had it been some sort of emotional trip for her, this being at the bedsides of the dying, whose effect was wearing off? But it had been boring: she knew what to do and she had done it. Robbie's mother and Simon and Mike and Trish and the doctors and nurses and carers involved would all think that she had been just wonderful. But it had been an achievement of practice and knowledge, not a triumph of love, as it should be. To walk to the doors of heaven with someone and then just let them go, let them fall free unencumbered not because that is virtuous but because you love them.

And she had not been there when he died. 'I won't go away, Robbie,' she had told him. 'I'll be here.'

Her voice quavered, broke up suddenly, and she started to cry, 'It's silly, Hugo, it's silly and selfish but I wish I hadn't gone home. I wished I'd stayed. I feel sort of cheated of something, as though he should have waited till I was there. Maybe he was pissed off at me, maybe he thought, well, if she's just going to push off . . . maybe it was the last thing he thought, a sort of despair because I couldn't do the distance. Or maybe he wanted me.'

Hugo petted her, 'Ellie . . .'

'I know, I know,' she said, 'but I promised him. I promised I would be there. And I wasn't.'

'You were. You were in every way that mattered. He wasn't that stupid, he knew that. He loved you and he knew you wouldn't have given up on him.' He grinned a little sheepishly. 'This may sound like a bit of sentimental crap but, Ellie, I think . . . we think people who go like that, like Robbie did, slowly, I really do think that they can choose, that they do choose. I've known people who picked the one moment when they were alone, for instance; you know, well-loved and well-cared for people, who just need a bit of privacy to get over the hump. They'll wait until their lover goes to the loo or something and then die. It must be choice. They never look like it was panic. Or people who wait for their lover, their mother, the priest, whatever their bag is. If Robbie had needed you, he'd either have died when you said you were going or he'd have waited until the morning.'

'Thanks,' she said a little shakily. Hugo had missed the point. If Robbie did not need her why on earth had she put herself through all that? If he had not needed her, at least wanted her strongly, then why had she stretched herself out on that particular rack one more time? If, on the other hand, he had needed her, she had failed him.

She was enormously comforted by Hugo's presence, by his love and concentration, by the very fact that he had come so quickly when he had heard, and by his arms round her now. He held her and then started kissing her, very gently on the top of her head, mussing her hair: a gift, she knew, because it was not his sort of gesture.

He stayed all day. Holding her hand while she made the inevitable long string of phone calls to all the people who ought to know, going with her up to Robbie's flat to see him and condole with his family. He insisted she ate, suggested she sleep and went with her for a walk in the park. He offered to take her home, afterwards, but they went back to the studio instead.

'This is silly,' he told her, 'do you need to be here? You're tired. You should be in bed. Do you want me to come and tuck you up?'

'No I'm going to work. There's something I have to do.'

'Oh Ellie!' He sounded exasperated.

'No, I said it wrong. There's something I *want* to do. Perhaps,' she smiled, 'perhaps I "just need a bit of privacy to get over the hump". Honestly Hugo. I want to be here . . . it's my place . . . I don't want to be at the house . . . I'll probably sleep here too.'

'Are you sure? We could go somewhere, or . . .'

'No. please.'

They smiled at each other. He was a little worried and very loving. She was totally weary. Then she pulled herself together, 'Don't go just yet though. Come in the office a minute. I'll make us some coffee.'

Megan had finished work, but she was still sitting at her desk, obviously waiting in case Ellie needed her.

'OK?' She smiled at them both. 'Ellie, if there's anything . . .'

'I know, Megan, thank you.' Ellie smiled gratefully. 'We haven't got a funeral day yet. Sometime next week. Will you want to come?'

'Yes, I think so.'

'Shall we close the shop?'

'The girls could manage, of course. Or . . . do you want to?'

'Mark of respect?' asked Hugo curiously, 'how sweet you two are.'

'Old-fashioned,' said Megan darkly, '"craft tradition".'

'Don't tease me,' Ellie interrupted.

'We're not, oddly enough,' said Megan, 'we're slightly admiring, and in my case, though not in Hugo's, slightly at cross purposes. It's my job to run a tight ship, take on commercial values and enable the Craftsmistress to be an Artist. And then

133

I find I really like the prissy and uncommercial things you do. It's not teasing.'

'Yes, it is,' said Hugo. 'Where's my coffee? No, not you, Megan, I wouldn't dare and you're obviously trying to leave.'

'I'm staying, Megan,' Ellie said. 'I'll probably stay all night, but if I leave I'll do the security. Are Patsy and Mary still here?'

'Patsy went. Mary's still up there. She was supposed to be checking the glass balls for packing.'

'I'll lurk here then, I can't face sheepish condolences.'

'She says you and Patsy say you can't do that gorgeous blue bauble on series.'

'She's right.'

'It's lovely, Ellie. Couldn't you take it down a bit, simplify.'

'I don't know, Megan; I think it would just look naff. We're doing enough others, aren't we?'

'Yes, but I like it. I like it a lot.'

'Present?'

'Ellie!'

'She always gets shocked when I give things away, even to her; she thinks it's wasting resources,' Ellie told Hugo. 'I even have to sneak Christmas presents out of the office.'

'Luckily for you,' Megan was smiling, 'but actually I'm going to make an exception for this one; yes, please, I'd like it. I'll keep it here for a bit, to encourage you, but its mine, and when I want to I will take it home.'

'Megan,' said Ellie touched and surprised.

Megan owned three pieces of Ellie's glass. Two she had bought herself at their full retail price and one, a huge pink and gold almost spherical vase, Ellie had made for her as a birthday present. It had been accepted reluctantly and only on the condition that Ellie never did so again.

'It's little enough, it has no commercial value on its own, it's one of the most beautiful small things you've ever done, and it's *you*. No one else could have or would have.'

'And Patsy,' Ellie said quickly.

'The studio then. It is hallmarked from this studio; only *we* could have made it.'

Megan stood up, carried her coffee cup through to the tiny kitchen space, and Ellie and Hugo could hear her rinsing it out. She emerged, carrying her coat. 'I'm off then. Take care, Ellie.'

'I'm not planning to blow.'

'That's not what I meant. Goodnight, Hugo.'

'Night, Megan,' Hugo said.

'Bless you, Megan,' Ellie murmured in her ear as they touched cheeks. Megan patted her gently on the shoulder, and departed briskly.

They were halfway through their coffee when they heard Mary coming down the alley. They saw her passing the window, glancing in, registering surprise. She poked her head through the door.

'I'm done. I was just coming to ask Megan if she wanted me to lock up.'

'No need. I'm going to work.'

'Oh damn, Ellie, I'm sorry; I've lidded the furnaces and everything. I didn't think you'd . . .' There was a pause, 'I'm really sorry about your friend, Ellie. I . . . should I have asked Megan?'

'She wouldn't have known.' Ellie was tender in her sadness. It made some people short-tempered, grief and tiredness together, but it made Ellie grateful, generous. She said suddenly, 'Mary, do you ever want to work at night. Do you have keys? Has Megan shown you the alarm system? I mean how to switch it off as opposed to on. You ought to feel free . . . except if there are lights on, it's me. OK.'

Mary blushed with pleasure. 'Thank you.'

'Ask Megan in the morning. If I forget to tell her; say it was my idea; you've been here long enough. Which reminds me, by the way, if you're counting the glass balls, can you remember the blue Venetian one? Megan's going to have it; it shouldn't go in with the rest, I don't want the packers mixing it up. They're coming on Friday.'

'Don't worry; it's not with the others anyway, they're all in the packing room, Patsy told me to put them out on the trays. I've just done them.'

'Oh, where is it then?'

'I don't know. Probably Patsy put it out.'

'Fine. Are you off then? Where's your helmet?'

Hugo said affectionately, 'You're so bossy, Ellie, like someone's Mummy.' He was then momentarily nervous that she would feel betrayed.

Mary said, 'I haven't got the bike today, I'm walking.'

Ellie glanced quickly at Hugo. She wanted to be alone. She could always trust him to get that sort of message.

'I'm on my way too. Are you homeward bound? Do you want company?' Mary nodded, pleased. Ellie went into her little room at the back to put on her overalls, and Hugo picked up the coffee cups and carried them to the sink.

Mary and Hugo walked together, and Hugo noticed that he had to shorten his stride for her to keep up.

'That was kind of her,' Mary said, 'I've often wanted . . .'

'To have it to yourself, the studio?'

'Yes, but . . . sometimes I just want time to think. To think about glass, you know. It's hard work. Ellie works you hard; she's a good teacher, and I really wanted to do it this way, but I'm learning lots of new things all the time, and I don't have a chance to pull it together. Sometimes I think maybe I'll go back to college, do some graduate work, but that's not quite what I want either. If, just sometimes, I could go there at night. Just be there. There's so much going on, I mean outside. Concentration, I find concentration very hard at the moment. I need breathing space, and she's just given it to me.'

'She's like that. Why didn't you ask?'

'Unprofessional really. Sort of etiquette. It's hers to give, I mean any studio boss's. That's why I'm pleased actually. She didn't have to.'

They walked down to the tunnel. When Mary saw the tunnel entrance, the neat round dome and little pointy top knobs, she laughed. 'Someone told me they were called Queen Victoria's boobs. They do look like tits don't they?'

'I suppose. I don't know very many real ones.'

'Ever had sex with a woman?'

'That is taking liberties,' Hugo said shortly.

'It's what they're there for, liberties.'

Hugo grinned, impressed. Mary glanced at him, not wanting to go too far, but curious. Do not, she told herself, do not ask him if he has ever had sex with Ellie. Just don't. Don't, because he will quite properly be angry; and don't, because even thinking about anyone having sex with Ellie is a very bad idea for you personally. She acknowledged the value of her own advice. And because she was so busy instructing herself, there was a pause in the conversation, which Hugo heard as respect, so he answered the question.

'Yes, I have actually. It was a long time ago. I was curious.'

'Is your sexuality driven by curiosity?'

'Probably. Anyway, I did it, and she was a very nice woman, and it "worked", but it was an error, for me, a misdirection, so I haven't bothered since.'

'Not one of these gay men who sleeps with women then?'

'Exploring my latent bi-sexuality? No thanks, I'm rather old-fashioned.'

'But you like women . . .'

'"Some of my best friends", etc. I like lots of things I don't have sex with – Matisse paintings, beer, smoked halibut, my grandfather. Do you? Sleep with blokes?'

'No. But I've done it with straight women which is probably even more of an error.'

They trotted down the steps into the tunnel, and walked along, comfortable and companionable.

Suddenly she said, 'I knew him too, you know.'

'What?'

'I knew Robert.'

It still took him a moment; he had never heard Robbie called Robert before.

'Not well . . . not like Ellie did, but . . . his sister was a friend of mine at school. He was quite important to me, when I was in the sixth form, working stuff out, you know.'

'I'm sorry,' he said. 'Why didn't you say? It didn't occur to me.'

'It wouldn't, would it?' which was entirely reasonable, but he could tell that she felt hurt somewhere. 'My first,' she said shyly, 'my first AIDS death.'

'And no one has comforted you?' She looked very young, and he heard his own voice sounding as though he was talking to a child which was not fair. 'It's shitty isn't it?' He put out a hand and touched her shoulder, and she turned towards him crying. He held her briefly, semi-detached against his chest.

'Tell Ellie,' he said.

'It seemed intrusive.'

'It wouldn't, not to her. Honest. She'd like the idea of his larger community. And . . . she's very kind, you know, Ellie, especially if you're upset, distressed. Sometimes that's annoying, that she pays best attention if you're miserable, but when you are miserable it's very nice.'

And even in her genuine sadness Mary felt a flicker of something like triumph.

'You must tell her, because of the funeral. You will want to go and she will feel terrible if you don't go and she asks you to work or something and then she finds out later. And . . .' he hesitated, not sure if what he was about to say would seem in appalling taste to her, or if she would hear it as the simple truth that it was, '. . . and the funerals are important. We've learned how to do that. The pay-off for an AIDS death is an AIDS funeral; and you can take that away with you to every appalling "proper" funeral you ever have to go to and there will be lots, and it will comfort you.'

Hugo felt old: he wanted quite suddenly not to be an Urban Bad Boy, an in-your-face queer, but to be a cardigan wearing-poof in the country with a West Highland terrier. He laughed at himself; it was too late for that. Instead he was extremely good at funerals; and had developed a detached way of speaking about sexual practices which was enormously factual, unembarrassed. AIDS is a bloody brutalising disease and it would be stupid to pretend he too had not been brutalised by it.

The awareness that there was no going back, only forward, made him feel loving towards this young woman.

'I'm meeting someone later on, but I need to eat first. Do you fancy something?' he asked her.

She was pleased. He enjoyed her pleasure. Suddenly they were in a unusual, soft mood – linked by a death that was peripheral to their emotions but central to their lives. She ate with a greedy enthusiasm that took him aback. She talked with a stunning candour about sex. She asked him why it was that the London lesbian community did not seem thrilled to bits to discover they were very unlikely to get AIDS.

'It ought to cheer us up no end, you know, and it doesn't. Why not? Because we all hate sex really? It's faintly disgusting, and any excuse to wear latex gloves is a comfort. I really do not understand it. For me it's such a relief, that research and . . .'

'I don't think so, I don't think it's just sexual repulsion . . . I have a theory that it's about underlying feminism.'

'You mean the big no-no on anything more energetic than stroking the cat and patting the puppy?'

'Would I dare? No. No; everyone knows that the sisters have

put in more than their share of bedside time – I mean the hard stuff, the work; but your politics say that you shouldn't be servicing *men*, even gay men. So it has to be your illness too because, if it isn't, you are just the old unreconstructed carers, nurturers and nurses you have always complained about being. So when someone comes along and says it is not your disease, you aren't building communities of need for yourselves, you feel foolish and it makes you angry.'

'Enough of the "you", please; say "they".'

'Not a feminist, then?'

'I suppose . . . yes, of course I am, but . . . to tell the honest truth . . . there's lots of sorts; and I'm not, I can't stand, there's something about a puritanism that calls itself politics. Like dressing badly is virtuous. For me it's . . . "If I can't dance, I don't want to be part of your revolution." Like that.'

'Hey, what is that?'

'Emma Goldman,' said Mary, 'the anarcho-syndicalist.'

'Ellie would love that.' He knew at once that it was not fair to bring up Ellie, but Mary just smiled and he let it go without apology.

She told him of her sexual adventurings in London. She was shrewd and self-mocking. He enjoyed it.

'Are you a pioneer or a settler?' he asked, and noticed, pleased with himself, that he had remembered not to mention that this was a game of Ellie's.

She looked blank, so he explained, expanded the concept. Then he asked, 'So – does it turn you on to do things that you feel are transgressive, or are you looking for a place to settle down?'

'It's odd,' she said, 'you might understand if you met my father, but I don't have any real sense of the transgressive at all. He is a man so wonderfully liberal that sometimes you actually try to say something that will make him angry.'

'Like what?'

'I did tell him once that I was joining the Conservative Party, just to bait him, and he only managed to look saddened. I could walk into the house with the proverbial black one-armed lesbian mother and her triplets and say, "Oh, Dad, this my new lover, we're into heavy S and M", and he would say, "Hi, do sit down, I'm just cooking. Are you a vegetarian because I'm afraid there may be some chicken stock in this soup?" And he would mean it. So I don't think that I get much of a charge out of sexual transgression. Shame really. Do you?'

'Yes,' he said.

'But you don't have sex with women?' She was teasing him, but he was having such a pleasant time that he admired her bravado, rather than feeling pissed off.

Later she said, 'I'm asking round. Do you know anyone who might want to father my baby?'

'Contact?' he asked.

'Some, I hope. Name, I'd like, and some background. Something to tell the little one when it asked. Put contact down as negotiable. But no financial responsibility.'

'Are you serious?'

'Yes, I told you before. Now I think I could hack it. I'd like to do it soon, because in London there's the support and things like that and later I'll probably go and live in the country some-where, because of having my own studio, so I'd like to get the baby bit in before then.'

'Me?' he asked. He was surprised, but not astonished at himself.

'Are you serious?'

'Negotiable. Contact. I would want contact, definitely. I'm not sure that I wouldn't want some responsibility with it. Not veto rights, not even birth certificate if you didn't want, but something. A right to care? Could I tell?'

'Who?'

'Whoever I wanted.'

'If you could tell, I could too.'

'Oh . . . well that sounds fair.'

'We'll have to talk more. Are you interested in talking more?'

'Yes.' There was a pause during which they stared at each other with a wild kind of delight.

Then she said, 'I have to ask . . . I'm sorry . . . everyone says "Ask early, ask soon, get it done with".'

'Do you mean about status?' That was not her vocabulary, he realised at once, so he went on, 'I mean you need to ask whether I'm HIV positive, don't you? If I knew I was I wouldn't have offered. I've never tested.'

'I'd have asked you to test anyway, even if you had already.'

'Yes.'

There was a pause.

'When are you thinking of . . .'

'Sooner rather than later. This year. Not tomorrow.'

'I'll test, OK.'

'Why don't you test and then if . . . if it's OK, if everything is . . . if we have anything to talk about, then we'll talk.'

'No, we talk first and then if you want to go ahead, I'll test. I'm not testing unless you're committed . . . and then I'll test again six weeks later, to match with your cycle. I'm not testing on an off-chance.'

'And in between the tests?'

'You'll have to trust me.'

'Shit!'

'You'd have to trust anyone.'

'I know. It's weird.'

'For me too. There's a condition: if I test positive, and I might well, you'd know that, you'd have to know that. You'd know my status. And I'd expect you not to tell. I'd have to trust you, because I won't be telling anyone else.'

They looked at each other, slightly awed by how far they have come in five minutes. For completely different reasons they both simultaneously thought of Ellie and wondered if the other one would tell her. And what the hell she would say. They did not share this shared thought, but grinned at each other, acknowledging the privacy of the other's mind.

Chapter Four

When Hugo and Mary had disappeared into the evening, Ellie gathered herself together. She had come here, to the studio, to make Robbie's tear for him.

Since she had been a student she had made a glass tear for all the people she loved when they died. No one ever saw them. When they were finished she put each one into a little red cardboard box and locked it in a cupboard in the small store room behind the drawing room. There were about a dozen of the tears now: some of them were so lovely that sometimes she was tempted to show them. It was important to face that temptation, important to protect it fiercely from logic, from reason, and from egotism. On each box was a neat white label with the person's name and the date of the death and *Jesus Mercy, Mary Pray* written in Ellie's tidier handwriting – she had two, a large sprawly scrawl which she had developed at art college, and a neat plain hand taught in the primary school of her childhood.

Tonight she had already decided what she wanted to make for Robbie. When Hugo and Mary left she had felt a deep sense of relief, because she was free to make it, but she did not go straight to work. She needed it to be dark, and so she waited out the evening's fading in Megan's office.

She rang Judith, and told her answering phone that Robbie

had died. Then she rang the machine again to let Judith know that she would not be at home that evening. She rang Robbie's flat to find out how his mother was. Shocked was the short answer, exhausted and shocked, but Robbie's father was coming down the next morning – did she, Ellie, have any idea whether Robbie had left a will, or any clear instructions, about his things?

'I'd ask Trish,' Ellie told her, not wanting this to be her business.

'Oh, she said to ask you. And is there anyone else I ought to tell.'

'The hospital, perhaps.' Ellie gave her the number. 'You should try and speak to Sue, she was his nurse, his and Tim's. She's lovely, you'll like her; she's a friend too, you know; it's been a long time.'

'I don't know how you all do it,' Robbie's mother said, moving audibly towards tears. It was not a good moment to say, 'with too much practice', so Ellie did not. Instead she asked tenderly if there was anything she could do, and was hit by a ferocious wave of relief on hearing that there wasn't.

She put down the telephone and fought off a wave of exhaustion, that small and deceiving part of her which said lie down now, Ellie, lie down and sleep, the tear can wait. The effort of fighting off the tiredness released the waiting anger. She was shaken with such an anger that she felt ashamed, and the shame was not strong enough to suppress the anger; a great lava-hot core of rage against whatever it was that was slowly and irresistibly killing everything she loved, killing love itself in her. Her growling ferocity was more like an animal than like the gentle and liberal-minded woman she had for so long aspired and pretended to be.

It was an anger so strong that she had to do something with it. In a moment of clarity picked up the telephone again and dialled her brother's number.

'Alan?' she said, when he answered. 'Hello, Alan; this is Ellie. I have thought about this very carefully and I think it is fair to tell you right now that I will not come up and stay with Mother this summer. I haven't got time and I don't want to.'

'Nellie?' he said, she had caught him unawares and that inspired her. She refused any longer to wait, dumb like a lamb before the shearers. She was even amused by her own biblical thought.

'But Nellie . . .'

No 'buts'. No 'Nellies' either, she thought but did not say. 'My first offer still stands – I will pay for her to go somewhere nice, or to have someone come in for her. Whatever. I am not undutiful, I am just unloving. I have better people to love. Have you got that?'

'Betty . . .'

'Good. Well I must get on now. Bye, give my best to Betty and the children.'

She hung up. He could not ring her back because she was not at home. The anger and the relief met head on and bred a sort of excitement. It was dark enough now. She got up, stretched, pulled her boiler suit from its hook and slipped down the dark alley to the old garage. She knew her delight was childish, but she was pleased with herself and in the mood to make something fiercely beautiful.

The burglar alarm lights go on as she approaches the vast doorway. She opens the little wicket in the huge doors, and slips in; the neon light from the alarm catches the glass shards around the water bucket, and like a child in autumn leaves she deliberately scuffs through the pile, crunching over diamonds towards the light switches. The vast darkness of the room, the glass jewel-like on the concrete floor flashing refracting light: a cavern, a dragon's lair where the great beast broods on the gem stones, for ever and ever, uncounted years, centuries, eons.

She can hear the low steady growl of the dragon's breath, purring out as the dragon broods, dreaming perhaps of a time long ago when the volcanoes hurled molten silica into the air to become vitreous.

The first flicker of the neon tubes in the roof high above her head is a blinding flash of lightning; it carves its way precise as rough glass against skin, a rip in the sky revealing the brilliance of heaven beyond, and it slices its forked path like a tongue down on to a beach of the great original continent. The great lightning bolt smites the sands of the beach and a tongue of glass lies where it struck and will be there for ever even though the drifting plates of the world push the beach, high up into mountain ranges, folding the strata of rocks as Ellie folds a fresh gather from her furnace, and still the first glass from the lightning bolt is there, folded in with the other layers. And she is reeling terrified by her own temerity and by the swooping passing of the galaxies and the long, long journey.

Then the huge cavern is flooded with artificial light; it shrinks, refocuses and is her studio again. The dragon's breath calms itself into the electronic hum of the furnace, the diamonds dim and disengage, retreating into broken glass shattered by sudden cooling, smashed from the end of the hollow blowpipe by being plunged into water and by a deft and practised flick of Patsy's wrist tapping it against the wall; and Ellie Macauley is in her studio in Deptford pulling on her boiler suit and scanning the wall rack for the little pontil which will make solo working easiest.

She seldom works alone, like this, and then usually at night. The very first glass blowers probably worked so, somewhere in northern Palestine, around the time when BC and AD met, alone and at minute furnaces, making little bottles, tiny hollow vessels, carried away by the magic of seeing the glass grow, swell, be inspired by human exhalation. They must have worked in faith, those Semitic glassworkers, for they made nothing that had not been made before and more easily by moulding and slumping and working, but this was a new thing that they did. And did the desert stars roar overhead? And were they struck with awe by night and sunstroke by day? Did they see angels and watch the bushes burn and burn and burn and yet be not consumed?

'Come on, Ellie,' said Angel, 'you're getting over-excited.'

'You sound like my mother,' said Ellie crossly, coming down to earth too suddenly.

'She can't be all bad then.'

Ellie pulled herself together. She was not planning to blow tonight anyway.

She removed the furnace door; the heat and light leaped out in a single pounce, still shocking. Then she was at home; and became stern, efficient and concentrated, plunging the pontil deep into the molten glass to make her first gather; a deft twist and the surplus fell off, dripping back into the crucible. Spinning the pontil rhythmically she carried it to the marver and rolled it into a neat sausage. She reached for the delicate narrow jacks she had placed ready to hand. Scale was the problem here, she did not want the tear to be more than about an inch and a half long, smaller would be better. When working at such a small scale, the distance she had to keep from the hot glass seemed unnatural. The jacks were slim, dainty, but they were long. She wondered without distracting herself if Mary might not be too small to work alone like this, not enough arm reach. Firmly, gently she squeezed in two deep furrows, down the full length of the soft sausage, and then swift and graceful she was back at the furnace coating her gather with another layer of the clear glass. Because of its viscosity the glass from the second gather would not flow into the furrows made in the first layer and air would be trapped there. Two narrow grooves of air sealed for ever into the glass itself. At her bench she started to roll the pontil; then, with a pair of pincers, she grasped the opposite end of the gather and pulled gently, twisting; the two narrow columns of air stretched into strings and twined round each other.

Heat until workable; work until cool. Heat means soft here, and cool means hard. And shaping the glass ball with the air twist embedded in its heart, into an egg, rolling it carefully into shape, pulling, twisting, like a child making toffee. A tear-drop, a crystal tear-drop, refracting light because of the lead, hard, clear. It is awesome, magical, that a measured mixture of roast crushed flints, bright red lead-oxide, tartar, borax, saltpetre – nothing fancy, nothing hard to come by – should melt together into something so soft, so flowing, so gently malleable; and should harden into something so strong and wonderfully clear, with an innate sparkle – something that would, quite unexpectedly, ring like a bell when it was tapped.

Now it was a tear-drop, with a perfect double helix inside. The double helix for life, the cooling into brilliant hardness, the air, the life, still trapped inside; and the two threads of life curving round each other, like DNA, and like love. Her tear for Robbie that was both mourning and celebration.

'Ah, air and angels,' whispered Angel, moved.

Ellie pulled on the huge gloves and picked up the tear tenderly. Something else about glass that she loved – her contact with it, while she was working on it was infinitely tender, intimate, maternal, but never sensual: it was fierce inside, this thing that looked so cool and smooth. It had to be kept at a distance, the distance of glove or pontil; not like clay which snuggled up to you puppylike, inserting itself into the gaps between the cells of your skin.

She carried the tear to the annealing oven, where it would cool slowly, and slowly harden. She watched it as it lay – should she, should she, she wondered irritated, have run the double helix, the hollows of air right through the tear so that instead of being enclosed within it they were open ended: so that instead of life, Robbie's life, being enclosed in her sorrow, her tears could be the channel through which life could drip.

'Next time,' she told herself and then stopped, appalled. No more next times, please, please God. Tears as pure as the glass one, as warm as the glass one, pooled in her eyes.

She had read somewhere once about the topology of droplets: gravity and surface tension were in conflict. A drop of liquid did not fall off the end of a tap or nose, or eyelash. As it filled – except you could not say 'filled' because the drop *was* a vessel-filled-with-water, it was not a skin, a membrane, it was . . . like a body isn't a vessel to carry the person, separate and emptiable – the skin, body, brain, memory, soul, personality was one, one together thing and should not be separated . . . dear God she was tired . . . as the droplet grew, its weight pulled downwards, larger and rounder on an ever-longer and ever-thinner stalk until the stalk snapped, not up at the top but well below the middle, and while most of the drop fell, the upper end of the stalk sprang back upwards, and so created the extra weight to make the next droplet.

Her thoughts were out of control. She suddenly remembered her history of glass professor laughing and saying, 'I don't think they suddenly learned to blow glass, learned how to inflate it in year zero; it wasn't an invention like that, it can't have been – all the moulding and folding, they must have known it would inflate for centuries; there are always bubbles in early slumped glass. No, I'm convinced that some smart-arsed Arab suddenly learned a very simple new technology, he learned how to get the damn bubble *off* his blowing tube. *Eh, voilà, c'est tout.*' The pontil.

. . . The pontil – transfer the glass from blowing-tube to pontil and later snap it off from there – all blown glass had a pontil mark, its navel, where it had been snapped away . . .

She was still standing by the annealing oven with the tears pouring down her face; she was soggy, blotched with tears, her lesions of loss. Then, gently as a mother who hopes her child is sleeping, but still ravaged by tender anxiety needs to see that safe sleep, Angel murmurs, 'Come, Héloïse, come on; bedtime.'

Tenderly Angel says, 'Come Ellie; it's lovely, you've made a lovely thing for a lovely man. Come now; bedtime, now.' And leaning metaphorical weight on Angel's non-material shoulder, Ellie, knowing she is empty, knows too that she must sleep, must sleep now.

She went upstairs to the divan in the drawing room, and lay down there. The weighting towards sleep stretched, pulled down, empowered by gravity, until the thin stalk of consciousness snapped and suddenly shapeless, Ellie plunged into chaotic sleep.

She woke in the grey pre-dawn when the yellow street lights of London look weak and fevered. She woke suddenly and abruptly; and waking, knew she had been woken – woken by something cracking, breaking perhaps, and by a cry so desolate, such a perfection of grief, that she had thought it was her own. Awake she knew, with the startling humility of those startled from sleep, that she was not capable of such a purity of sorrow. This made her sad, but all the same someone, *someone* had been that grief-struck and had expressed it, here, in the upper room of her well-secured and well-ordered studio, and she was alarmed.

'Who's there?' There was silence and she knew she had known there would be silence. She knew there was no one there.

Neither the toughened Presbyterian child nor the impassioned Catholic adult was allowed to believe in ghosts; so ghosts did not occur to her. But someone had cried out in grave sorrow. She got up, crossed to the doorway and switched on the light. Outside the window it was suddenly black – the night blanket protecting the grey pre-dawn from the garish lighting inside. There was the long drawing table, scattered with sheets of paper, sketches of angelic glass windows, and additionally dotted with Mary's dirty coffee cups – Ellie managed, in her regal and demanding glance that swept over the room, to narrow the corners of her eyes in passing annoyance, and then to widen them again with pleasure at the sight of the sketches for her own Haven charger. There were the three shelves of 'reference library' and a cork-board pinned with cards, technical notes, torn-out pictures – including some fabulous striated fish from the *National Geographic*. There was the divan piled with old soft cushions, dented where her head had lain, and there . . . Ellie was confused.

There was no one, no one there, only the room, brightly lit, bright harsh lighting and she had known there would be no one there. And in the corner, near where her head had lain, another different source of light, an iridescent, soft opaloid light, of no colour, of all colours, prismatic – neither shimmering nor glowing but something in between for which Ellie did not even know if there was a word: like ice or phosphorescence, but not cold – warm, coloured. She walked towards the light, enchanted.

The light and its source was something lying on the floor. A shard, no something finer than a shard, a thread . . . but barbed – a barbed thread of . . . she bent down, picked it up, it was firmer in her hand than it looked, rigid, not soft – a splinter of a barbed thread of glass, but so fine, so attenuated, as though from a coloured cane . . . finer than any glass she had ever seen, and it was barbed, minutely delicately barbed like . . . like something, but Ellie could not think what . . . and, turning her wrist slightly, she saw it was so shot with colour, and inward light and there were only two glassmakers in Britain who had such mastery of colour, and she was one of them and she had not made it, and – she knew almost peevishly – could not have made it.

And even as she looked, both awed and anxious, she could

see it was devitrifying, crizzling, breaking down into crystals, into specks, and its lights went out into dust, and it was gone – there was a faint glimmer on her hand, a fine powder shot with distant glitter; then the warm softness of her still sleepy hands, her own sweat, absorbed it, or a breeze from her breath dispersed it. There was nothing there.

Ellie stood still, quite still.

'Angel,' she called, and her calling was as soft as the exhalation which had vanished the . . . the . . . She knew what it had been – the filial, one strand from a feather, a peacock feather, but made of glass, and barbed to link it with the next, so that the air could not break through, an angel feather . . . and created . . . what was it, what was the quotation that she always applied to good work, her own good work and other people's . . .

and this is the truth of the pervading intricacy of the world's detail: the word is not a study, a roughed-in sketch; is supremely, meticulously created; created abundantly, extravagantly and in fine.

'Angel,' she called more commandingly, but Ellie could not command Angel, who had no obligations, or not to Ellie. Angel came and went according to her own free will and freely-willed obedience, neither confined by nor bound to any time or space.

'Angel,' repeated Ellie, and even as she did so thought how lucky, how lucky that Judith is right and fag-hags have a deficient sense of social shame even before their naked selves or else I could hardly stand here at about four a.m. in the morning trying to summon the attention of a non-person in whom it is probably psychotic to believe.

This unwanted return of her clever intrusive self made her cross, so she said, 'Angel, stop fucking about. I can't cope with it.'

Silence.

'Is *this* . . .?' She looked at her empty hand, her confidence draining away and her irritability with it. '*Was* this a . . . a feather from your immortal wings?'

Silence.

'Angel, please. I don't understand. You told me you had no material presence.'

And shockingly deep inside her left ear, well inside the spiral that was as haired and barbed as Angel's wing shard, she heard Angel's voice say, with a kind of weary bitterness, 'Yes, well, and Thomas Aquinas told me that angels were infinitely secure in regard to the attraction that any created reality can exercise on us, whatever perfection it may possess. Ha, bloody ha.'

'I don't understand.'

'Oh that just means that that overweight, shifty, neo-platonic Dominican and I were both wrong.'

'Angel, what's going on here? What's happening? Am I finally cracking up?'

'Let's hope so; because, if not, I am, and that's infinitely more serious.'

The feather, the tiny strand of feather had cracked and crizzled in her hand, had died of glass sickness; the world was devitrifying in her hands.

'Go to sleep,' said Angel, sounding tired. 'You go to sleep and I'll try and get this sorted out. I'll try.'

Ellie stumbled back to the bed. This was a dream, it had to be a dream, a bad dream. The light was still on, but the outside world was recovering its greyness. She swayed, more tired and distressed than she had known. Even as she fell back into sleep she was aware that Angel had been sad, and she didn't understand why, but she did know that it was a sadness that made her own loss and grief look like a sulking child's whose toys have been taken away.

Inevitably she slept later than she'd planned and woke

confused and baffled, uncertain as to whether the now full morning light was more or less real than the grey half-dawn. She was, she acknowledged ruefully, too old to sleep in her clothes; she felt stiff, dirty, old and simultaneously infantile. If she went over to the office to shower would Megan be severe because she was late – if she was late – or tender because Robbie had died, or that Megan-like mixture of both? Megan had, so long ago, introduced her to adulthood; but, perhaps a symptom of ageing, time's supposedly inexorable arrow seemed to have gone into reverse with her: more and more, and not without adolescent guilt, Megan became her mother. Come to that, she thought, startled, Henry had become her father.

And was it shame, or simply a rush of hormones pounding their independent way through her veins, their veins? She began to burn again; strange and familiar every time, the sweat on her neck, in her cleavage, on the inside of her thighs, armpits, forehead, burning, melting, rose-red blood flowering on her body – and she did not need this, she did not need it. When would all this bloody stop so that, uninterrupted by her body, she could ask herself when and how the two people who had allowed her to escape childhood and enter the world of the grown-ups, had been made over into parents? Did her high, bold sense of choosing, claiming, pretending, a family amount only to replaying the old Freudian game in a more volatile, if more ego-enhancing, way?

Somewhere deep in the recesses of her imagination, and semi-repressed, she had a flash of a fantasy of Megan and Henry together, her parents, of Megan as Henry's 'real woman' who turned to him not to be cuddled and comforted but for hot sex, for desire and inspiration; and the idea of it, appallingly, turned her on almost before she knew she was thinking it.

So now, she thought crossly, she needed three showers –

one for her feet and hands and hair and stiff shoulders from the sofa night; and a second for her breasts and belly and neck and thighs, still sticky from flushing; and a third for the sudden softness in her labia. 'Go wash your brain out with soap,' she told herself. Her mother had done that, had handed Ellie a bar of soap and a tight-lipped look.

Ellie had left her watch downstairs in the studio so she could prepare herself for Megan *en route* to the shower – the degree of guilt, and of apology, related to how late she really was. She glanced swiftly round the drawing room, searching only half-consciously for clues to the events she had not yet dealt with. First she needed to wash, to become unglued.

The night before she had planned to remove the glass teardrop from the annealing oven before Mary and Patsy arrived. She had forgotten about it, so that when, halfway down the staircase, she heard Patsy's voice, she did not make the connection.

'Put it down, Mary, it's one of hers.'

'It's lovely, isn't it?'

'She won't like you playing with it though. She must have done it last night; it wasn't here when I cleaned up.'

'How does she do it? Why is it so sad when it's so pretty?'

Ellie still hadn't made the connection, was still wondering what the hell time it was, when she stepped into the studio. For Mary though there was a shock – the sudden appearance, less than a yard away from her, of her somewhat dishevelled boss, hair wild and unbrushed, all red and witchy – and with Patsy's reprimand in her immediate ears, there was sudden guilt too. It was an accident, but an accident that should not have had a chance to happen.

She dropped the tear.

And, because it was a glass tear, it broke.

It did not shatter, but the thin stalk where the tear had hung despairingly to the lower eyelash of the mourner, snapped off. The fat globular body, now more nearly spherical, rolled bumpily across the floor towards Ellie. Without moving her feet she bent and picked it up – as she had imagined last night the two air tubes that made the double helix were open. She would have been wrong artistically she realised, looking at it; the power in that embracing coil should be closed off. It was the end of the line for Robbie's genes; they had not been selfish enough; they had failed to get themselves passed on – they had failed to protect themselves from invasion.

There was a prolonged silence.

'I'm sorry,' said Mary quite quietly, for what she had done had indeed been dreadful. She had picked up someone else's work for curiosity alone and dropped it. In any glass studio it was the dropping, slipping, bungling moment of ungrace which was the sin and had to be, because the breaking was so nearly inevitable.

'I'm sorry,' said Mary and waited for the storm to descend.

Ellie looked at her in silence.

'I'm sorry,' Mary repeated, 'I shouldn't have been holding it, and, as I was, I should have been more careful.'

'OK,' said Ellie, calmly. 'OK. It was an accident. It doesn't matter.'

'But it was lovely!'

'So I should hope,' said Ellie; 'I made it.' Still smiling she walked across the vast room towards the half-open yard doors. She stood there briefly, blinking at the morning.

'I slept here last night,' she said. 'Slept over and overslept. I'm going to have a shower. Can you two get set up? See if, between you, you can work out a routine for this morning. I'll do anything that's simple. If in doubt, ask Megan what would suit her best. Let's just do some work. Give me ten minutes.'

With a tidy gesture she chucked the remains of the tear into the bucket which stood as always within the charmed circle of glass fragments – it plopped satisfyingly as it hit the water, and the sound was followed by slightly sharper tones as the thrown up droplets followed the glass ball down into the depths.

'Oh, shit, shit, shit. You stupid cow,' said Patsy when Ellie had walked out of hearing range.

'Why didn't she get angry?' Mary asked, frightened.

'She was.'

'She didn't say *anything*.'

'She never does. Not if she's got something real to be angry about. How could you?'

Suddenly Mary felt aggrieved; still high on the decision she and Hugo had moved towards the night before, she wanted admiration or at least drama. She had wanted to tell Ellie and see her admiration and even delight, a mirror for her pride. This scary calm burst the bubble of her excitement.

'Well, I said was sorry.'

It had been an accident, she did not want Patsy's criticism, and even less Ellie's cool forgiveness.

'And she said it was OK. So. Come on, for God's sake, just do what she says; let's get some work done. It'll make things better.'

But for Ellie things did not get better.

They got worse.

Her house seemed bleak and empty, its prettiness revealed as pretext. She wanted Henry back. She found excuses that even she knew were pathetic to contact him, to ring him up, to force his hand. But Henry's control was impeccable. She could not reach him; she could not shake his serenity. She could not make him cross, or even impatient. She could not break his perfect manners and his distanced composure. She wanted him to behave badly. She wanted him to complain. She wanted him to do something, anything, that might suggest he had any doubts, any second thoughts, any conflicts.

He only wanted one thing from her and that was a divorce;

he wanted her to agree to a quick and simple divorce; until she did, he would punish her by his indifference. And if she did, he would still be gone, she would gain nothing, nothing, except her own damnation. He had gone, and she was alone.

Knowing that, she still plotted. What if he were ill? she would catch herself thinking. Or, better still, what if she were ill? She caught herself examining her breasts with a morbid optimism; she had a smear test and hovered over the post in the mornings, waiting for the results. She despised herself, but she was not sure she could survive without him.

Dear Miss Stephanie Landsdowne,

I am sorry to have to inform you that your mother is extremely ill. The doctors all feel that only you can save her life. Although of course there is nothing that can be done to compel you to take this basic responsibility I am hopeful that you will return immediately.

yours sincerely

She found herself picking up teenage magazines which had articles in them about how to keep your man, or win true love, or maintain a long-term relationship. They mainly recommended more experimental sex and not taking Him for granted. She had failed on both counts, she realised and snivelled through long sleepless nights.

In her head, she was furious. In her head, she had long fights in which she berated him, punished him for his treachery, for his stupidity, for his meanness. In her head, she went over and over the clear moment when she had slashed his face with the fish knife; it became a high point, a victory. She repeated it in technicolour fantasies, but the anger stayed inside, churning her up; face to face, or more often voice to voice, with him she was craven, sugary and selfless. She did not like herself.

Her friends were no help. No one actually said, 'What's new?' or 'About time too,' but she felt that they were thinking it. She was afraid she would exhaust their patience, she would bore them and they would abandon her too. Judith was wonderful, tough and robust and very funny: she had enterprising plans for further fish knife attacks; she referred to Annabel by a series of ridiculous names, always speaking of her as though she were indeed the bimbo that Henry denied. Ellie would laugh for a while and then find herself sniffling into her food and getting appallingly drunk. She loathed herself and did not seem able to do anything about it.

Late one evening she found herself parked outside Annabel's house – watching, snooping, spying. At last the downstairs lights went out and one upstairs light came on. She saw Henry come to the window and draw the curtains. She felt a wave of pain, followed hotly by a wave of unlovely lust, and then she had to scramble to open the car door to throw up in the gutter; she was sick with self-disgust and terrified that he would come back to the window and see her there. She fled into the night: three times round the M25, stopping only for petrol and cups of coffee in plastic service station restaurants; looking at the other waifs of the dark, the flotsam of the night. She was repulsed by herself, and tired and desperate.

darling Steph – please come home. I need you. Mummy.

dear Stephanie, you have given me no reason to believe that you care in any way about me, but I am still appealing to you in the hope that there is some vestige of good will remaining, love Mummy.

Stephanie – you and your father are a pair of identical shits. Ellie

Ellie would not write, would not give in, apologise, repent. She knew she would be finally unable to bear it if she so humbled herself and was rejected.

And if she wrote, she would have to tell Stephanie that her father had left her. Her daughter had left her, her husband had left her. There was something wrong with her. She was not going to give that power into her daughter's hands. She did not know if Henry had written to Stephanie. Stephanie had already denounced her as an interfering, dangerous bitch. If she wrote and that was still what Stephanie thought, then she would take Henry's side and Ellie would die.

Her brother rang repeatedly, pleading and accusing. He was trying to undermine her moment of clarity and self-assurance. She suspected that he would in the end succeed. Her submission would be worse than if she had gone to Scotland quietly and obediently in the first place. She did not tell him about Henry either. Alan already had a moment of startling rudeness to hold against her; she was not going to give him her personal failure and wickedness as a further weapon. She clung with desperation to her refusal, but was frighteningly aware that her despair was drowning her clarity. She knew she would dislike herself even more if she gave in to his shameless bullying, but at the same time it was hard not to feel that she was so wretched anyway that how could things be worse. She discovered a self-punishing monster inside her and she was terrified by it.

Nothing was the right shape. Angel would not explain what had happened in the night in the drawing room above the studio, but since then there had been something different and strange in Angel's presence: a sort of inattention, that offered no reassurance.

Ellie could not make a new tear for Robbie – she could not

bring herself to; it had been such a glorious moment, a triumph of her own art. Later in the day that it was broken, when there was no one else in the studio, Ellie had fished the shattered remains out of the water in the bucket and put it in its box and locked it in the cupboard. She was not certain if that was right.

Then one morning Judith rang sounding distraught. 'Meet me after work, Ellie, please. I have to talk to you.'

'Are you all right?'

'No, I am bloody well not.'

'What's the matter?'

'I'll have to tell you. It's not telephone stuff. *Please* Ellie.'

'Of course.' She could not bear to hear Judith sounding plaintive. 'Of course. Where?'

Where was inevitably the West End and Ellie had to struggle into town weary and miserable. Judith was late and when Ellie saw her approaching, she was panicked: Judith was as immaculately dressed as ever, but she was pale, almost gaunt; her slimness suddenly deteriorated into emaciation and her eyes were bright with an evil self-mockery. Ellie instantly realised that she worried about Hugo's health and worried about her own health, but she never worried about Judith's. She had had lunch with Judith a week ago and had been so full of her own woes that she did not even know now whether Judith had looked like this then. Now Judith had the transparent look of someone with cancer. And Ellie knew that her first response was not love and compassion, but an entirely egotistical self-pity.

'Darling,' she said immediately, rushing into speech, to silence her own unlovable thoughts, 'what is it?'

'Guess.'

Ellie did not want to try and guess. She felt sick. 'I'm not guessing Judith, I'm not fooling. You look like hell. Come on. Just tell me.' What would she guess, when she already knew what she feared – bankruptcy? pregnancy? the dog has died? 'I don't want to play. You just tell me. Please.'

'La Carissima is getting *married*.'

'What!' Among all the dreadful thoughts that had filled her mind she had not even thought of this.

'She's thirty-three she tells me and it's time she was settling down, so she's marrying some unbelievably posh and rich bloody Italian aristocrat, and she says it isn't going to change anything. Just a touch of Lavender she says. Oh, yeah. Then she rings up to say will I wear something extra glamorous for the wedding because she has told her fiancé so bloody much about her fabulous best friend. She hasn't told him. She hasn't told him, Ellie. Can you believe it? She says there is stuff he doesn't need to know. I'm *stuff* he doesn't need to know.'

'Perhaps it won't make any difference.'

'Don't, Ellie. I didn't say "Perhaps it won't make any difference" when Henry presented you with Little Miss Lollipop.'

'But lavender, presumably he's gay too.'

'Then why isn't she telling him? That's the whole point. She still loves me to distraction, she says. She still wants to have sex with me, she says. She just doesn't want to tell her intended that she's a lesbian. *I'm* a lesbian, Ellie, I'm a goddamn dyke, and she is my lover, my sweetheart, my girl friend, my *numero uno*, and so on and so forth *ad nauseam*. *Mia Carissima*. I'm forty-two years old and I thought this would hang about fairly effortlessly until I was too old to care. I thought I had it made. I feel like a complete idiot quite apart from . . . well . . . quite apart from the fact that I'm soft on her, and I never bloody knew it until now. So I feel like an idiot in spades. And I don't know if I'm mad or sad, or even if I ought to be glad to get the little trollop out of my life.'

Although she wanted to, Ellie could not say, 'Bloody men' in the patient maternal voice that heterosexual women use with each other when their men are bloody.

Nor could she say, 'Well there you are then, that makes two of us. You thought you were so much damned cleverer than I am. And there's no difference.'

Nor, though she was tempted, could she say, 'Judith, you are not allowed to be distraught. I can't cope if you are going to get distraught. I'm the distraught one; you are the worldly one. You are the tough nut. Just do that for me.'

Instead she said, 'Poor Judith,' which turned out worse than any of these.

'Pity, you see, that's what I'll get – pity.' Judith was getting louder, not in the flamboyant style that Ellie was used to and loved, but in a crazy-lady way. 'The boys will laugh pityingly, and my women friends will love me pityingly and they'll all think, See, she thought she had it made. Pity. For God's sake, Ellie, I'm the one you're meant to envy. I don't want your bloody pity.' Then she burst into noisy tears.

Ellie found to her own self-disgust that she was embarrassed; and the fact that Judith had endured scenes infinitely more embarrassing from her, without turning so much as a hair, did not help. She wished she had Judith's skill at taking moments of potential degradation and with a single low-pitched gravelly sentence, magically remaking them into hilarious episodes.

Later Judith herself was embarrassed and apologetic.

'No need, no need, please, Judith. I've done far worse.'

'But it suits your style and it doesn't suit mine.'

Just when she needed her most, Judith was not available to Ellie as succour and support.

'Ellie,' said Megan one morning, 'what do you want me to do about this?'

'This' transpired to be a letter from Friedhelm, an enthusiastic letter full of confidence in the design concept and greedy for another meeting on site.

'Perhaps Mary could go,' Ellie said.

'Read it, Ellie. Mary has been talking to him, writing to him, working with him and neither you nor I knew a thing about it. What the hell is going on, Ellie?'

Ellie paid attention because Megan so seldom swore. 'It'll be an accident; she doesn't think. It's not a big problem, Megan, I'll speak to her.'

'You aren't paying attention, Ellie. You are not Mary's mother – you are not her teacher or her patron. She is your apprentice. She is using that to steal your authority, and if you don't take some grip on that then it is going to change the balance of this studio in more ways than one. I am not having these windows become Mary's project rather than the best most prestigious commission you have ever had.'

'It's OK, Megan. I don't mind.'

'Well I do. And I happen to be a director here the same as you. Get your self together Ellie. Please go to Germany.'

'I can't,' said Ellie and burst into tears.

Megan comforted her, but Ellie sensed that she was not satisfied. Megan was right anyway; she shouldn't let Mary go to Germany on her own again. The shift in power was too dangerous, not to her advantage. She could not feel that she cared, but she still knew that there would come a day when she would, and she did not want it to be too late. But she could not go to Germany.

'Megan, I can't. I just can't go. It won't help. I'll just cry. You go.'

She thought that Megan would argue with her; it was not the sort of thing that Megan had ever done, but now Megan smiled crisply and said, 'That's a good idea. I'll arrange it. I'll keep her in her place.'

Which meant that Megan thought the situation was serious, and that she did not trust Ellie to manage it. Even Ellie's professional competence was challenged.

She did not even ask Megan what she had said to Mary. The

results were horribly obvious: Mary sulked, and the sulking made her clumsy.

Ellie tried to ignore it, pretend that it had nothing to do with Mary feeling thwarted, unable to get her own way. Clumsiness just happened sometimes, Ellie knew it happened, particularly if one was thinking hard about technique. There was an innocence, a naïvety before technique; and there was a grace of practised skill beyond technique, and in between there was an awkwardness. Ellie tried to blame herself: she was not being patient enough, rhythmical enough to sustain Mary. Mary had too much on her mind; she, Ellie, had given her too much responsibility, was working her too hard.

Or of course Megan was right and the sly little bitch would not work on anyone's stuff but her own. She had plotted to go to Germany on her own and was punishing them all. Ellie found an anger, that for the first time linked Mary and Stephanie consciously in her mind: they both just wanted their own way and would throw her and her feelings to any handy wolves in order to get it.

Oddly the thought of Mary as malevolent comforted her for a couple of long evenings. But when Patsy complained she found herself defending Mary.

'We've wasted an entire bloody morning, Ellie; she doesn't pay attention, and she doesn't seem to care.'

'Come on, Patsy, you know it happens; we've just lost it for a bit. I'm not doing so well myself as a matter of fact. I don't know what we'd do without you, you know, you seem to be the only person with two hands and the right number of fingers around here just now.'

'She's sly,' said Patsy suddenly.

'I thought you liked her.'

'I do actually, Ellie, but she's . . . sly isn't the right word, I don't know why I said that, but she's not team, she doesn't know how to do team.'

'She'll learn.'

'You have to leave yourself outside and she doesn't.'

'You have to leave . . . what makes you think that, Patsy? I think the opposite really; that you have to bring all of yourself inside.'

'OK, but she doesn't do that either. You do one and I do the other. I hang me up with my jacket most mornings; you carry you like your underwear. She's neither one.'

'She's good though, Patsy, you know it. She's better than anyone we've had before.'

'Well, I wish she'd get her act together.'

'Me too.'

Please, God, don't push it, she wanted to say to Patsy. I need you, and I don't need Mary; but I love Mary and I don't love you. So don't make me have to do anything about it, just leave yourself outside hanging with your jacket. Please. And please, please, don't complain to Megan, because I both love and need her.

But the rhythm of work was disrupted. Apart from anything else they were spending too much time on the older technologies of window glass. It was fun to do: blowing long cylinders of glass, annealing them and then, slicing them along their length with red-hot shears, then reheating and flattening them into sheets. Ellie became half-obsessed with the learning of the new skill. No one blew flat glass any more, but it was an ancient craft. Other work fell behind, even the supposed matching altar vessels, the chalice and paten which would symbolise the reality contained within the bread and wine, semi-transparent layers and within all the layers the invisible truth. But the making of ritual vessels had given way to the making of window glass: she was back in the Dark Ages where the priest had raised the glass chalice to his damnation. Vessels were forbidden here, and the glassworkers turned to windows, encouraged by the Church: did even God prefer Mary's glass to Ellie's?

Despite Patsy's cross complaints, Ellie began to feel that she too was shifting loyalties, aligning herself with Mary's windows. One day when she went upstairs for something, she found Patsy reading one of the glass history books and smiling delightedly. 'Hey, Ellie, did you know that there were these monks at some place called Jarrow who made millefiorí flat glass, in the seventh century, for windows. Could we do that, even if we can't do those Italian bowls? Please.'

Ellie was delighted; it was the first time she had ever known Patsy to be inspired with an idea, a glass idea of her own. But she was also scared; why could Mary provoke this creative enthusiasm when she could not? She was torn, uneasy, uncertain even here at work, the place of refuge.

She had a fight with Hugo.

It was a painful, stupid fight, and not about anything real. They had, of course, had fights before, long serious arguments about politics and sex, and wonderful noisy contretemps which always had an element of the theatrical about them. Fights that were always half a joke, decorated with extreme verbal abuse, which was partly generated for the pure pleasure of shocking other people. Occasionally, in their excitement, these would tip over into real fights, before they knew what was happening. Once they had had a fight at the vegetable counter in Sainsbury's about whether or not they were going to serve quail with slices of starfruit on them at a dinner party they were giving. It started playfully with her saying it was naff, and him saying she was a Calvinist and soon after that she was screaming tearfully it was typical poofter-cooking, and that he was a poncy asshole. By that time he was telling her that she had a dour Presbyterian soul, regardless of her fancy Catholic pretensions, and she was acting like the worst sort of nanny, and that the reason she never got laid was because she was frightened of getting mess on the sheets. They were collecting an audience of shoppers both impressed and appalled by the time the manager came and suggested that they carried on their fight elsewhere. They found themselves outside the shop, laughing, but tremulously, each shocked at their own angers, each faintly apologetic.

'I suppose,' he said to her later, 'that it is a bit of a relief to know that you can, under pressure, say homophobic things, otherwise the political theory would break down.'

'Likewise sexism. Oh, I am sorry.'

'Don't worry. Me too. And anyway I still love you to pieces.'

Those sorts of fights, however passionate at the time, they reconstructed quickly into episodes of their own self-mythologising. They displayed them with a certain ironic pride, aware that while their friends would say 'they're impossible', they'd say it with affection and some admiration. 'Showing off' her mother would call it, but she was far away in Ayrshire and would never know.

This time was different. This time she needed him too much, so that what started as a cheerful brawl about whether or not it was politically OK to accept funding from a particular multinational pharmaceutical company, whose record was dubious, grew poisonous. Hugo resigned from the committee which voted to accept. Ellie said he was being Manichaean, a preposterous purist. It should not have become so important.

It did because Ellie was feeling so insecure. If Henry could stop loving her then Hugo easily could; she held him by nothing more than wit, comfort and money. She hated herself for even thinking like this. The saner bits of her knew that it was simply not true. But she felt deserted. She needed him, and let it show, becoming tearful and humble before his anger instead of meeting it with her usual bold intelligence.

He was frantically busy; she never saw him. He was organising some big conference in the north-east, and was constantly commuting up and down. He wanted to come home and play, and she was not playful. And he felt guilty because he had not told her about Mary and him becoming friends, becoming – at least in a dream which developed steadily and sweetly – co-parents. He intended to, but she tried to tell him about the complexity of the studio and her feelings about Mary, and he felt disloyal because he was hearing the other side and Mary's side was, at that point, so much more energetic, attractive, joyful, that it was easier to believe it. He wanted to have Mary's baby and he did not want to have an HIV test. He knew he should tell her all these things, but instead of giving him space to do so, Ellie just bored on about her own misery. He was cross with her because she made him feel guilty.

Then one day, in the drawing room, while she was looking for some pictures Ellie chanced on Mary's open diary. On the Wednesday, scrawled casually in red biro, was *Supper – Hugo*. Of course, she thought quickly, there were lots of people called Hugo.

On the Monday of that same week she and Hugo were supposed to be having supper themselves. He rang shortly after six o'clock and cancelled. She could not question him about his Wednesday date because she should not have been looking at Mary's book. But it was all too much and quite suddenly she lost her temper.

'Ellie, I'm truly sorry,' he repeated, but she could hear him being annoyed too.

'It's my bloody turn,' she said. 'I'm not some rich bitch you can just use and dump.'

He hung the phone up on her. He was ashamed of himself. He had felt a sudden overwhelming need to retreat; guilty, he told himself he would make it up to her in a little while; that tomorrow he would send her flowers and an apology. He had gone too far. Then before he even had time to calm down, she rang, weeping, to apologise. Her self-abasement in the face of his rudeness frightened and somehow disgusted him. He lost his temper and told her so. Then he put his answering machine on and refused to return her calls; he was afraid of the tide of his own anger, and wanted not to have to deal with her vulnerability.

But she was left shaken, depressed, trying to persuade herself to be reasonable. She knew how hard he was working. She knew he was sympathetic, he just did not have time. He was still coughing; perhaps he could sense her concern about that, although she tried to be enormously careful; perhaps he could sense her concern and simply did not want it, and why should he want it? What was so terribly wrong with denial anyway if what was being denied was unbearable. Alternatively and just as convincingly she was neurotic and over-anxious and he was fed up with that. Just like Henry was.

She decided wilfully to take a grip on herself. She would start because it was the easiest thing, by being nice to someone else.

'Judith, darling, would you like to put on something ultra chic and come with me to a private view do?'

'I don't feel chic.'

'Listen, hon, in your baggy school knickers you'd be chic. This one will be fun and we'll look divine and everyone will say, "Dear God who is that stunning woman with Ellie Macauley? How does the old bag find such gorgeous friends?"'

'They won't,' said Judith darkly, 'they'll say, "Why hasn't she brought someone pretty for little me to play with?"'

'No they won't,' said Ellie, bold in her affection, 'all the brighter people, those who know enough even to think that, will say instead, "Ellie Macauley? I never knew she was *that* way inclined. That explains a lot." And my stock will rise and I will be able to buy you presents as wonderful as the ones you buy me.'

'Flattery, Héloïse Macauley, as you very well know, will get you just about anywhere. OK. You're on. Where and when?'

So they went to the private view, looking indeed wonderful and depending on each other, grateful and affectionate in their need. It was fun. It had been great fun, until, for one moment alone, Ellie was looking at a rather wonderful green glass vessel, inspecting it, admiring but critical, observing the richness of the green, wondering how it was done and also where had she seen just that colour before, somewhere – a depth of green, not at all like the German *waldglas* where, so satisfactorily the soda from beech ash created a glass exactly the colour of spring beech leaves seen in the sunshine; this was a different, deeper green. Enquiringly, she reached out an admiring finger to touch it. And she saw that the finger that touched it was not hers, not her strong white hand, with the sprinkling of freckles . . . but long, chocolate coloured, more elegant, ringed heavily and all the rings are of different coloured glass, and the vessel is not on the white table cover but in the hands of small dark woman, kneeling at her feet, offering her a great green bowl.

It is the *sacra catina*, the great treasure of the Cathedral Church of San Lorenzo in Genoa. The Queen of Sheba receives it from the hands of the glassworkers of her court and her dark eyes sparkle in its refractions: a rare gift from her to Solomon, Son of David, King of Israel and Judah. This bowl is a gift from the Queen of Sheba to Solomon, and in all his glory he has no treasure so green as this and he accepts it from her in silence. She is laughing. He is astonished because no one laughs at him, but she laughs like a bubbling stream, like a child laughs. Solomon's wisdom is deep and solemn, but she is laughing at him with the laughter from the world's beginning. She is laughing because he loves the green dish as a child loves a toy and because he is awed by it, by its greenness, by her, by the beauty and the laughter.

Is the Queen of Sheba laughing because she knows her green glass basin is a treasure to the House of Israel for ever, though lost like so much when the people are taken to captivity in

Babylon and found again when the temple is restored? Is she laughing at the dubious House of the Herods who will claim it as royal treasure, not temple treasure? Is she laughing because John the Baptiser, the madman in his cell, will sense the great green dish near him as he sings through the night and infuriates the Tetrarch? Is the Queen of Sheba laughing because she realises that through the green glass his blood will look black when his head is carried round the hall and Salome will pout like a sulky child when she thinks that she should have asked for the lovely green glass and not the ugly red head?

Is the Queen of Sheba laughing because she sees a harassed Jewish housewife in Bethany trying to prepare Seder for her Nazarene friend and his disreputable gang, picking up the green dish which John's disciples had stolen from the palace in his honour and hidden in her house? Is the Queen of Sheba laughing because she is now placing in Solomon's hands the same bowl as this peasant woman will set on the table so that the Nazarene will use it for a blessing cup – and it will become the Holy Grail, the great treasure of the Cathedral Church of San Lorenzo in Genoa?

Or is the Queen of Sheba laughing just because the bowl is beautiful and in her wisdom all beauty fills her with joy and the joy spills over into laughter like a mountain stream?

'Ellie!'

And she was standing, just touching the lovely green vessel that her colleague and rival is exhibiting with one finger and laughing like a maniac in the middle of a public gallery. Judith was looking slightly anxious. The glassworker who had made it was moving across the room, not so much nervous as curious.

Ellie drew a deep breath, shaken. She leaned on a long-practised charm, backed up by the rigorous discipline that her parents had taught her for lesser occasions than this a long time ago.

'Oh Brian, it's wonderful. I was laughing because it is exactly
the same colour as that bowl in Genoa, the one they call the
Holy Grail, and I couldn't place it. I don't suppose you're going
to tell me how you get the colour?' And catching out of one
unfocused eye the little red sticker, she became bolder. 'I want
it, Brian, you clever thing. Will you sell it to me?'

'You never buy, Ellie; you're famous for not buying other
people's glass.'

He was flattered, delighted. Then he too noticed the red
circle, 'Damn; I'd adore for you to have it, but I'm afraid it's
already sold.'

'Oh dear,' she said. 'Well I'm not surprised.'

'Let's get out of here,' she whispered to Judith less than two
minutes later, 'I'm going insane.'

'What was that about?' Judith asked her later.

'I don't know,' said Ellie. 'It was scary. I lost it. I didn't know
where I was, or what I was doing. It's happened before, but not
in public. I'm frightened.'

'Stress, darling.'

'Judith I . . .' but what can she say? *I thought I was the Queen
of Sheba.* For God's sake . . . 'Perhaps it is the menopause,' she
said gloomily.

'Don't you adore it?' Judith said. 'Don't you just adore
expressions like "a woman of a certain age". I am a woman of
a certain age.'

'You're not,' said Ellie, 'you're far too young.'

'Well, I will be soon,' said Judith, 'and I can hardly wait. It's
such a wonderful example of the typical euphemisms used to
keep women in their places. I know, you know, we all know,
that anyone who says "a woman of a certain age" really means
"We all know she's menopausal but we're not going to use *that*
word." It reveals the same slimy mentality as the enchanting
custom of putting sanitary towels into a *PLAIN* BROWN
PAPER BAG, which in these days of advertising is exactly the

same as pinning a button on a woman announcing in neon letters "I'm bleeding vaginally". If you see a woman carrying a plain brown paper bag you know perfectly well she's menstruating.'

'She might be unusually efficient and her period hasn't started yet,' Ellie tried to enter into this high-spirited flamboyance.

'Granted,' said Judith graciously. 'In the second place, it means the opposite of what it says – what it means is that the speaker is uncertain how old I am, into which category I fall and how the hell to treat me. He really thinks I am a bit too old to be wearing skin-tight leggings, or a mini-skirt, or no bra, or whatever; or he thinks I'm a bit young to be "letting myself go", but he will very generously forgive me because after all I am at *that age* and minor eccentricities or misunderstandings of my social status are only to be expected, poor little me.'

'The trouble is, Judith,' Ellie said, 'you don't know what the hell you're talking about. It simply isn't fun. It takes your head apart as well as generating a flourishing moustache.'

'Really?' said Judith with childlike curiosity. 'I didn't know that, let me see.'

'I pluck,' said Ellie, covering her upper lip with the back of her hand.

'Don't worry about it,' laughed Judith and then added, 'or about being insane. We're all insane. Look at me. I've decided to go to Venice to the wedding and make a fool of myself.'

'It's the fag-hag's deficient sense of social shame at work again. What wildly inappropriate plot have you cooked up this time?'

'I want to go.'

'Will you have "just cause or impediment", all Jane Eyre-ish?'

'Do they have that in Italy?' To Ellie's relief they talked about Judith's painful resolution for most of the evening.

Only as they parted, when Ellie said, 'Look, if you're really going . . . just, take care. You want to still like yourself next week,' did Judith refer in any way to Ellie's peculiar behaviour.

'Don't split infinitives,' she responded. 'And as to taking care, you too, Ms. Macauley. Don't think I don't notice. And, by the way, you did a nice cover-up job, no one but me will ever guess you are completely barking.'

Which was comforting in a way. They hugged and parted.

Ellie was exhausted and confused. She reached her car with a sense of relief, unlocked it and got in, reaching mechanically for the belt. She put the key in the ignition and glanced automatically into the rear-view mirror; there was a flash – no, a passing – of light, reflected from the back seat. Iridescent, pink perhaps, or blue and crimson lustre, crimson and gold on glass, and . . . she swung her head round violently and there was nothing there. But Angel was present in her head.

'Angel, was that you?'

'Probably.'

'But I saw . . . I saw you in the mirror.'

'Well, I'm not a vampire,' Angel said. 'As a matter of fact, we do tend to manifest in mirrors first.' But before Ellie could say anything Angel went on, 'It was a blunder, all right? I don't mean the manifesting, I mean what happened at the gallery. I was incompetent. This time it really was not you going insane, it was me getting out of order.'

'What ever do you mean?'

'Well, you know, angels may have problems with matter and time, but we have none at all with order and hierarchy. Placement, etiquette, decorum, whatever you want to call it. Or we shouldn't.'

'Angel are you apologising for something?'

'I don't think we can apologise. We're inerrant, we can't be wrong, so presumably we can't ever need to apologise and because we're supernaturally economic, we don't do what we don't need to do. No, I'm explaining.'

'So what happened? Angel, it was so strange. It was my hand, I saw my hand, my . . . it was my hand, but it wasn't, it was quite different. I mean it was the hand that was part of the person who was doing the seeing, and I, me, I was doing the seeing, but it wasn't my hand. That doesn't make sense. And there was all this stuff that I don't know about, but that me did know. Angel, I was fucking frightened. And it's not the first time, only in public . . .'

There was a pause.

'I can't explain, not now,' said Angel, 'I can only comfort and reassure. I am telling you, with complete authority, that it had nothing to do with you.'

'But it did.'

'No, it didn't.'

'Please.'

'Just believe me,' and with such speed that it gave Ellie a headache Angel flowed down her hunched spine and evaporated.

Because there was nothing else to do, Ellie drove home. 'Just believe me.' Just believe that although you have had a totally weird and slightly schizophrenic experience, you can rest serenely in the knowledge that it has nothing to do with you, and is all the fault – no, not fault because Angels do not sin . . . It is all the *cause* of your guardian angel who has assured you that an angel is not a vampire. Ellie did not find this a satisfactory or even very comforting explanation.

What, though, would be better? Easier to cope with?

Menopause?

Menopause was completely horrible and it prevented her from knowing whether she was feeling any of this at all or whether it was just her hormones surging about and her body destroying her mind. Or she really was going insane. Was it insanity? Hormones? Tiredness? Or beauty? She lost the dividing line. It was perilous.

Then just when Ellie was beginning to believe that things could not possibly get any worse, the crucible cracked. The raw glass inside the main furnace was kept constantly molten in a huge earthenware pot called a crucible. In the end the glass corroded the pot, eating into the clay until it cracked; the molten glass then pushed its way through the cracks, widening them, until, like lava through the fissures in the earth's surface, it poured out in a slow river. When you cooled the furnace in order to remove and change the crucible the glass of course cooled too and sealed the old useless pot to the floor. It always happened in the end, inevitably at the worst possible moment, and every time it was unexpected, infuriating, frustrating and hard work.

Ellie arrived at the studio one morning to be confronted by a tearful Patsy.

'What have you broken?' she asked with a smile; Patsy, probably because she was so careful, was always reduced to tears by any accidents. Ellie had a brief vision of a tray of shattered decanters and herself explaining to Megan that it was just one of those things, it could not be helped.

'Not me,' said Patsy; 'we've got a crucible crack.'

'Fuck,' said Ellie. After a pause, she asked, already knowing the answer 'How bad?'

'Bad,' said Patsy. Now Ellie was here, Patsy no longer felt responsible, and was restored to her own calm self, the person who is good in an emergency, who does what is needed and does not make a fuss.

Ellie did not want to take it on, she was too tired.

There was no choice.

'Have you told Megan?'

'Not yet.'

'OK. Turn down the power, check the new one. Oh, damn, we did not need this. I'll go and have a word with Megan.'

She went back to the office. Megan was on the phone and when Ellie came in she looked up startled, as though caught out. Ellie hovered undecided in the doorway.

Megan said, 'I'll tell her. Yes, don't worry. Goodbye then.' She hung up. 'Ellie,' she said.

'We've got a bloody crucible breakage,' Ellie said.

'Ellie,' Megan said again.

'The whole thing, completely gone, there's metal everywhere, it's a nightmare.'

'Oh Ellie,' said Megan, 'not *now*.'

'It's always *now*.'

'Ellie, I'm sorry, but that was Henry on the phone.'

Ellie struggled to refocus. 'Henry? Is he OK?' and she could not avoid noticing the many layers of her own reaction. Fear, fear that he was ill and a secret springing of hope that something had happened, something important enough to make him change his mind.

'He's fine. Your brother just rang him at the hospital. Your mother died this morning.'

Ellie looked at her blankly.

'Last night. Betty took her breakfast in this morning and she had just died, in her sleep, quite peacefully they think.' There was a pause. Megan was not entirely sure what to say next; she realised that she did not have the least idea how Ellie was going to react. 'I'm sorry, Ellie.'

'Shit. Shit and damn and all the other things. Oh shit.' And then after a pause she yelled, 'She did this, the fucking witch; she cracked the bloody cauldron.' For a few moments Ellie was entirely somewhere else; outside herself as she had been when she had cut Henry's face; she was shouting without knowing what she was saying. 'She did it to punish me, to punish me. I hope she bloody well burns in hell.'

179

'Ellie!' Megan moved round her desk with extraordinary speed. She held Ellie in her arms tenderly but her voice is stern. 'Don't. Just shut up. Don't talk like that. Be quiet.'

It was a return, a return to the experience of mothering that Megan had given her when she had run away from her parents and come home to Megan's house. She flopped her head suddenly on to Megan's shoulder and began to cry, as she had done the second night in Megan's house thirty years before.

'She hates me,' she cried, 'she hates me.'

Megan knew better than to deny it.

'She may hate you, though you will never know that, but she did not crack the crucible. She's not that powerful. She was an old and disagreeable woman, don't give her power.'

And later when she had calmed down and gone outside to walk up the street just to be on her own for a little while, Angel endorsed what Megan had said. Her mother was not a witch because witches were necessarily powerful and glamorous and creative.

'If you want to think about witches,' said Angel, 'think about your daughter, not your mother.'

Ellie was shocked and angry.

Angel said firmly, 'You only don't want to think of Stephanie as a witch because you have negative views of witchcraft – and for someone who works with magic I find that very interesting. You ought to be proud.'

Diverted from her anger and grief, Ellie tried to focus on Stephanie in this light.

Now Stephanie was in the jungle; now she grows playful, and in her playfulness she grows powerful.

In the jungle Stephanie encounters a people who loved her seizures, who honour them as the presence of the Spirits. She is everything wrong – she is white, and a woman and young and noisy, but the spirits stamp down between her shoulders and with scuds of foam on her mouth she raves – the spirit mothers can enter her body and reveal their wrath and love. She can let the ancestors through and the people are grateful. Not often, but sometimes, here in the jungle, Stephanie does not take her drugs.

If she times it right, which is not too difficult, her fits can come upon her not as a curse but as a blessing; a divine blessing from the spirits. The people are grateful and honour her. Her expedition leader, who is not privy to her powerful trances, is grateful to her because he sees that the people honour her, and this makes the whole expedition easier. The interpreter, who comes originally from this very tribe, and has not in his heart moved as far as his American accent suggests, deliberately confuses the leader about what is happening: a white woman, he explains, was lucky; a young white woman so round and fair would bring them all good luck. These people have not seen a white woman before and they find her glamorous. 'Do not be afraid,' he says, 'they will not hurt her, they will not . . .' his hands express sex more vividly than the expedition leader likes to think about.

When Stephanie speaks with the spirits the people protect her. Here she writhes not on the hard surfaces of British hospitals and pavements, but on the soft mulch of the jungle floor and so there is little danger in the thrashings; and she has a small bone, an ancestor bone, that they wedge between her teeth as she falls forward and so she is safe, and safe she is powerful.

She knows it is risky and foolish, and she does it half knowing that and taking the responsibility of risk, and half at risk, giving herself as a gift to the risky gods of shamanism and so her witch power is freed in her and indeed she could crack her mother's crucible, the cauldron of her mother's magic, half a world away, if she so chose, but she does not choose.

One day she will have exhausted all her anger, and learned to live with her seizures and manage her power and then she will go home and give this up, but not yet; she walks safely in the jungle and touches the heart of her own power.

Ellie's daughter was a witch. Ellie did not know this, but

encouraged by Angel, she sensed something of it. Her mother's death freed some space in her imagination and for the first time in months Ellie found herself thinking about Stephanie, not about her, Ellie's, relationship with her daughter. Comforted, Ellie turned her attention to the heavy, messy, physical task of hacking out the old pot and installing the new one.

Ellie went north to the funeral on her own.

It was the same weekend as Judith was going to Venice. Ellie did not even ask her. She knew that whatever was happening to Judith was far more important than her mother's funeral: it was more important to her, never mind how important it was to Judith. They had purchased together an immensely witty and frivolous hat for Judith to wear to the wedding – it would be entirely unsuitable for a Presbyterian funeral.

'I could not bear it if you wasted that hat,' Ellie had teased Judith.

'Well, if I happen to murder either of them, will you come and visit me in prison?'

'It's a promise. I'll buy a hat even smarter than that one, and dab my eyes with a lace-edged hankie as I walk across the Bridge of Sighs and descend to your dark dungeon.'

'I don't think they use it any more.'

'Damn!' She drove Judith to the airport the day before she went north herself. She did not park, but did get out of the car outside the terminal. They hugged each other very carefully, very warmly.

'Just take care,' said Ellie, 'and come back safely.'

'Venice is no further than Ayrshire – nearer in fact. You come back safely.'

Ellie felt as though a major prop had been snatched away from her.

'Megan,' she had asked, 'will you come to the funeral?'

'No,' said Megan.

Ellie was a bit surprised. 'Please,' she tried.

'No,' said Megan. Then after a pause she explained, almost tentatively. 'I hate the place. I got away. I don't want to have to see my ex-husband.'

'But Megan,' and now Ellie was curious rather than pleading, 'you had supper with him only a couple of months ago.'

'Here in London, yes. Up there is different.'

She did not ask anyone else, none of her gay friends. There were a number of reasons why not and she was aware of most of them. She did not want any of them to see the cold and horrid town that had created the boundaries of her childhood, to hear people calling her 'Nell' or even 'Helen'. She would feel diminished, exposed, nullified by the assumptions that would shape her while she was there. She did not want them to know her like that.

There were other things too. She wanted to behave well and knew she would not, knew she would giggle and joke if she went with anyone who would giggle and joke with her. She wanted to act with perfect dignity, a dignity which would not quite outweigh her final evil in having refused to go home this summer, but might be held in the balance against it.

. . . And damn it, if she had not lost her head the night that Robbie died, she would not have had to have that mark against her; she would have been able to put off the decision until there was no decision to be made . . .

She decided not even to ask herself how much she did not ask those friends because they would offend a group of people that she thought she did not mind offending. She would not insult them with the homophobia of the cold lowlands.

So she went alone, on the train from Euston.

She had agreed to stay two nights. She must have been mad. Two nights in Betty and Alan's house, where there would be no alcohol, no warmth, and no wit. Cold. Rigid. Unbearable.

'Do you have to dress like that?' Alan said when she came down for the funeral; and she could not but remember the pleasure, the comfort, that her hat, black gloves, lovely coat, high-heeled shoes had given people at Robbie's funeral, even as they themselves wore old jeans and leather jackets.

'A mark of respect,' she said, and felt immediately ashamed. Alan, very properly, gave her a nasty look.

They walked from his house to the kirk.

They sang Bunyan's pilgrim hymn slightly too slowly. The minister preached on discipleship and how her mother had afforded them all an almost biblical example.

Ellie thought about Robbie's funeral and Mike Turney's speech full of jokes about Robbie's lesions and stubbornnesses; and Robbie's mother, rather shakily thanking them all for the privilege of knowing them, not even insulting them by thanking them for the care and love they had given; and Mary and Robbie's sister holding hands like schoolchildren and singing with the tears pouring down their faces; and the coffin piled with inappropriate gifts, from a poster of Stephan Edberg to a pink chiffon scarf.

She watched Alan shake his head quietly but firmly at his own daughter when she cried for her grandmother's death. She remembered Robbie's father, carefully dressed in his black suit and tie, liberated into his own grief by the blatancy of other people's, turning unthinking to the person next to him and laying his neatly brushed but balding head on the chest of a strange man with a leather jacket and a pierced eyebrow and sobbing, letting himself be hugged, even petted for a brief and blessed moment.

She watched her own gloved hand being taken in sympathy and shaken kindly for her sad loss, when almost every one of the reaching paws must know that she had not seen her mother in ten years although there had been nothing whatsoever to prevent her catching a train for the living as easily as she had caught it yesterday for the dead. For Megan's sake, she smiled and shook hands with Megan's ex-husband who expressed warm sympathy and did not use the occasion to make any reference to his ex-wife whatsoever.

Then, just when she was feeling securely superior to their small-minded lives, she glanced at Betty and saw in her face an agony of loss that was as real as Robbie's keening at Tim's funeral. Had Betty loved her mother? Had she lost something, some claim to identity? Ellie knew suddenly that it was not Robbie's sort of loss that she saw in Betty's face, it was her own – it was how she felt about Henry. Caring for her mother had given shape and meaning and therefore joy to Betty's life – it was the thing that she did, that made a framework, and out of that doing something, that might as well be called love, had indeed been formed, and now it was gone. She found that she had no words of comfort for her sister-in-law; that she, warm-hearted, tender, kind, understanding Ellie, to whom her friends turned in their distresses knowing they would find comfort, was just a minor snob who gained gratification by being the woman who understood queers.

As they walked from the grey kirk to the village hall for a nasty selection of sandwiches which she had not cut, she saw suddenly a little child, a little girl with wanton red curls cut off short, running up this very street. A little girl in a place that, even if it was not much fun, was perfectly safe, a child fed, organised, educated, cared for. She saw a woman, not laughing or joyous, but solid and brave and honourable according to her own rules, a woman of rigour and not unuseful. Ellie neither loved nor liked that woman; that was sad, but it was not the whole story. Betty had loved her. Alan had loved her; her granddaughter had wanted to weep for her in the cold morning. For all Ellie knew Stephanie had loved her. She was even, briefly, glad that she had come.

This did not last. After they had driven to the cremation, sharing a car and driving behind the hearse so that the whole thing took hours longer than it need have, and driven back again and eaten some thin soup too obviously made with cheap stock cubes, and everyone had thanked Betty and said there was nothing more warming than good soup, was there? . . . After all that, they trekked out to the lawyer's office for the reading of the will. The old woman in a final, punitive, wicked act had left everything – everything carefully listed: money, personal effects, a good deal of the furniture that Alan and Betty used daily – she had left it all to Stephanie.

It was an insult to everyone. To Alan and Betty, who had cared for her so faithfully; to their children who had been real grandchildren, taking with the tolerance of the young all the inevitable disruptions and restrictions to their own lives that sharing a home with the elderly must bring. It was an insult to Ellie and Henry too, implying somehow that they would not, or could not, provide for their child. She had instructed the lawyer to write it in full, the precise words: *To my beloved grandchild, Stephanie Elizabeth Landsdowne, because I have been given so little chance to see her, and because she will need it most.*

To make it worse Alan and Betty were extremely noble about it.

'This is ridiculous,' said Ellie, 'I'm sure Stephanie will . . .'

'It was all hers,' said Alan.

'And Father's,' interrupted Ellie; 'it's not right and he wouldn't have thought so.'

'He left everything to her, absolutely; it was hers to do what she liked with.'

'I'm sure Steph wouldn't want . . . I'll speak to her.'

'Please don't. We didn't look after her to get anything out of it.'

'I'm not saying you did. I'm saying that it isn't fair and Steph will agree with me.' And why was her daughter thousands of miles away instead of here to back her mother up. 'Surely you . . .' she looked to the other grandchildren who could not be that unselfish '. . .there must be at least something personal, something you would like. I think you could contest the will if you wanted.'

'I'm sure they would not,' said Alan, obviously holding on to his anger with some difficulty and therefore furious with his sister, 'Are you suggesting she was not of sound mind? You wouldn't know, Nell, because you haven't been here, but she was entirely sane, right up to the end. She won a game of Scrabble against Robbie the night she died, I'll have you know.'

'This is not sane. It is not just and it is not fair.'

'That's for Stephanie to decide. I'm sure my children are not as avaricious and greedy as you seem to want them to be. I would be delighted for them if she had left them . . . Why aren't you pleased for Stephanie?'

She wanted to say that she did not want to be grateful, and she was not grateful. It was ridiculous. Stephanie simply did not need it; Henry, Henry and she, were rich, rich beyond a degree of comfort and security that Alan and Betty did not even probably know how to imagine. And, with Stephanie on another continent and not communicating with her, there was nothing she could do; it was not even her inheritance to be generous with, to assuage her guilt and allow justice to happen. She disliked her mother with such clarity that she could hardly speak, and Alan loved her with such discipline that he could not allow his very proper anger any expression. He was proving himself the virtuous person – she could only hope that this would be sufficient comfort to him.

'I'll get in touch with Steph,' she managed, 'as soon as possible. And in the meantime don't do a thing. Please.'

'We must do what we think right, Nell.'

'Yes, of course.'

There was nothing to do except eat supper, go to bed and catch the train back to London in the morning.

Somewhere south of Carlisle, rising through her tiredness and ill will, she heard Angel say, 'I think you should make a tear for your mother.'

'No.'

'Yes.'

'Angel, they're for love.'

'And for loss.'

'Can you have loss without love?'

'Certainly.'

A black tear, plain, perfectly smooth, obsidian, as hard and tough as her mother. A loss. There certainly could be loss without love.

She would also have to write to Stephanie. This filled her with an odd pleasure. She would have to write. Without loss of pride she could write to Stephanie. No emotion, just business.

Darling Stephanie,

Your grandmother died last week. I am sorry to upset you with this news, and would have left you to your chosen isolation, except that she left you everything in her will. I think this was rather unfair to Uncle Alan and your cousins; although of course it's up to you. Since you presently own their dining-room table (among other things) I'm afraid I have to ask you to let me know what you think should be done about this. Your uncle is so outraged that he is being stubbornly legalistic. It really does need sorting out.

love from Mummy.

dear daughter – your grandmother, who hates me as much as you do, has left you rather a lot of money in her will. Now, even in your selfish greed, you will never have to deal with me again. A bit of luck for you, for both of us. your mother.

A few evenings later, she went to the studio to make a tear for her mother. The black glass she used was so dense, so opaque that she inserted a secret lead weight into the centre of the globule before marvering it. The weight of it was important suddenly, it had to be heavier and darker than any glass. When it was done she saw that it was beautiful, it was perfect; despite her efforts at solidity, which had been successful, it had a reflecting quality that came from the glass itself. You could not see through it, but you could see into it. It gave her technical pleasure and made her cross. After she had put it in the annealing chamber, she had a great longing to make a new one for Robbie, clear and filled with twists of air, like before.

She went upstairs, through the drawing room and into the little room behind it. She unlocked and opened the cabinet, and picked up the top box, Robbie's box, slightly uncertainly, not quite sure whether this was right or not. As soon as the box was in her hand she knew it was too light; with hasty care she took off the lid. As she had already known it would be, the box was empty.

She did not open the other boxes, but she lifted each one, weighing it on her palm. They were all heavy on her hand, except one: Mark's tear had been blown, thin and fine, almost without any weight, so its box felt empty, but when she shook it very tenderly she could feel the tear inside shift just enough for assurance.

She had, definitely and without any question, put Robbie's tear in this red box. Equally definitely it was not here now.

It had been broken, not something to steal.

It had been in a box, in a locked cupboard, not something to lose accidentally.

That was one too many things.

They were all small and all unusually lovely, special: the fused cube, the tiny millefiorí bowl, the perfect glass sphere containing blue wrought canes *façon de venise*, Robbie's tear.

They had something in common, she realised: they had all been technical experiments where the perfecting of the technology had produced something better than she had planned.

Very slowly she went round the whole studio with her eyes wide open, looking for absence. It was hard to remember in the clutter; there should be a small round ball, with a flat bottom, a potential paperweight perhaps, which she had made last winter when thinking about cameo cutting: a crystal ball dipped into blue glass which she had then cut away; the opposite of the Portland Vase but a similar technique. She had never much enjoyed cold cutting and had not developed that idea any further, but it had been a success – the blue tree visible from both sides, once flat, and through the glass distorted by the roundness, both abstract and three dimensional; the right size, very satisfying, very lucky. She had left it in the cutting room because she knew that Megan would like it, but once Ellie knew she could do it, she did not want to have it. She could not find that now.

Beyond that it was hard to tell. Dear God, they had a lot of bits and pieces hanging around. They must have a spring clean; she did not want to think about the things that were missing . . . stolen . . . lost . . . taken.

Accidents happen.

But Robbie's tear had been locked up. In a box. No one could have shoved it somewhere unthinkingly. Perhaps she was really going mad. She would search her house at home. Megan wouldn't . . . And as soon as she had thought 'Megan wouldn't' she stopped herself. If she was thinking that, then she was also thinking that someone else would, or might, and she did not want to think it. Mary, Patsy, Sally the cleaner, the packers, prospective clients – sometimes they came into the studio, if both she and Megan liked them, or they were paying enough or . . . They never came up here.

The packers were easiest, because she knew them least. She

tried to settle on a slightly demented packer who arrived on Friday mornings with kleptomaniac tendencies – undiscriminating except by size.

That was stupid.

But the whole thing was stupid. She did not want to think about it. It was too weird. She would think instead about a new tear for Robbie – at least this new confusion ended the old one: she would have to make him a new tear. Not tonight. Tonight she did not want to think about it. She wanted to go home.

She went home. But she could not clear the losses so easily from her head.

Chapter Five

'I must say,' Megan said, as she and Ellie sat in the office drinking coffee, the day after Mary and she came back from Leibnitz, 'that she behaved impeccably. Charming and venerative. Much more the privileged apprentice than the rising star. I was impressed. Friedhelm was impressed too, of course, which was probably the point. He was also worried about you, Ellie, why you weren't there. It is you he wants, he really does.'

'You don't trust her, do you?'

'Not exactly. But it's complicated.'

Megan wanted to say that it was complicated because she was muddled. Mary reminded her of Ellie at the same age, except that Ellie had needed her then and Mary abundantly did not; a big difference. At the same time she knew she was jealous of Mary; until Mary came it had always been Ellie and her and their work-force. Mary was different; she could be a partner for Ellie, a colleague. Megan felt that this got in the way of her clarity. Her real interest was the good of the studio and Mary, pushing Ellie, making demands, being ambitious, was good for them all.

'Patsy called her sly once,' Ellie said. 'Does that fit?'

'Yes . . . no. I don't know. "Sly" would be deliberate. I don't think she plans it. Why?'

'Well why is because we all seem to have forgotten that I want to do these windows. I keep forgetting that.'

'You've had a lot on your plate.' Megan smiled. Ellie was obviously beginning to recover.

'Megan, there is something weird going on in this studio, and it only started when Mary came.' Megan looked baffled. 'We keep losing things, Megan.'

Megan looked startled. 'No, think about it,' Ellie said, forcing down her rising panic, her own desire not to think about it. 'The oxidised cube, the little bowl. And unless you took it home without telling me, your blue glass bauble.'

'Oh.'

'Well I can't find it. And, other bits and bobs – a little paperweight I made, cold cutting . . . and I keep some stuff in the cupboard in the back, upstairs. I keep it locked, Megan.'

'And you think Mary . . .?'

'No. No, I don't "think Mary"; I just don't know what to think. Not you. Not me. Not Patsy. I can say those. I can't say "Not Mary" and I don't like it. And . . . and it's very intimate blowing with someone . . . and something has gone wrong; two months ago we were great, and now we're not. She's clumsy; I'm all over the place; Patsy's getting peevish.'

'Start with you, Ellie, not with them. You take control here and everything will be OK.'

'Am I being ticked off?'

'A little, yes.' Ellie was about to protest, but Megan went on, 'I just don't believe anyone is running around nicking bits of glass; it's ridiculous. We'll have a big spring clean later this month and they'll turn up. The only alternative is to sack Mary, and neither of us for very different reasons want to do that.'

Ellie knew that was true of herself anyway. As Megan spoke her heart sank and rose within the one sentence.

'I know you have had a bloody miserable time, but frankly,

Ellie, you're not going to solve it without some effort; and you have no right to take it out on me. I don't mean personally, I mean thanks to you this studio is my security, my job, my life, mine. I'm not going to let you throw that away, because you're too busy feeling sorry for yourself to manage one talented but spoiled brat.'

'Megan!'

'Oh dear,' said Megan, 'I'm sorry. Sometimes I act like your mother.'

'Sweet Megan, you are nothing like my mother.'

'No, no. I mean I feel like you're my daughter. I chose you for my daughter. So I'm allowed to tick you off.'

Ellie's eyes filled. Then suddenly they were both giggling at this improbable exhibition of emotion.

It was true, what Megan had said, true for both of them, chosen mother and child, but what was as true and more important was work: they were bound together because of their work. Megan had the right to defend the studio; the right to such a demonstration. Her conviction was a solace not a wound to Ellie. It shifted things forward.

Hugo and Ellie inevitably made up.

When he stopped being cross with Ellie, Hugo felt guilty. He knew how much he owed her. He knew that he had not been around for her. He did not like in himself the thought that he took but did not give. He had genuinely been busy, hard driven, and he had spent several evenings with Mary testing the boundaries of possibility with her, and Ellie had been all over the place, and rather to his surprise had not asked him to go to Scotland with her for her mother's funeral. And, of course, he loved her. As soon as she stopped trying to make-up their fight, stopped phoning him plaintively and apologetically, he started worrying about her, then missing her, then needing her.

In the end he rang her. He did not even need to apologise, just ringing was enough, Ellie was more than ready to forgive, indeed he was fairly certain that she did not even acknowledge that he needed forgiving. She took it all on herself. But he knew she was trying too hard to be chirpy and jolly with him; she did not even enquire, as the terms of their friendship required that she should, whether he was making up just because he wanted to go to New York.

Within a couple of days it was as though they had never fought. They met for a drink one evening. Hugo arrived scowling sardonically, 'I suppose,' he said, 'that you have one of these.'

It was a formal wedding invitation. He fanned the card with its silver copperplate print under his nose, with a gesture of disdain.

'Jim and Stuart's?' Ellie laughed at his petulance.

'How dare they so insult us?' He was half joking, half genuinely put out.

'They're our friends,' Ellie said.

'Doesn't mean I have to believe in it. This aping of heterosexuality.'

'Oh come on, it's ironic. Satirical.' The invitations had been issued in the names of their cats.

'No, it's for real; it's just dressed up a bit camp.'

'We like camp.'

'We do not like promises of everlasting monotony. We don't like cosy, at-home, mortgaged happiness . . .'

'. . . in the place of a risky joy.' She had smiled at him, 'Different people have different risks. Commitment can be risky too.'

'Couplism,' he grinned darkly.

'How old-fashioned. I suppose this means the spring romance is now off.'

'Of course. I could not bring myself to abandon high political principle even for his totally adorable bum.'

195

Then suddenly he wanted to do something that would make her happy. He needed to make some reparation.

'But none the less, you need cheering up.'

'I'm fine,' Ellie said quickly.

'Liar. And anyway on this occasion I think we should abandon high political principle and go.'

It was more than important, it was necessary. It was less generous than it seemed. He needed Ellie. He was going to take an HIV test. Once he had reached that point, he knew, almost to his surprise that he could not do it on his own; that meant he would have to tell someone, whatever he had said to Mary, and the someone would be Ellie. He needed her to hold his hand.

Ellie grinned, knowing none of this. She had already decided to go to the wedding, even anticipating Hugo's objections. She had, in fact, already booked the hire of a morning coat and top hat, and had agreed to read a lesson at the ceremony.

'I'm not giving them a wedding present, though,' he said firmly.

'I am.' She had made them two glasses; lovely, solid fluted wine glasses in dark blue glass with ebullient and witty scarlet prunts, mould formed with their initials, and even Megan had smiled indulgently.

'Yeah, well you would. You're a softy. Next thing is, you'll be thinking that this brainy Blairite scheme to provide state dowries for the daughters of the poor is a good idea.'

He smirked malevolently. She took him more seriously than he had meant. The preposterous accusation made her brave.

'Of course not. And, of course, *you* ought to be given a darling Italian *cappuccino* machine, or whatever the trendy culinary device for the chic pink-pounder is just now, and possibly if you'd get a decent kitchen, you'd get one from me. Have a not-wedding-party and invite all the people you've ever given wedding presents to. The trouble is that you're turning into a queer fundamentalist: there's lots of ways of doing things, and laying claim to a wedding, more stylish and more fun than the heterosexual version, saying "Look we can do even this better than you can", if you happen to be the sort of person for whom that sort of commitment makes sense . . . There's nothing wrong with monogamy, there's only something wrong with valorising it, making it obligatory.'

'Wow,' he said, mocking, 'it will be Valentine cards next.'

'I never send them; you do.'

'Ironically.'

'There you are.'

'Well, I've said we're going anyway.' After quite a short pause he looked at her quizzically and said, 'You were going to go in any case, weren't you?' And when she nodded, slightly embarrassed, he laughed and said, 'Your cowardices are always in the wrong place. Oh Ellie, I do love you, you know.'

The wedding seemed to provide Hugo with a perfect opportunity. They would be together and with friends; they would have a wonderful time, and be happy. After the party they would go out to dinner and he would ask Ellie if she'd come with him when he took his HIV test. 'If.' Without arrogance he knew there was no 'if': she would agree, that was one of the reasons why she was the person he wanted to ask.

The week before the wedding Hugo had a drink with Mary, a thing they did quite often now. Mary was in a buoyant mood, almost completely satisfied with her life. Her fears that Megan might not like her had been allayed by her terrific performance in Germany. She was working well. She was moving forward; not just here in the studio, but in life as well. Hugo had agreed to test. If all was well there she would try to get pregnant this autumn; perhaps she would have a spring baby next year.

She liked Hugo, she thought he would be a delightful parent, with just the right amount of responsibility and presence. And, she thought, he would bind Ellie into her life. She wanted that. Entangled in her own ambition and Ellie's professional authority, she was both needy and greedy. Competitive and starstruck. She sensed that Ellie was manageable. Her feelings for Ellie were those of a daughter, powerful and confused, but she had never had a mother so she did not know this.

The way she felt she did not want to have to deal with anything difficult that evening.

When Hugo asked her, apparently casually, if she had told Ellie about their procreative plans, she said 'Yes, yes'.

In fact she had not done so. She was going to . . . but . . . there just had not been the right time yet. And anyway it was Hugo's job. Hugo was Ellie's friend. He should tell her, if he thought it was any of Ellie's business.

Right at the beginning of all this Hugo had told her that he would not tell anyone except her about the result of his test. This had made her feel slightly smug, self-contented, and so she had remembered it with more clarity than Hugo had. When he changed his mind and knew he wanted, needed, Ellie with him when he tested it did not occur to him to tell Mary. To her it seemed a tiny lie, a social convenience to keep the evening running smoothly.

He didn't ask her what Ellie had said because he considered that Ellie's business. Since Mary was casual about it, and Ellie did not mention it he assumed that it was not a problem for either of them. Some friends arrived in the bar and the conversation moved on to other things.

At a curious level Mary was innocent. She really did not know that she was a manipulative user: it was an unexamined habit. She had an essential weakness because she had been so securely loved as a child. It was not that she thought the world owed her a living; it was that world had consistently given her one.

On a bright Saturday afternoon Ellie and Hugo went to the wedding together. She wore the hired morning suit and the swagger of it made her feel good. So did the house when they arrived. Silvery balloons, helium inflated, bounced against the ceiling and their long gold ribbons trailed a moving veil against the guests' faces as they walked through the front room. The continuous movement of the party kept the balloons bobbing and drifting gently.

There was pink champagne. In the kitchen there was a feast, a witty banquet of canapés. Ellie was tempted to be offended that they had not asked her to make something, but speedily discovered that the food was a wedding present from a professional catering friend of theirs, who now simpered beside his table, nourishing himself on compliments.

'I especially,' said Ellie to him, 'admire those,' she smiled and pointed to the slices of beetroot cut in heart shapes, with tiny mayonnaise arrows piped on to them. She could not have bothered.

At the centre there was the wedding cake, in tiers, beautifully iced, and on the very top of it two tiny plastic grooms twirled together. Did one, Ellie asked herself, have to buy two sets and throw away the brides, were there somewhere two tiny dollies all in white plastic lace seeking partners and finding each other? Perhaps she should throw a separation party, with a single bride dancing alone on the summit of an ice mountain. She realised even as she thought this that she had accepted something inevitable. She had better not get too drunk; this was not an occasion for sitting on the stairs weeping, which was what would happen if she didn't take care.

It was a lovely party. Stuart and Jim weren't children, there was nothing naïve in this celebration, but there was something innocent. All love was innocent love, Ellie knew sharply: any love was devoid of harm for the beloved, it was just that love never came pure, it came packaged in people who were lots more and other things than lovers – gluttons and sadists and egotists and God knows what other toxic beings; was there, she wondered, such a word as 'nocent'?

The wedding ceremony was mocking, gay, exhibitionist and joyful. It clearly meant different things to different people – street theatre and touching triumph and political sign and reactionary indulgence. Even the ceremony itself was a scoffing finger stuck out in the face of the law, since a solicitor friend of theirs represented the registrar dressed in Nazi gear. There was a confusion, for Ellie at least, as to whether this was a comment on establishment homophobia and oppression or a personal sexual proclivity; whether it was funny or in dangerously bad taste. But then her own outfit, in which she felt so good and for which she was receiving admiring compliments, was like all women's drag, valorising establishment masculinity. Damn.

Jim and Stuart vowed to share the onerous duties of maintaining the cat litter tray in a hygienic state; they vowed to try and forgive each other future infidelities; they vowed to have fun and to stay together for as long as possible. A few people wiped proper middle-aged wedding tears from the corners of their eyes. A few people had not bothered to leave the bar, or could be heard in the kitchen still screeching. There were four bridesmaids. One was Jim's thirteen-year-old niece, delighted by her own sophistication, and already nervous about what version she was going to give her school friends on Monday. The other three, identically dressed in matching frilly white frocks, were interpreting their roles variously: one seriously cross dressed, looking sweet if exaggeratedly feminine; the second equally properly dressed, but with his beard unshaven; and the last closely resembling a pantomime dame.

'Would you call this blasphemous?' She looked down at Stella, another old friend of the grooms and, especially valuable in these circles, another feminist fag-hag.

'Yes, but God thinks a bit of blasphemy in a good cause is just fine,' Ellie whispered back.

She had thought about what lesson she would read. She had thought about it quite hard and carefully; she wanted something that was celebratory and not too silly. She had been appalled to discover how little gay literature was appropriate: all the love songs, from David's lament over Jonathan onwards, were about death not life, about separation and tragedy rather than love and hope. She had wanted something contemporary. Something by a woman.

When the time came she intoned in a splendidly churchy voice, 'Here beginneth the Second Lesson:

and you held me and there were no words
and there was no time and you held me
and there was only wanting and
being held and being filled with wanting
and I was nothing but letting go
and being held
and there were no words and there
needed to be no words
and there was no terror only stillness
and I was wanting nothing and
it was fullness and it was like aching for God
and it was touch and warmth and
darkness and no time and no words and we flowed
and I flowed and I was not empty
and I was given up to the dark and
in the darkness I was not lost
and the wanting was like fullness and I could
hardly hold it and I was held and
you were dark and warm and without time and
without words and you held me.'

In the middle her voice wavered; she was almost embarrassed, it seemed an excessively sexy poem, out of keeping with the irony and mockery she had promised Hugo, and then as she read on she ceased to care; it was a sexy poem for a sexy occasion.

The lawyer gave a Nazi salute and intoned, 'I now pronounce you man and man together and what this party has joined let no asshole put asunder.'

They all clapped. The couple kissed. Stuart was considerably smaller than Jim; they were wearing matching dinner jackets and bow-ties, formally effected except for neon pink socks. They started with a mocking cheek-to-cheek peck but, stirred by something, turned it into a moment of desire and in front of a hundred people found each other's mouths with a tenderness and intensity which silenced the raucous gathering for a breath.

Then the party spread out through the house. Ellie felt light and inflated; lots of wine and lots of kisses. She felt at home. Descending to the kitchen for some more wine she heard her name called.

'Ellie! Ellie will know.'

'Know what?' She joined a small group, acknowledging Stella who had called her, and a couple of other women and a very young, very tattooed man she did not know.

'Who are the women that gay men are having sex with?'

'What?'

'Well, you know all this chatter about gay men who have sex with women? We hear lots and lots about them, but who are these women? They never get a mention.'

'Well not me,' said Ellie, laughing, 'if that's the question. Personally I don't believe in it. I'm too old; identity has to have some relationship to activity. Let's ask . . .' her eyes swept the room. 'Let's ask Phil. Phil, come here.' He came over, kissed Ellie and smiled complacently.

'I hear and obey, oh queen.'

'You're a gay man who has sex with women.'

'How do you know that?'

'I know it too,' said Stella, 'everyone knows.'

'Damn,' he said.

'Well, who are these women?'

Now his eye swept the room; he had the grace to look a little sheepish. 'No one here,' he said.

'We don't want names,' said one of the women, 'well actually we probably do, but really we want to know why gay men who do it are treated as glamorous, when women who have sex with gay men are treated as fucked-up, afraid of their sexuality and generally a mess.'

'Fag-hags,' said Phil, 'that's different.'

'Real fag-hags,' said Ellie firmly, 'don't have sex with gay men, they have fun.'

'And sex isn't fun?'

'I think it's simpler,' said Stella, 'I think that gay men and lesbians and some straight women and some bi-sexuals, but no heterosexual men, can simply be group-identified as queer and that within that context object choice doesn't count.'

Ellie felt old. She glanced around wondering if she was the oldest person there, and was reassured to observe that she wasn't.

She took her drink upstairs, vaguely looking for Hugo, or for anyone else who did not make her feel like a grandmother. On the stairs there was an animated knot of people waiting for the loo.

She heard someone say slightly plaintively, 'I don't understand exactly what post-modernism *is*?'

Then she heard the wonderful, unmistakable, even though she had not heard them for over twenty years, gravelly tones say, 'Post-modernism is heterosexuals trying to get a handle on camp. Not too difficult to grasp once you know that.'

She jerked her head round and there he was. 'Neil!' she squeaked.

'Ellie Mac-effing-cauley!'

They were in each other's arms, despite the narrowness of the landing, and kissing mouth to mouth and someone putting an arm out to stop them falling down the stairs.

'Do you two know each other then?' There was more laughter.

'This is my first true love, and I haven't seen her in quarter of a century.'

They had been at art college together, in the giddy sixties, and they had been friends. Back then, back before feminism, before Gay Liberation, they had briefly been lovers, but more importantly colleagues, companions, siblings, chums, teachers, pupils, friends.

'This woman taught me everything that makes me so uniquely and wonderfully me,' Neil said, exuberant, over the top. She remembered him looking at her with wide-eyed joy, one day, in their last year at college and saying, 'One in twenty and God chose me.'

And now, 'Sweet gorgeous Héloïse Macauley. I have found you, oh woman of my dreams.'

'Do I get jealous?' someone asked.

'No, John,' said Neil, 'but you do push off and let us do some radical catching up. Are you still married to him? Did you have some sweet babies? Are you still inflating transparent supercooled liquids.'

'Barely, just one and yes of course,' said Ellie, extracting herself from his arms but holding on to his hand.

'Come upstairs, right now,' he commanded. 'They've set up something that resembles a quiet place. Why didn't I recognise you when you were reading that incredibly sexy poem? Whose is that divine voice? I thought, why does it remind me of my youth? But there was quite a crowd. I couldn't see your bewitching hair,' and then after a pause he said, 'Oh Ellie.'

'Tell, tell,' she said. 'Where the hell have you been? Why are you here? What are you doing? Are you well?'

There was the tiniest pause after she asked that and they both know why.

'Yes,' he said, 'I'm well.' She squeezed his hand tighter in relief. He was a wildly active gay man in the USA before anyone knew they had to be safe, be careful. He had left for the States soon after they both graduated. They had almost been going to go together, and then she had married Henry. They had corresponded for a while but they weren't letter writers, and he had been doing whatever he had been doing and she had been married and had Stephanie and been working . . . It had drifted, the friendship, just drifted, and now tossed up on a beach again it could just be picked up casually, and the oceans of time had scarcely corroded it.

One of the bedrooms had been arranged with piles of cushions and drapes, like an exotic tent. They collapsed together, shifting back two decades so that he sat against the cushions and she sat between his legs and leaned against him. He rolled a joint and smoked it, holding it out occasionally for her; she took it and inhaled the occasional puff.

He was thinner, his body, his hair, his fingers, all thinner. Just as she was fatter. But there was no difference.

'So, how's things?' she said.

He hugged her and told her about going to the States and stopping painting and moving into arts administration and gay activism, and back into art history, sort of, and being here doing some research: representational theory really. Eve Sidgewick and . . . They talked very little about their student days, their shared past; they talked about new things since then, so they knew that it was still a friendship, not merely a nostalgic delight.

'Sidgewick? You have turned into a theorist, haven't you? I can't read that stuff . . . but why were you being so dismissive of post-modernism, down there on the stairs? Though I must say I liked it.'

'I wasn't being dismissive at all, Ellie. Just so much hooey is talked about post-modernism. That kid . . . even you, are afraid of it, scared you're not up to it, and I hate that. It's meant to be fun. Do you still believe in fun?'

'Absolutely, though I haven't been having a lot recently. Go on, we'll do me later.'

There was a bad bit in the middle, he told her, too many drugs, too much sex and everyone dying. 'I was lucky. And I felt bad about being lucky. I felt outside; I was a foreigner; I was too lucky; I wasn't at home.' He had crawled out of that, and now things were good; John-on-the-stairs was a doll. He was too old to be in love, he said, but he was happy. 'I'm so happy to see you,' he said, and stroked her hair.

'It's not as red as it was,' she said.

'It's fabulous,' he replied, 'like Rapunzel's.'

She leant against him, slightly drunken and very strongly connected, not just to him, although that was wonderful, but to herself and her own history.

'Don't be sad, Ellie,' he said suddenly, 'that's the wrong way round. I'm meant to weep intensely and you're meant to bounce around saying sod the lot of them.'

'Sod the lot of them,' she said, 'I'm not usually sad, Neil, just the last few months. People die. Henry's dumped me.'

'He dumped *you*!'

'Got himself another woman.'

'Stupid idiot. Tell me about the glass.'

She did not feel treacherous with Neil, because he had known Ellie when she was young and hopeful and Henry had been huge and fierce and it had all made sense. She talked about her work, about oxidisation and mirrored glass, and he responded quite knowledgeably.

Later John came in and sat down beside Neil. Ellie tested the muscles of Neil's arm and could feel no sign of him wanting her to move. She liked that.

Dancing started downstairs, the house was vibrating gently. Necking started upstairs. Neil leaned forward and kissed her gently, then kissed John.

Hugo arrived, looking for her.

'Ellie?' She opened her eyes and smiled. 'Ellie, I'm off now, are you coming?' It was an enquiry not a request.

She reached out a hand and he pulled her upright. She shook herself like a dog coming out of water. 'I've left my tail-coat somewhere,' she said, 'and I'd better say "Goodbye-and-thank-you-for-having-me" to Bun and Deedles.' Neil looked up, interrogatively. 'Their cats,' she said, 'our kind hosts of today.'

'Hello, Hugo,' said John.

'Do you know each other?' Ellie asked, then laughed. Of course they did. 'Neil is my oldest friend. When I was still a sweet young thing, and he was a disturbed adolescent.'

'You must tell me about her,' said Hugo to Neil.

'Hugo, does this mean you have John's address? Phone number? Save us all looking for pens and things.'

'Neil's an American, more or less,' said John, 'he has cards.' He extracted one from Neil's wallet and gave it to her.

'I do too,' said Ellie, 'but not on me. I'm coming Hugo. I'll ring, sugar-plum. Soon.'

After they left the party, Ellie and Hugo walked along the street together. Ellie was alight with pleasure. She loved Jim and Stuart, she hoped they would be happy. She had loved the party, felt high on it, and she had found Neil, a pure delight. She was walking down the street with Hugo, after a long day of pleasure and everything was wonderful.

Hugo said, 'I'm not now going to pass any comment on that extraordinary reading, but thank you.'

'Oh,' she said surprised. They walked on in silence for a while.

'Ellie,' said Hugo, suddenly uncertain as to how to begin, which – since uncertainty was an unusual state for him and he was therefore unpractised at it – meant that he was clumsy, a clumsiness amounting almost to brutality. 'Ellie, I need to test; will you come with me?'

She had said, 'Yes of course, sweetheart,' to the question before she had even absorbed the meaning of it. When the impact hit her, she stopped walking, poised, one foot in the air, for a whole breathless second; and then with a kind of distanced disciplined rigour she was walking, still calmly, beside him. Her hand tightened round his.

He was thinking of the practicalities, of his own fear, and of the baby. He left the request in the air, knowing her generosity and assuming her goodwill. They were more distant at that moment than they had been for years.

When she was breathing normally again she said, as lightly as she could, 'I thought we didn't test. I thought we believed that status should not be allowed to affect behaviour. I thought we did not fancy life as a suffering AIDS victim and would ride out the storm of doubts and curiosities until we were ill.' Then, not liking the tone of that very much, she said, 'Oh, my darling.'

Only a few weeks ago she had said to Judith, 'Enough, Judith, enough. I've done my time with this bloody illness. Any new friend has to present me with a negative status certificate taken out in front of a public notary; I'm not doing it again.'

Somewhere far down inside her belly, the slow beginning of anger: anger, rage, pain. A complicated anger. She was angry because homophobia in the rest of the world made anger impossible. She was not allowed to be angry. She was not permitted to ask furiously: Why haven't you been more bloody careful? Why haven't you taken responsibility? Why should I have to take this on? Why am I going to have to be good and calm and sweet? Why are you so sodding selfish?

Despite the fact that there is no allowance for this, despite the fact she is unable to articulate this anger, none the less the rage is true. It is true and at the same time it is only one tiny bit of what is true, and it will be the bit that once again will be set aside, because the other bits – that she is not angry, that she is not judging, that she simply does not want her friend to be ill and to die, and that it is hard to live in a world where the gap between being criminal and being terminal was shorter than twenty years – are more important and therefore oddly even more true. There is no intimacy in the world like the intimacy of dying, and she knows that she is privileged that he will ask for that intimacy if he needs it. She knows too that she would be furious if he had asked someone else to hold his hand while he tested. She suspects that this may say something about herself that she really does not want to know.

All this is too much for her, too much for this pretty street, this slightly tipsy walk away from a party which had given her so much ease and pleasure.

He withdrew a little, away from her arm which clearly would like to embrace him and which he did not want. He wanted her to be more practised, smoother, more accomplished at this; he wanted her to take it over, to organise it, to let him be a child for once. Even as he wanted this he was perfectly aware how irritating he would find it if she did.

He said, answering her slightly sarcastic response with a slightly offended one of his own, 'Of course I'm going to test. I do have some sense of responsibility.'

They were still walking down the street. But muddle, failed communication, had lumbered between them as irritating and inconvenient as a clumsy puppy.

Light dawned for him first. 'Hang on,' he said almost laughing, 'you're missing a bit here, and it's my fault. It's about donating.' And then, unless there was still any confusion he went on bluntly, 'I want to have a baby.' It was the first time he had said it out loud and he was thrilled by the sound of the words. 'I have to test.'

'Yes,' she said, scrambling to reorientate. She was nimble, though still wary. 'That's sweet. You've wanted one for a long time, haven't you? A dear little claim on the future without having to do the nappies. No, that sounds mean. You'd probably be good at nappies.' She was talking desperately, gabbling, covering up the fact that she did not know what to say. 'Do you know that you'll almost certainly have a boy: have you noticed how they nearly all are, the A.I.D. babies?' She heard her mouth say the initials and notice what they spelled and paused. This time it was he who stopped abruptly.

'Artificial Insemination by Donor,' she said, 'I'm sorry. What an odd coincidence.'

'Shit,' he said, 'I'd never noticed. Very Freudian.' He mimicked a teutonic accent, not entirely successfully. They were both a bit shaken. Rallying valiantly, he essayed a tone of irony, 'Makes you bloody think, doesn't it?'

'There's too much going wrong here,' said Ellie. 'We need to start all over again. Let's find a place we can talk. Shall I buy you supper?'

They both sighed with relief. Almost sheepishly they looked at each other. And, like a sign from heaven, despite the quiet and out-of-the-way nature of the street, a taxi turned the corner ahead of them, its orange sign a beacon of light in the darkness. All efficient, Hugo stepped into the road between two parked cars and hailed it. A small black cat ran out from under one of the cars and almost across her feet. She could not help but smile at this token of good fortune. A black cat and a taxi when you wanted it. Angel was probably hard at work. She felt calmed.

They climbed in, and filled a couple of moments working out where they might go. Not too expensive, not too noisy, the usual easy discussion at the end of which they came to the usual easy answer: the small bistro round the corner from his flat where, under such, and many other circumstances, they usually ended up eating. They had also to explain to the taxi driver where it was, which filled the time, and so, agreeably for once, did listening to his banter.

Hugo put his arm over Ellie's shoulder, so that it lay along the back shelf of the taxi, half touching her but not entirely; it was a discreet way of saying 'We blew that one, but it doesn't matter'. She responded by tucking her shoulder into the inverted L-shape his armpit now presented.

Without warning she felt the most appalling weight press down on her neck, as though someone had lowered a sack of grain on to the top of her head . . . No, not the top . . . just forward of that . . . between her crown and her hairline . . . heavy, unspeakably heavy. So heavy her head toppled sideways under the weight of it, flopping against his chest. At that exact moment the taxi driver, instructed by Hugo, spun the car abruptly into a corner. Perhaps it was that that threw her head against him, although she knew that it was not.

'Ow! Ellie!' And then, to the driver, 'Hey, careful.'

'It wasn't that sharp,' the cabby said without rancour.

Ellie knew that Hugo had felt the weight too; but even as she struggled to think of a way of explaining, the weight lifted and she heard Angel's voice, very quietly saying 'Sorry'.

Ellie was distracted; it had not hurt exactly, but it had been the most extraordinary and shocking physical experience. It left her shaken, wobbling between the worlds, disjointed, and so, just as the taxi was approaching the restaurant, she said, without thinking, 'So, who's going to be the mother of your baby, then?'

Hugo heard it as a continuation of the conversation. He had planned to tell Ellie in his own time, tenderly, carefully, when they were seated at their own usual table, wine glasses in hand. He was suddenly angry. There was something exploitative in

making him tell her when he knew she already knew. He was
angry at his own need of her, his fear, the acute weight of her
head crashing painfully on to his chest, her never letting him
do anything in his own time – he wanted to punish her. He
wanted to punish the world, and she was the bit of it nearest to
hand. Ellie was punishable, always too punishable. It brought
out all his well-repressed meanness. So he said with a studied
off-handedness, 'Don't fuck about, Ellie. I know Mary told you.'

And the taxi stopped and he jumped out, paying through the
front window as he always did.

Jealousy hit her, a great green monster, unexpected, sudden,
unmistakable, like the breaking of a dam. She had half risen,
her own weight shifted forwards to the very side of the taxi
seat, and she felt knocked backwards, although she continued
the necessarily ungraceful movement upwards and through
the door and on to the street.

She knew exactly what it was she felt.
Mirror, mirror, on the wall,
Who is the fairest one of all?

A green glass mirror, the strangely pleasing mirrors that Mary
had been working on. Green ice. She would kill him. Her hand
tightened round her fish knife although it was miles away in
the kitchen in Greenwich; she had left it that morning, lying on
the draining board, in easy reach of her hand, and her fingers
tightened round it. Quick, quick as a fish in water, she would
slit his guts open.

Or her own wrists perhaps.

Or Mary's smug beautiful face. Thief. With the broken edge
of Robbie's egg, that Mary had so casually, so stupidly, or so
meanly dropped; she would hold it in the palm of her hand
where it would fit smoother and cool, and she would use the
broken edge, jagged and sharp, like a laser, down the side of
that little dyke's perfect profile.

She stood poised on the pavement, while Hugo joked with the taxi driver who could not find the right change. Then he turned away from her and crossed the pavement into the restaurant.

Ellie eyed the door, less than ten feet away, in a kind of reeling terror. They will go through that door, they will say hello to the manager, who is from long years of regular dinners, almost a friend, and he will check if anyone is sitting at the table that they usually use, and then they will make some small talk with him as they walk to the table and sit down and he will bring them their usual bottle of white wine and two glasses and pour for them and make some comment on the menu, and by that time she will have to have recovered.

If she tells him how she feels, he will be angry. If he is angry, then she will get angry too. And they have fought too recently; any fight they have now will get attached to the last one and there will be no going back. His anger is distant. Hers is not. When angry he disengages entirely, and has to choose the moment for re-engagement himself. But now he needed her. He needed her because he is going to have to go to the hospital and take a test which, for whatever reasons he takes it, cannot not be frightening him. So the ice of his anger will be further refrigerated by the shame of his need.

She, on the other hand, gets miserable and pathetic when she's angry; very swiftly on the heels of fury she hits a place where the anger is over and she is just a molten quivering pleading drizzle, and her nose gets snotty, and she shamingly pesters the person she has fought with to forgive her.

And if both these things happen this time there will be no going back. It won't be either of their faults; it will just be so.

She wants to kill him.

She wants to kill Mary.

Mary is a thief.

She has stolen everything.

Mary is a thief. She has stolen Ellie's beloved friend. And this is what They all say, that straight women who hang about with homosexuals have weird sexual longings and she had always denied it, denied it with a laugh because it was ridiculous, but now apparently it was being made true. And she is older and wiser and she knows the extraordinary, and beautiful, passion that gay men have for their children, because such babies come as pure gift, beyond the proper expectations of life and happiness. Therefore such fathers have always an awed madonna-worship for the mothers of their babies; and Ellie could not bear it if Hugo looked at Mary like that.

Mary is a thief. She has stolen a place in Ellie's heart. Stephanie had gone when Mary arrived. Mary has eased the pain of Stephanie's departure. That pain has diminished, has nearly vanished. Mary has stolen the one thing that Ellie can still offer her vanished daughter – the purity of a unique emotion.

Mary is a thief. She has stolen Ellie's fertility. Ellie knows it is too late for her; she cannot compete, she cannot have a new baby. That belly swelling, that beautiful, fearful fluttering, sexy above the pubic bone, of the foetal child quickening. Mary can do that, and doing it Mary has turned her into the witch, the evil stepmother, the hag.

Mary is a thief. She has stolen Ellie's craft; she has lurked in the corners of Ellie's studio, watching, spying, seducing Ellie's loyal team. Mary has wrenched the studio away from its own tradition and towards the architectural glass that Ellie had repudiated so many years ago. Henry, for whom she had made that decision has left, and Mary has snuck into the vacuum, undermining Ellie's decisions, making windows not vessels, ways out instead of safe containers. Mirrors instead of translucence. Soon – very soon – Mary will make better glass than Ellie does. She hates Mary.

Mary is a thief. She has stolen . . . Ellie stopped. She made herself stop; it was too preposterous. Not just the technology.

a bowl: *millefiori* with star canes
a fused cube with oxidised lightning trapped within it
a Christmas tree bauble: blown crystal encasing blue
    filigree *façon de venise*
a paperweight: small, cameo cut
a tear-drop: with double air-twist and its neck broken
    off

Oh, come on, Ellie, she told herself sternly. But she had nearly said it to Megan. Why was it any more preposterous than the notion that Patsy, tidy, careful and devoted, had simply misplaced all the smallest good work that Ellie had done – had lost them *all*? Stop, she ordered her overcharging imagination, stop it now.

They were already halfway across the dining-room, dodging tables; and Jon was admiring her tail-coat and she was waving at Lisa who was working her way through art college and put in long hours here as a waitress.

They had reached the table; Jon was pulling out a chair for her, making a gesture of it; he was saying, 'I'll get the bottle, while you inspect the specials' board.'

And he returned with their wine and the glasses and smiled, and put the glasses on the table and fussed with his corkscrew and teased Hugo. She hated Hugo. She hated Mary. She hated them. She hated him. And Jon poured the wine, for her to taste, with a smile, and she smiled back and flapped her wrist half-laughing, and sipped and nodded, and he poured Hugo's glass first as they had taught him ages ago, and then hers, and then he pointed out various items on the board – smoked halibut with scrambled eggs, such heaven.

And she was so angry and confused that she was going to have to tell Hugo about it, and then the waiter disappeared and

Hugo picked up his glass and wrapped both hands round it, and she did the same and then she met his eyes and he was smiling and looked scared and she loved him so simply and purely that none of all this mattered.

It was all true and none of it mattered. He was her friend.

His smile changed abruptly, 'She didn't tell you, did she? The lying little bitch.'

And she was tempted, tempted on the pinnacles of the temple to say, 'You need to watch that one, Hug; she's a sly little trollop, no better than she ought to be; and Megan and I think she's a thief as well.'

She resisted the temptation. If she said that she would force him to choose, to choose between them, and in the choosing either she will lose a friend and an apprentice or he will lose a friend and a chance to have a baby. He wanted to have a baby she knew that. She willed herself to be generous, and at once it became not so very difficult.

She smiled back and said, 'Just a muddle I should think. OK. Let's deal with the big things. You want to have a baby, so you'll have to test. Are you scared?'

'You make us sound like a bloody couple or something. *Mary* wants to have a baby. I've agreed to sperm donate if suitable.'

'Contact?'

He had the grace to look a little shamefaced, 'Yes, of course, contact.'

'Financial support?'

Pause.

'I don't know, we haven't discussed it.'

'Yes, of course, financial support.'

'I want a child, Ellie. I really do.'

'Yes I know,' she said, 'it's all right. I understand that bit.' How odd, she thought, he could have had mine; not now of course, but when we first met. But she would never, ever, have chosen him as a father of her child.

'I understand that bit,' she said, 'but, do see it from my point of view; I can't help being a bit pissed off with Mary.' This let off some steam safely. 'She's the best bloody apprentice I've had in years – ever, now I think about it; she's lured me into an immense amount of new work, a new sort of project – and she's off to have a baby. Women. I ask you.'

'She'll go on working though; I can't imagine her not.'

'Yes,' sighed Ellie, 'yes, she will. And I'll cover for her like mad in the name of feminism, and Megan will be cross with me and Patsy will be jealous; and when the little darling starts at nursery school Mary'll refocus. She'll have had three years to think about glass within a context of perfect security; she'll have kept up the technical skills and she'll be better than me.'

'Is that how it was with Steph, when she was little?'

'Actually yes, that's exactly how it was, although I've never thought or said that before. But it's not exactly how it was, because I was the pregnant person then, and I'm the boss now. And I've never worked out until just now why Tony and Jerry were so fucking pissed off with me.'

Of course that was not exactly how it was at all; it was not remotely how it was – the utter wearisomeness of the early years of maternity, the sense of going insane. Insane if you thought about work, because to think about the child and think about work were too many things to think about and you were exhausted all the time. Insane if you didn't think about work, because work was so central to being that not to think about it was to lose yourself somewhere in a welter of chaos, and being a mother without being a self was an invitation into the chasm of disintegration. But she must not think about that now. She has let him divert her.

'Yes,' she said, 'yes, of course you have to test.' She did not ask which of them, Hugo or Mary, had first raised this delicate point, because there were some things that she really did not want to know. There were also things that she had to know:

'Are you scared?' she asked again. She had wanted, even expected, it to come out tenderly, with just a hint of humour, a mere soupçon of irony. For some reason it didn't work, it sounded too challenging.

'Yes,' he said, 'yes, of course I'm bloody scared.'

When she heard him respond to her intention, not to her tone, she knew both that he was indeed bloody scared, and that he loved her very much. She took both facts in at the same level; but her heart soared in response to the second. She would never doubt again: put your fingers into the wounds and know, was what he had said to her. She forced herself to respond at the most pragmatic, least emotional level she could manage.

'Do you have much to be scared about? I mean, which sort of fear is it?'

'Bitch,' he said, smiling at her.

Jon hovered. They both ordered, quickly, absent-mindedly.

'Rough day then?' Jon smiled. Often they could spend fifteen minutes deciding what to eat, changing their minds, changing each other's minds.

'Yes.' They said it simultaneously, and laughed. Jon laughed too and left them.

'Scared or scared?' she said quickly, before he could change the topic.

'Scared,' he said.

She drank her wine and waited.

'This is not a confessional,' he said, 'and you don't know just how much I hate condoms.'

'I'm not absolving, Hugo, but only because I'm not judging.'

'No,' he relaxed suddenly, 'it's me; I'm always ranting on about taking responsibility.'

'You can take responsibility and take risks – you just have to take responsibility for those risks. No whining. Like the Lloyds losers. They took the profit, they have to take the losses.'

The starters arrived. She picked up her fork and looked into the heart of a fried mushroom.

'Do you know,' she said, 'that I'm the only heterosexual woman I've ever encountered who has never made a contraceptive blunder, and I put that down to low libido, not high responsibility.'

He looked interested, 'But you're a Roman Catholic.'

'So? Oh, I see; well, that might be why actually, along with my libido problems. If you're going to be bad, you have an obligation to do it well.'

'So obviously I don't feel much guilt about being a sexually active gay man.' He was not in too much distress if he could do that so quickly, she comforted herself. Or very distressed indeed, of course.

She stabbed the mushroom with her fork and wished she had had less to drink at the party. He pushed his scrambled egg around the plate, extracting the scraps of smoked fish and fiddling with them.

'I'm frightened,' he said, drawing a deep breath, 'I'm frightened because I think I'm positive.'

'Yes,' she said. Perhaps her heart will break. She wished she did not know so much; wished she had not seen the horrible disease run its horrible course so many, too many times. She put her left hand on the table, while eating another mushroom with her right. It does not look entirely casual but not, she reckons, too oafish. On her little finger she wears a tiny obsidian scarab, mounted in gold. Henry had given it to her for her fortieth birthday present: a genuine ancient amulet; a charm to bring tomorrow and tomorrow. After a pause he put down his knife and with his index finger just touched the middle of the hand, firmly, pressing down slightly; then he picked up his knife again and went on eating. Sometimes he acted like a comfort virgin. He would hug her easily to comfort her, but became as sensitive as a nine-year-old when he himself needed comfort. She had learned this the hard way, and was careful. She left her hand on the table, palm upwards, for a while.

'I've been coughing all winter; I can't get rid of it.'

'Yes,' she says, her fear rising now, the fear that she had not even let herself think about.

'I've done stupid things, Ellie.'

'Fun things,' she said firmly, not even thinking, stupid idiot. 'Fun things; you're a grown-up, you know the dangers, you're entitled to adventures if you choose them knowingly, and run with the tide. You taught me, Hugo.'

'You told me a Dorothy Parker poem, a while ago, about burning candles at both ends, do you remember? Say it again.'

She said it at once:

> 'My candle burns at both ends;
> It will not last the night;
> But ah, my foes, and oh, my friends—
> It gives a lovely light!'

She smiled for him and his eyes filled with tears. Hers did too. 'It's not Dorothy Parker actually; I said it was but I was wrong; it's Edna St Vincent Millay really.'

'Damn,' he said. Then, 'I haven't tested. Not just because of the politics – though I believe that stuff – that status shouldn't affect behaviour and so on, but more because I just don't want to know. There was one time when it was chic, you know, and a secret putrid corner of one . . . of me,' he said with an effort at a hideous honesty, 'actually wanted to be in the gang. But now, it goes on and on and on; and I don't like it; it isn't good for people, I mean it wouldn't be good for me, saying all the time one is not a victim, not suffering, no, and at the same time expecting the whole world to love you because you're positive. I just don't want to know.'

She did not ask, simply because she was not and did not wish to become his therapist, she did not ask, why the hell did you tell Mary you'd do it then? She understood only too well those strange mixed motives, the way she deliberately trapped herself into having to do what she did not want to do; or wanting to do what she did not want to do; and in his case also winding himself up to run wild risks because without them he was not himself, which was of course why, cautious, almost cowardly by nature, she loved him so much.

Once, early in their friendship, she had asked him something about morality, and he had made a fabulously vulgar gesture and said, 'God can go spin on it!' She had been secretly delighted that anyone *dared*. He was brave where she was brassy, and bad where she was only naughty.

She accepted the moment. 'If you want me to come when you test, I am honoured.' I am sick with fright too, but he did not need to hear that.

'Please,' he did not beg, but he definitely asked.

'Can you please, please, please, do one of those one day ones?'

'Of course.'

'When might suit you?'

'Whenever, sweetheart.'

'Next week?'

'Have you booked?'

'No. I wanted to talk to you first.'

She did not allow herself to be delighted.

She was delighted.

The next morning she rang Henry. 'It's all right Henry. I consent. I don't like it, but you should feel free. I've been silly.'

She did not like it, but she consented to it, with an effort of the will. 'He dumped *you*?' Neil had said disbelieving. She wanted to find herself as he saw her, a person of worth and dignity. Brave as they were. A queer woman, regardless of sexual practice.

Far from being instantly delighted, Henry was almost tentative. 'Divorce?' he queried hesitantly.

'If that's what you want. I would like it if we could be friends.'

Even as she said it she knew it was lie; this was not a man she wanted as a friend; he was her husband or nothing. To her own surprise she felt relief, a fine shard of release that underlay the struggle and the defeat and the sadness. A sense that was enhanced as she noticed that Henry was not overwhelmed with delight: had she stolen a grudge or forced his hand? It must be good for the middle-aged male ego to have two women who both want to be married to you.

Finally he said 'Thank you,' and let her fall free.

'Thank you,' he repeated. 'Take care of yourself.'

She did not want to take care, she wanted to have fun. There did not seem a high chance of that.

'Pray,' said Angel, 'just try prayer. That's fun.'

Since Angel was now present, Ellie, emboldened, asked, 'Angel, that business in the cab, when my head went so heavy, was that you?'

She could sense a snuffly angelic embarrassment.

'What was it? What was going on?'

The snuffling continued; it took Ellie several moments to realise that Angel was . . . crying. Could angels cry? Angel was quite definitely weeping, sniffly, awkward, unpractised tears, that made Ellie more embarrassed than sympathetic.

After a while Angel disciplined herself and tried to explain. Because of the gap, almost though not completely unbridgeable, between time and eternity, it was very difficult for Angel to explain how it is for angels.

'I fucked up,' said Angel; or perhaps in the present tense, 'I am fucking up.' Time, Angel struggled to explain, does not work for angels as it does for humans. Angels abide in eternity and penetrate into time, but since their concentration is perfect at the moment of penetration they are completely present. Like good sex, says Angel, groping. Time, for angels, struggles Angel, has no linearity, no determinative arrow. It comes in discreet, non-sequential moments, each one perfectly fulfilled in itself, but not connected to any other. Thus as guardian, an angel may be acting in relationship to a number of souls who are not living within the same moments in time.

There should be no confusion. But sometimes an angel becomes confused. The experiences of re-incarnation, for example, that humans assume to be about themselves, are in fact angels getting confused, a striking angelic indiscretion.

Usually, Angel told Ellie, it does not matter; sometimes it could even be useful. It could give individuals a sense of being a part of a continuity that transcended the present moment, the particular and tiny speck of Now.

But sometimes . . . sometimes it became more serious. Time-pounces they call them in heaven, when Time, chronology, pounces on an angel's consciousness too much, too often.

The child drowning, weighted down by the green glass ingot from the harbours of Sidon.

The apprentice girl on the run, wet from the lagoon, driven towards the weightier glass of the north countries.

The forbidden chalice shattering in the night while the barbarians howl and the gates and the blood and wine spill out red on the tile floor.

The Queen of Sheba laughing in the court of Solomon, laughing through the history of the western world.

Ellie was quicker to leap on this last than she should have been.

'That can't be right, Angel,' she said, 'because all that stuff about the Queen of Sheba and the Holy Grail – it's not true.

223

The *sacra catina*, that green bowl, everyone knows that it's first century Roman work. It was not made for the Queen of Sheba. It's a myth.'

'So are angels,' said Angel. 'That doesn't mean it isn't true. Who is everybody? Half of Genoa believe the bowl is the Queen of Sheba's gift to Solomon, and is also the Holy Grail . . . More than half, really, far more than half, if you take it across time instead of just in the present.'

'But that doesn't make it true. There's not the remotest chance that we, I mean people now, that we're wrong.'

'You don't think in infinity, Héloïse,' said Angel, 'I'm always telling you. In history the remotest chance is long odds, but given an infinite amount of time everything that has any possibility at all will happen. That's what infinity *is*.'

'But . . .'

'You're dodging,' said Angel, 'you're distracting me. Now is not a good moment for post-modernist demythologising. I'm trying to explain about time-pounces, about me. Can you, please, listen.'

'I am trying,' Ellie said.

'I always . . . I always have glass connections. I always have, from before the beginning,' Angel said now, with a deepening voice. 'For eternity I have carried that responsibility . . . I really love glass . . . its transparency, its brittleness, you know. And it should have been all right, because as well as being a transcendent medium, glass is, after all, one of the best insulators in creation. But I got carried away; I started getting confused. Too often.'

Angels, contrary to belief, get sick. 'I am sick, Ellie,' said Angel, with great sadness. Angelic illness is like a virus – not quite a biological virus, more like a computer virus. Like crizzling inside the early lead glass, once it's started it can't be stopped.'

It is a sickness like addiction; once you're addicted you *are* sick, but earlier, before you are sick, before you are addicted, there is a moment, a moment of consent. 'I consented,' said Angel, 'and now I am sick.'

Ellie heard the sadness, but she did not understand.

'Angels love,' said Angel. 'Angels love and we are meant to love, but we are not meant to fall in love. I have fallen in love with matter, with flesh. It is a great danger for angels . . .

'. . . if an angel falls in love with bodies, wants to have one, wants to feel what they feel, to be where they are, it is not lust, but it is desire. If we desire we develop a sickness: we call it Angeloid Incarnational Delusion Sickness.'

Angel paused.

'NO,' shouted Ellie. No and no and no. She refused to hear.

Angel wept again. Ellie could feel that irrepressible, bonded-into-the-veins maternal sentiment that could not let another being just cry.

'Oh Angel,' she said.

'We're all vulnerable to it,' said Angel, and for the first time sounded resigned.

'This will make you laugh one day,' said Angel, though with a sort of half choke, 'but we call it Weights – when we are . . . infected . . . involved, we . . . angelic thoughts are so real, that what we *think* has substance, has reality. So we might, for example, start to manifest – have visibility. Or we weigh, we start to weigh like all matter weighs . . . heavy . . . that was what happened in your head in the taxi.'

'And the feather strand?'

'And the feather. But you saw how quickly it devitrified, crizzled. Angels aren't meant . . .'

Angel began to cry again. So did Ellie. They wept together and could not comfort each other.

After a while Angel said, 'It's not your fault but . . . you, the glass, Hugo, Judith, Megan, the glass windows, the mirrors . . . so much . . . so much delight. And a world that could delight with you and your kind, chooses instead to hate; or at best to try and change you all. And still the glass. Fragile and tough. Hard and soft. It got to me in the end. I loved it too much. Then I wanted it too. So: I'm positive.'

Ellie did not think that she could bear it.

'Hugo. Is he too?'

'You know I can't tell you that.'

'Not both of you. I can't bear it.'

'You may have to.'

There was a long and absolute silence inside Ellie's head. It stretched out, and out into the darkness. From very far away she heard Angel saying, 'I'm being recalled.'

'For punishment?'

'Of course not. I'm an angel. I can't sin. I can't be punished. For . . . assessment. For testing. Let me go, Ellie. Please, help *me*. Let me go while I still want to be well. Please.'

Almost she could not. Almost she set her will to bind Angel, to seduce her, but . . . Ellie drew a breath and said, 'Bye for now.'

She stopped herself saying 'Take care.' Instead she said, 'Have fun.'

She knows a moment of perfect emptiness. Because she has given everything away she experiences both loss and freedom, she sees improbably and certainly . . .

. . . a small dark northern Palestinian girl, poised precisely between child and woman, takes a hollow iron tube from beside the furnace and dips it into the cauldron where the blue glass shines molten.

The sky is blue. The land is hot gold brown. The shadows on it are black.

She blows down the tube and into the glass. The glass swells, stiffens on the tube and begins to inflate; it is round, round and perfectly smooth. It is as round as a baby's head, as round as the dome of the temple, as round as a tear-drop. As she blows the bubble bigger the blue fades, paling like the evening sky, paling as clear as the water in the lake. Through the bubble she can see the hot blue sky, the hot gold sun, the hot brown hills and the cool blue lake where the fishermen go out to catch the shimmering, light-refracting, translucent fish.

She breathes into her glass bubble and is inspired.

She does something very simple that has never been done before. With a deft movement that surprises even her, she transfers the bubble of blue glass to a different rod, she smoothly closes the air hole and removes the blowing tube. She gives the rod one sharp tap. Lying on the leather that covers her hand is a sphere, her glowing blue, light-refracting, light-distorting bubble, free of the rod, free and filled with inspiration. It has a navel, a small round scar, that joins it to her and to history, but she has set it free.

She hears a tender, mocking, everlasting angel-voice say to her, 'Do not be afraid, Mary, for you have found favour with God.'

She is pregnant, breathed into, inspired by the spirit. This is the annunication.

There is a silence at this conception, as intense as the sun, as deep as the blue lake, as translucent as glass, and deep within the blue there is a flash of lightning . . .

. . . Ah, sobbed Ellie, and she was open, open and unafraid of her own openness. She wanted, almost to her own surprise, to have sex, to make love, to open, open herself up for . . . for . . . it was not for anyone and she would not do it, but she who never wanted to have sex wanted it now. She learned how to receive so that receiving was a gift, a gift of fearlessness, of power and love.

On Tuesday, while it was still early, Ellie pulled her car into the curb outside Hugo's flat. It was a morning of quite exceptional loveliness: pale, with the sky so high and far away and delicately blue that it looked like a painting.

Dear Stephanie,
I'm sorry I behaved so badly.
much love, Mummy.

She had left home too early because she had woken too early, and because she had wanted at all costs to avoid the tunnel in the rush hour. So for once she had enough time. She smiled, got out of the car and walked back towards the corner and the post-box, carrying a white envelope with three stamps on it, addressed to Stephanie Landsdowne, in Borneo. She pushed it through the narrow slit. Only going too far was far enough.

Dear Stephanie,
I'm sorry I behaved so badly.
much love, Mummy.

She walked back; it was still too early so she climbed into the car and sat waiting until it was late enough to make a move.

The terror that had been waiting all week, the terror that he might be positive pounced. With that terror came other fears: the fear that she might burst into tears, might carry on, might in some way interrupt his moment of self-acceptance. The fear that she would be so determined not to get in his way that she would be distanced, indifferent to him. And underneath that the real terror – the fear of the long haul, the long wearisome waiting to be ill, and then the long wearisome being ill and then the long wearisome business of putting yourself back together when someone you love very much dies.

She laid her head briefly on her steering wheel. She was here for him. She told herself this in different tones – sternly, to make herself behave; lovingly, to make herself feel more loving;

proudly, because he had wanted her; firmly, because she needed telling; ironically, because it was not true; so, finally, amusedly, because it was true – the fact that she was here for herself, meant that she was the right person to be here for him. Then she did relax, head down and hands floppy, for a brief moment, drawing what strength she could find in the contented certainty, just for those few quiet moments, that her strength would be enough, just, and absolutely. There was not much else.

Finally, she drew a new breath and straightened up. She turned the rear-view mirror so that she could inspect herself, patting her hair and squinting to get different parts of her face into reflection. She turned round to pick up her hat from the back seat. She had bought it on Saturday; a chic little pill box with some rather smart jet bead work on the side; she wore it tipped very far forward and with her hair as smoothed down as she could get it to be. It felt extraordinarily important that she look good – for his amusement, for her own succour, and for some sense that this was an important occasion.

She stepped on to the pavement and stood up; she tightened the belt of her rather wonderful 1940s' jacket with its enormous astrakhan collar. Judith had given it to her a few Christmases ago – 'Sod sheep sentimentality,' she had said firmly. 'This little lambkin was dead before I was born; surely its life would not be further disenhanced by adorning you rather than a dustbin.' And then, admiring her own generosity and good taste added, '*and* you look utterly fab in it.'

Ellie panted up the four flights of external stairs to Hugo's flat. She tapped down the open-sided balcony that ran along each floor and knocked on Hugo's front door. There was a long silence and she knocked again, harder. She reached out with one hand and nipped a dead flower off the nasturtium that grew in his window box. There was a Labour Party poster in the window advocating a candidate for some up-coming local election; the nasturtiums did not obscure it.

She heard some shuffling inside and finally the door opened. Hugo was wearing the tartan towelling dressing-gown she had given him last Christmas; she could not help but feel pleased.

'I'm not that early,' she said, giving him a quick kiss.

'No, come in. I overslept.' She felt an internal flicker of outrage – she had been fretting half the night.

His hallway was as always a tiny shock after the slightly dingy climb. Hugo's flat was painted throughout in the most unexpected and radiant colours: the hallway walls were coral pink, and all the woodwork including the floor was shiny dark blue.

Once inside she was aware of noises off. 'Someone here?' she tried to make a statement into an enquiry, but probably did not succeed.

'Do you want coffee?' he asked, grinning a little wryly and looking very young. They went into the kitchen. 'Does he know? About today,' she whispered. He shook his head, while saying, 'Put the kettle on, Ellie, will you? Coffee for three.'

The noises off had taken themselves into the bathroom.

'Do I know him?' she asked.

'I doubt it, I don't.'

'You're not getting breakfast in bed then.'

'Were you going to do that?'

There was an abrupt pause. Both of them reheard her trying-to-laugh voice saying once, long ago, 'No, let me do it. All fag-hags love taking gay men breakfast in bed, but unless they're ill it's so tacky that we have to resist.' She had been carrying a tastefully laid-up tray down the corridor to Mark's room when Hugo had arrived to collect his washing. It was the first conversation they ever had. 'You came out before I did,' he had teased her since. 'Before I said I was gay, you had said you were a fag-hag.' 'I didn't want you to think I was his mother,' she had replied, 'and you didn't need to say.'

With considerable grace she pounced on the uncertain, awkward memory and said, 'Oh, are you ill, I thought you were just hungover?'

They grinned at each other, both made horribly aware how edged their sensitivities were, how long and how difficult a day it would be.

She turned to the kettle even as they both heard the loo flush. The noises off were proceeding down the hall. 'Are you decent?' called Hugo, 'we've got company.'

The noises off appeared – young, very blond and just about decent, in as much as he was wearing boxer shorts. He had a smooth chest, reasonable gym muscles, and two silver studs in his eyebrow.

'Morning,' he said, taking in at a glance her improbable attire.

'This is Ellie, she's a friend of mine and she's here a bit earlier than I'd planned.' Hugo did not make it critical of either of them. For so radical a man, he had surprisingly good manners.

'Hi,' said the stranger, unfazed. 'I'll be on my way then.'

'Coffee?' she enquired.

He glanced at Hugo before answering. Hugo nodded briefly. 'OK, yes then.' After a tiny pause, he added, 'Please,' and then, 'I'll go and get dressed,' and vanished.

'Golden youth,' she commented, extracting the coffee tin from the cupboard.

'Don't be taken in,' said Hugo, 'he is a filthy-minded little thing.'

'Goody, goody,' said Ellie, but her sense that she was in control of the day evaporated.

She made the coffee. The golden youth departed. Hugo went to shower, 'And, while I appreciate it enormously, you needn't think I'm going to emulate your elegance.'

'Clean knickers,' she said, 'you might have to go to hospital.'

'Quite likely, if you're driving.'

It was a consolatory ragging. When he emerged, hair still

damp, shaved, cleanly, even neatly, dressed in jeans and a shirt, she said, 'Not bad for a poofter who's been shagging all night.'

'I'm aiming for an out-but-still-respectable look.'

'You, respectable! If that was the intention, you've failed dismally. It's more a leader-of-the-gay-community-taking-responsibility-for-his-own-life-let-it-be-an-example-to-you-all effect.'

Which pleased him.

They drove across London in the rush hour. She disciplined herself not to glance at him at every red light. She looked often enough to know that he was frightened and not wanting to show it.

There were children going to school, swinging down the street in their uniforms; or, smaller, holding Mummies' hands and skipping. There were people, people on the move, people going places.

'Why does everything look so radiant this morning?' he said suddenly.

'Because we're brave,' she said, 'because you are brave.'

Like a benediction he just touched her shoulder.

Yellow silk pyjamas, she told herself; if he is sick I will buy him primrose yellow silk pyjamas. And, with very little shame, she acknowledged to herself that she was excited. She was thrilled. Nervous would be more appropriate, she amended in her own mind, but it did not really change the truth. Challenged then, that was better, challenged to do this thing right; to discipline her reactions and to meet his needs; to hope without being totally certain what it was she hoped for. She was curious too. She wanted to get it right. There was a kind of clarity – he needed her, it was her that he needed. To become not her, to become someone who would get things right, would be to fail, because he needed her to need him. Taking her hand off the gear stick as she revved up the hill, she patted his knee.

They parked the car and walked up to the hospital. He

stopped outside and she stopped with him. He reached into his pocket and took out a cigarette packet.

'You quit,' she said indignantly. They had quit together, gone away together for a long weekend to Cromer in Norfolk of all unlikely places and inhaled and exhaled together in the sweeping cold of the East Anglian wind.

'I unquit, last night,' he said. 'Do you want one?'

'Not those,' she said, eyeing his Camel Lights packet with greedy longing.

'I thought about it,' he said. 'I stood in the shop last night and thought if I get Gitanes she'll give in and smoke with me. So I didn't. Wasn't that unselfish of me?'

'No. You don't like them, and they make you cough.'

But the very mention of the cough was an error; he chucked the cigarette away and turned to face the hospital door.

'Sorry,' she muttered, cross with herself.

'Don't,' he said sharply; 'I'm scared, I'm strung up tight and whatever you do, you're going to get things wrong. I personally guarantee it. Just don't apologise, all right? I shall hurt your feelings, and I don't want to have to feel guilty.'

She felt guilty. She repressed a further apology. She drew a breath and said as acerbically as she could, 'Fine. But you have to say when I blunder, not waste good nicotine and make me jealous.'

Then suddenly he put his arms round her, hugging her, tight, tight, her face was against his neck, his skin both soft and bristly where it was shaved. She risked a delicate kiss, more for herself than for him, and then extracted herself.

'Come on,' she said. And they went into the hospital.

A Case Conference in the Courts of Heaven.
Angel no 376,974,115,082.
What can such an assessment be?
Angels have no bodies, so it is not medical

Angels have no sin, so it is not judgmental
Angels have no morals, so it is not situational
Angels know all things, so it is not investigative
Angels are supremely free, so it is not coercive
Is it more like having the piano tuner in?
like an orchestra tuning up, up, up until the oboe sighs
    with joy,
A, pure A, an A, oh, ah, of satisfied desire.

Angels assess Angel. Apostles, martyrs, doctors, virgins and the power of the Holy Spirit on the face of the waters assess Angel. There is justice in the courts of heaven.

Words are timebound. They must come in order, first one and then the next. In heaven there is no time. So in the courts of heaven, in the timeless day of eternity, there is no language.

Bad luck, then, to the mystical voyeurs. It is impossible to speak of Angel's assessment.

Then Angel says, 'But it's too late.'

All those heavenly beings who dwell without terrestrial contact are completely confused, since neither late nor early have any meaning here, in the place where there is no time.

From within the feathered folds of Angel's immaterial garments, from under her glass-feathered wings Angel draws out . . .

. . . and the whole of heaven judders and shakes as it has not since Eve bit the apple and the world was tilted 23.5 degrees on its axis, causing seasons and famines and grief and children's sobs for ruined picnics. The courts of heaven lurch; the adamantine walls crack, refract, and crizzle . . .

. . . draws out:

a bowl: millefiorí with star canes
a fused cube with oxidised lightning trapped within it
a Christmas tree bauble: blown crystal encasing blue
    filigree *façon de venise*

a paperweight: small, cameo cut
a tear-drop: with double air-twist and its neck broken
   off

So now there is matter in heaven. The material has penetrated the immaterial; mass and matter and time have crashed the perfectly constructed barrier between their own appointed spheres and the ever-ranging, spaceless, placeless zones of eternity.

Angel is alone in an enormous space and looks down, down through the vast vacuity and knows the fear of falling. Because there is community and sympathy in the courts of heaven, all the heavenly hosts are looking down, up, over, round, out, in the same immeasurable and non-dimensional emptiness. There is a thrill of perfect fear.

Then the Word is with them all; the Word that need not have been spoken but was and is in the greater necessity of the passionate love of God.

Peace be with you says the Everlasting Word and raises wounded hands. Deep within each wound is a plug of black obsidian, glass from the heart of the volcanoes that were soldered into those hands when hell was harrowed.

'I will never forget them. I have branded them on the palms of my hands. So first,' says the Word to Angel, 'you can go and put them back. Which is more than I have been allowed to do.'

The eternal Laughter of the Word pours out over Angel who is drowned in the delight of laughter. Then all things are well for Angel, in the silence of heaven, and the love of the body and all its ways.

The massed bands of victory play out boldly, a blare of trumpets, the tinkle of harps and the giddy scratchy sound of kazoos.

It was, as it always was, arid inside the hospital. There were all the pleasantries of fine prints and pot plants that were meant to

235

disguise the fact that it was a hospital. It reeked, not nowadays of disinfectant, but of a designer trying to 'do' soothing colours, with efficiency, on a restricted budget. There were too many discreet notices with arrows directing them to a thousand places they did not want to go. She could not see any for where they did want to go, and they didn't much want to go there.

But he knew the way. How many people had he held the hands of here? Why was he not holding one of their hands now? Because she was safe – she had not had sex with anyone for so long that she was as safe as a nun. That was why he wanted her, she did not need protecting. And because he loved her.

There were two very young nurses in the lift, who got out the stop before they did. She could hear her own heels tapping on the linoleum floor and then the sound change because the unit's reception room had a carpet.

The counselling session made her want to laugh. Some of it did anyway. They wanted to know whether she wanted to test. If she was with him . . . the thought of being his lover seemed hilarious. They assumed she was his lover and she loved it. Responding to direct enquiry however made her feel coy.

She wanted a brassy tone, 'Why ever would I want to fuck him?' 'I'm his fag-hag not his shag-bag.' 'For God's sake, he's queer.' Queer, gay, too young, too sexy actually, too bold, too rough for her.

Instead she sort of tittered. 'No, I don't need to test. Whatever his status, I don't need to test.'

'I'm gay,' he said firmly. But he was planning to make a baby.

Ellie let her mind drift, because she did not want to hear the next bit. She, who had thought she had an infinite, even a prurient, curiosity about other people's sex lives did not want to hear the list of risks run. How dare he? He ought to know better. He did and still he dared and that had to be part of why she loved him. Oh damn, damn, damn, she thought.

But he, he did rather well. He addressed the counsellor throughout as a fellow professional – an open exchange of necessary information. He was not supplicant, but colleague.

They went later into another room where they prodded him a bit and took his blood sample.

'Come back at four-thirty,' said the smiling nurse.

'Louis' next,' he said boldly as they left the hospital; but he lit another cigarette and his hand shook, just slightly. 'For cakes that come from heaven via Vienna.'

'Yes,' she said, smiling modestly because that had originally been her joke.

They walked up to the top of the hill for cream cakes and coffee. There were old men who had survived concentration camps before either of them had been born, sitting reading their papers and doing the crossword puzzles. There were young, and rich, really rich, Hampstead housewives, if so dingy a word could describe these exotic butterflies.

'What's the common noun for debutantes?' he asked her.

'A fritillery, I should think,' she smiled, 'a fritillery of debutantes, sort of military and trivial at the same time. But Hugo, these aren't debutantes, and never were; too glamorous, and international.'

'He's an actor,' whispered Hugo, 'and that's his agent. He didn't get the part so he doesn't get lunch.' A rather beautiful man was sprawled in a chair in a suit, his blond floppy hair too closely modelled on Hugh Grant's.

'No,' said Ellie. This was a game they often played. 'His agent wants him to do something faintly pornographic and he's promised his wife – sorry his Lil . . .'

'Lil?'

'Live-In-Lover. Anyway, he's promised her that he won't, but he doesn't want his agent to think he's henpecked. So he's talking about his Arrrrt. But he's very vain, so of course he sort of wants to do the sex scenes because then she'll fancy him even more.'

'And his agent too.'

'He's not gay! You can't have everyone being gay, it's no fun.'

'For whom? And those two' – he picked two wonderfully prosperous looking women in their late fifties who were discussing the proposed marriage of the daughter of a friend of theirs, just slightly too loudly – 'are dykes.'

'They are NOT,' Ellie shrieked, even louder than the two women. They laughed.

'Oh sweet Jesus,' said Hugo, who was sitting facing the door, 'Mm-ermmm.' Ellie glanced over her shoulder to inspect whatever it was that Hugo was so blatantly admiring.

She grinned, 'OK, you win that one. Yes he is.'

'Ellie, darling! Goodness, you look fabulous.'

'You must learn not to sound so surprised, dear one; I always look fabulous.' She put up her cheek to receive his kiss. 'Do you know Hugo?'

They nod at each other, accepting connection with Ellie, and a small, socially appropriate level of mutual admiration.

'How's Jamie?' she asked him.

'Great. He'd have sent his love if he knew I was going to bump into you. What are you doing so far from home?'

'Business.'

'With Hugo?'

'Don't be so nosy,' she said.

'Well,' he was not offended, 'I'm doing equally secret and confidential business with him . . .' he indicated a table further down the café, 'so see if I care.'

He gave her another kiss, raised a smiling salute to Hugo and passed on down the room.

'Shit, Ellie, who's that?'

'Richard? Old friend. I like you better, Hugo,' said Ellie.

'So I should hope,' he said, reassured. 'Can we go for a walk? On the Heath.'

'Yes, good; then I'll take you to lunch.'

They walked up to the Heath in the brightness of the morning. He pointed out to her where one went to pick up trade among the trees and the underbrush, and he expatiated on the wild delight of stranger sex in the dark. Further on she showed him where she had lost her virginity.

'I blew it, you know; we had both, for rather different reasons, pretended it was the love that conquered all, despite my fundamental uninterest and his sexual proclivities. It was a long time ago.'

'Doesn't sound like blowing it.'

'No, not that; not the sex. He was rather a sweetie actually, it was just that we didn't remotely fancy each other, we just wanted to fancy each other and thought that was enough. No, when I say I blew it, I meant . . . his was the first coming-out speech I ever heard and I didn't find it a big deal. I just said something like "Oh, I know," or "Yes, of course," and he so badly wanted a drama. He'd have liked it best if I'd swooned or something; and it seemed so unimportant to me.'

'Didn't it surprise you?'

'No, of course not. He was a real honest-to-God homosexual, you know; I should think everyone but him had known for ages, but that's no excuse for stealing his thunder.'

'If you knew . . .'

'Oh, don't, Hugo; I was very young. Not that unselfish anyway; I wanted, needed, to have a lover – I was an art student, for heaven's sake. Virginity was worse than BO in those far-off days. And,' she paused, 'and I think I thought it didn't matter. I was quite naïve. Very naïve. I thought it was, well, like preferring the colour blue to green, not something integral, just something by-the-way. It still is for some people, you know.'

'Ellie, there's something wrong with you.' He was smiling at her, but she put up a hand to ward off a blow.

'I know,' she said, 'you don't need to tell me.'

'Hey,' he put his arm round her, 'I didn't mean that. I meant . . . you've got a bit missing, you're a mutant, you simply lack the homophobia gene.'

'What do you mean?'

'I know lots of heterosexual people, especially women, who've come a long way; learned to love poofs – I mean really love and appreciate and support, but they sort of had to learn it. That's OK, lots of gay men had to learn it too. But you haven't come any way at all. You just never had any gut repulsion. You're a freak of nature. I've wasted time admiring you.'

'Now that would be an interesting thing for those genetic scientists to investigate.' Her smile was a little wobbly. She was meant to be taking care of him, and he gave her this gift. 'Because if there's anything in it we could engineer for homotolerance and then there wouldn't be a gay problem.'

'If there's anything in it, you should have bred like a bunny,' he teased her.

Perhaps she could best take care of him by letting him be generous. They walked on across the summer grass. With a sudden inspiration she took off her shoes and wriggled out of her tights and handed them all to him to look after.

'How many?' he said curiously at one point, 'how many blokes have come out to you first?'

'Not that many,' she said; 'it's not my hobby. Now I'm old, I prefer people who've done that already. I don't like to deal with guilt any more – I have accumulated quite enough of my own.'

There was a pause. She held up her hands and pretended to count on her fingers. 'Maybe half-a-dozen, a few more.'

'Is it ever a surprise?'

'Not often, my gaydar is very finely tuned. Once it was a total surprise; but he was very young, a friend of Steph's. I hadn't sort of focused. He pinned me up against the fridge and called me Ms Macauley throughout.' She smiled remembering his sweet earnestness, while his friends were playing noisy music next door.

'Do you ever fancy us?' he asked idly. There were still hours to fill in and he did not want to have to measure them. He had concocted a strange place of intimacy, and, rather boldly, decided to use it. She was, he knew, at his mercy in some ways: she was wide open. Things she would not normally discuss, she would now.

'You're such an narcissist, Hugo,' she said, but smiling. 'No, I have never fancied you' – which was more or less true – 'at least not if you mean have I ever wanted to have sex with you.'

She wriggled her fingers out of his and pushed both hands into her pockets. 'More vague yearnings? Yes, of course, some-times. But not you, mostly not the people who are my friends – the people who bring out my tenderest fag-hag qualities aren't the sort of men I fancy. But look, fancying people isn't the point, is it? It's sort of incidental, something you handle like . . .' she giggled almost girlishly '. . . like wanting to go to the loo in the middle of a grand public lecture by a good friend of Henry's. You handle it, that's all, it's not the point.'

Suddenly she wanted him to understand something.

'Look, Hugo, sex, as such, just means something different for you and me. Sometimes I do fancy someone, usually totally unsuitable. I have a soft spot, I mean a kind of sexual soft spot for febrile, delicate gay men who ideally are alcoholics. Well I *mean*! I may fancy them but I'm not *stupid*. So it's possible to make quite clear choices about that. I want friends, I want you to be my *friend*.'

'I am, I am,' he said, reaching for her, but she dodged.

'No, listen to me, it's important. Because of basic homopho-bia any relationship I have with a gay man is assumed by gay men who are sexist *and* heterosexuals who are homophobic to be somehow contaminated by my improper lusts. You'd be outraged if I asked you if you fancied me.'

'That's not what I asked, Ellie.'

'Near as damn it. Look, it's a political issue.'

'Everything is.'

'That's why I like you,' she said.

And suddenly the earnestness evaporated, they were hugging each other, hugging each other against the world, the flesh and the devil. Hugging each other with a desire that was real and vast and entirely non-sexual.

'I love you to pieces,' he said.

'Thank God for that.' She buried her face in his shoulder and suddenly they were both overcome with sadness, and anxiety and the comfort of each other's arms.

With remarkable discipline she broke her clasp before he did. 'Race you to the bottom,' she shouted, giving herself a ten-yard start as she hurled down the steep grassy slope. They were children, running and laughing, innocent and loving. They were adults who carried bitterness and fear and complexity as close as their skins and now tossed that all away for the delight of chasing each other down a steep hill on a spring day.

She did beat him to the bottom. Just, and swung round to laugh; his coat was flapping and he swerved so as not to bump into her. The ground was still damp and he slipped, tumbled, still laughing and fell heavily. Out of breath from the exertion he lay face down in the short grass gasping painfully.

'Oh God,' she cried, suddenly sounding like a mother, 'are you hurt?'

He wanted to say no, no he was fine but he was struggling too much with his inability to breathe. She knelt down beside him, preposterously worried. 'Sweetheart, are you all right?'

He twisted his head up, smiled at her and said. 'I'll live.'

The glorious moment was abruptly over.

He stood up slowly; she brushed him down and, holding hands, they walked on silently.

After a bit she said, 'Much more important than your casual sexual encounters, this is where I taught Steph to ride her bike, when she was about four.'

Strictly speaking this was not true; she had taught Stephanie this childhood skill, the one you never forget, further down on the Highgate side, but it was a new topic of conversation and had the right flavour.

They walked back towards the village. She found herself touching him, petting him, more than she usually allowed herself to. She found that he accepted but did not return her gestures of affection.

They had lunch, in the end, not in an expensive restaurant as she had planned, but in a noisy bistro; the street remained very near and the volume of music and voices, the public feel of the whole place prevented any perilous intimacies. They drank rather a lot and he smoked.

When he went to find the toilets, she practised relaxation and concentration. They were on a cliff edge, a place where it was difficult to maintain good manners. For the first time she found herself thinking about what a positive test would mean, in this crazy AIDS world where positive is as negative as you can get. When he came back she found herself almost blushing: she had been rearranging the house so that he would have a lovely place to die in. She had redecorated Stephanie's bedroom and considered installing another bathroom, so that he could have one of his own. She would, she had been thinking, be allowed to bring him breakfast in bed.

She would cook him tiny nourishing meals, so witty and so tastefully garnished that they would whet even his failing appetite.

She would wake up in the night and sense his loneliness; she would go to his room and hold him while he sweated and sweated, or coughed and coughed. She would hug him and remind him that they had been here before and that though death was a tricky bastard there was no need to be frightened.

She would have long tender chats with his friends.

She would come in from the studio in the evening and his face would light up; she would cheer him with outrageous gossip and withdraw discreetly and understandingly when his ex-lovers came to visit. At first he would look lovely and later he would not and it would not make any difference to her. She would be *wonderful*.

She had just reached the point of deciding to buy him a Japanese kimono as well as yellow silk pyjamas when he returned.

'I'm scared,' he said. 'Can we have another bottle of wine?'

'Dutch courage?'

'You bet.'

They stayed a long time, drinking, gossiping, shoring themselves up.

'I'm divorcing Henry,' she told him.

'Really?' He sounded pleased and slightly surprised.

'Yes, it got stupid.'

'You noticed?'

She winced slightly, but knew that that was a conversation that would have to wait. 'I have a new plan. I think Judith is going to move in with me.'

'Really?' he laughed. 'Fabulous. What's brought that on?'

She said, 'She came back from Venice in a bit of a state. She says she behaved impeccably and I bet she did. But she came back . . . sad . . . defeated. So, being Judith, she was really aggressive and uppity. It was her idea. She said it would give all the heterosexualist bastards something to chew on. She said, and I quote, "Shall we pretend you are my lover, and really piss-off Henry and the Snake-bitch Contessa?" I should tell you that *La Carissima* is henceforth to be referred to as the *Contessa*. I haven't a clue if she really is one.

'She's hurting, Judith I mean; I'm hurting; but we adore each other, and we will both recover. Don't you think it would be a good idea?'

He was a bit taken aback; so was she. It was true they had talked about it, but she had told Hugo mainly for something amusing to say, and was slightly surprised to find that it sounded entirely convincing and desirable. 'Of course we'll have to redecorate the whole place. You can't imagine Judith living with all that *Homes and Gardens* prettiness. We'll end up with a ghastly minimalist Italian kitchen, in which she'll never cook.'

'Sell it, and get something that would work for both of you. Like joined up flats.'

It was a real possibility. She felt giddy with promise. She did not tell him what the scheme would be if he were going to be ill.

He looked quizzical. 'Did you tell her? I mean about today?'

'I was tempted, but I resisted,' said Ellie. Discretion not being one of her greater virtues, she had been severely tempted, but quite apart from Hugo's needs, Judith had been so volatile and distressed that Ellie had known that this was not a good time to entrust her with someone else's secret. 'Who have you told?'

'Well . . .' he hesitated.

'Mary,' Ellie filled in for him, managing it casually.

'Only in general. I've said I'll test, but not today, not you.'

She felt a thrill of pleasure which she repressed sternly. She said instead, 'It will be a staggeringly beautiful baby, won't it?'

He looked smug, and then doubtful and frightened. Quickly Ellie started to report on the post-wedding-bliss supper party she had been to at Jim and Stuart's. He told her about some work he was doing, and, encouraged she talked at last about the windows and why they frightened and excited her.

'Mary and me wasn't such a good idea then?'

'Not brilliant timing.'

He would never apologise, and indeed had nothing to apologise for, but he grinned ruefully, as near an apology as he was likely to manage. Then his attention went back to himself, which was where, just now, it belonged. She refilled his wine-glass for him, and he took an over-generous swig.

At the appointed hour she paid and they turned down the hill and walked back to the hospital. After a not unreasonable but completely unbearable wait, a nurse called his name. He took her hand and they walked into the inner sanctum. She could not read the face of the doctor who sat there.

The doctor told him he had tested negative.

'Are you sure?' he asked. She could hear that he was unconvinced.

'Quite sure,' said the doctor smiling.

Joy. Pure, unalloyed joy. She could hardly identify the feeling, it was so rare: not relief, not happiness, just this bubble, this inspiration of disinterested, pure joy, transparent as glass and as lovely. She rejoiced and was glad because her friend was well. There was no prettiness in her joy and she knew it; it was a joy as pure as her sorrow would have been if the doctor had said the opposite. And he had given her this.

Love.

And she had given him the chance to give this to her.

Love and joy.

They thanked the doctor politely. They went out into the passageway. There were still tense, anxious people waiting there. They were sensitive, careful.

As though walking on thin glass, thin transparent glass which was none the less strong enough to carry their weight, they walked down the corridor and through the clinic's door.

They turned there, standing quietly and put their arms round each other. They held each other tightly, exhausted, they leaned on each other and the weight was heavy with lucky love.

'I want a cigarette,' she said, once they were outside the

hospital doors. He took out his packet and offered her one, without comment. But when he struck the lighter and held it out towards her the little flame trembled slightly. She leaned forward, a fraction too far. Her nose glowed golden pink and she jerked her head away. There was an acrid whiff of singed hair. She was very conscious of inhaling; she had managed to forget how much she liked the taste.

They started walking back to where the car was parked. He said, quite unexpectedly, 'Once you told me . . . you described yourself as a gatekeeper – and you didn't mean it kindly.'

She must have registered her surprise as she struggled for the connection.

'A gatekeeper; I'm sure you said "gatekeeper".' Then she remembered and nodded.

He went on, 'But you're not, you know; you're a night-watcher, a lantern bearer.' He smiled very sweetly, the blue of his eyes deepening now the fear was over.

'Like bloody Florence Nightingale,' she said, dangerously moved.

'I'm not needing her just yet,' he said and then repeated it slowly and lit a cigarette of his own. 'Don't be so camp.'

They put their arms round each other's waists and walked faster. When they got to the car he released her, and walked round to the passenger side; she opened her bag and rummaged for the keys.

Her fingers touched something unexpected, cool, smooth and she pulled the opening of the bag apart to look. In the bottom of the bag was a glass ball, a Christmas tree bauble: blown crystal encasing blue filigree glass, *façon de venise*: a technical mistress-piece, a truly beautiful thing. She was shocked into immobility.

'Don't tell me you've lost the keys. Just don't,' he said, slightly teasingly.

'No,' she said, 'they're here.'

As she straightened up she saw her own face in the window of the car, a shadowy mirror reflecting darkly but truly. They must keep the mirrors of the windows dark like that, so that the passer-by will never be instantly certain whether she sees herself or a shadow of heaven or both.

The glass ball is smaller than, but very like, the joy bubble in the hospital room. It is the same colour, exactly the same colour, as the one she had seen the Virgin blow in her vision. All three of the balls inspire her.

She unlocked the car door, got in and scrambled her arm over to lift the lock on his side. He got in too. Suddenly the whole evening shifted. It was over, that long day. They ought to celebrate.

'Let's go dancing.'

'Till the break of day?'

'Yes, And if there's a piper I can pay.'

'We'll go back to Greenwich then,' he said, 'so you can change.'

'No,' she said decisively, 'I can't be bothered, and I look terrific.'

'You can't go to the Duke's dressed like that,' then lest he should have offended her he added, 'everyone'll think you're a tranny.'

'Perhaps I am,' she said, 'and you never guessed.' They are playful.

'Can I be your baby's grandmother?' she asked boldly.

'My baby is not having a fake transsexual for a grandmother. You can be the fairy godmother instead.'

They begin to laugh.

'Fairy godmother? It's good,' she said, 'it's very good. Better than fag-hag, really.'

He caught the pun and laughed louder.

She switched the engine on and over its initial cough she felt her cranial cavity fill up with knowledge. Her other missing glass pieces were, right now, sitting on the table in the studio drawing room. Robbie's tear was mended. Hugo was well. This time next year Mary would be nursing a little girl child. Nothing would get any easier. Lots of things would get harder. Hugo was well. He was her friend. They would have a big fight soon because this much dependency would make him fretful.

He was well. She rejoiced and was glad, because he was well.

Then her head emptied, drained completely. She was sitting in the car next to her best friend grinning like a child. She heard Angel's infuriating snigger and felt Angel, a little sadly, kiss her farewell.